UNCONVENTIONALLY,

UNCONVENTIONALLY,

Elle

a novel

JOURDANA WEBBER

EVERWILD PUBLISHING

NEW ORLEANS

ISBN: 978-1-966884-01-9 (Paperback)
ISBN: 978-1-966884-00-2 (E-Book)

Library of Congress Control Number: 2025900830

Any references to historical events, real people, or real places are used fictitiously. Names, characters, and places are products of the author's imagination.

Book design by Ashley Santoro

Printed in the United States of America

First printing edition 2025

Everwild Publishing
201 Saint Charles Ave. Ste. 114 #713
New Orleans, LA 70170

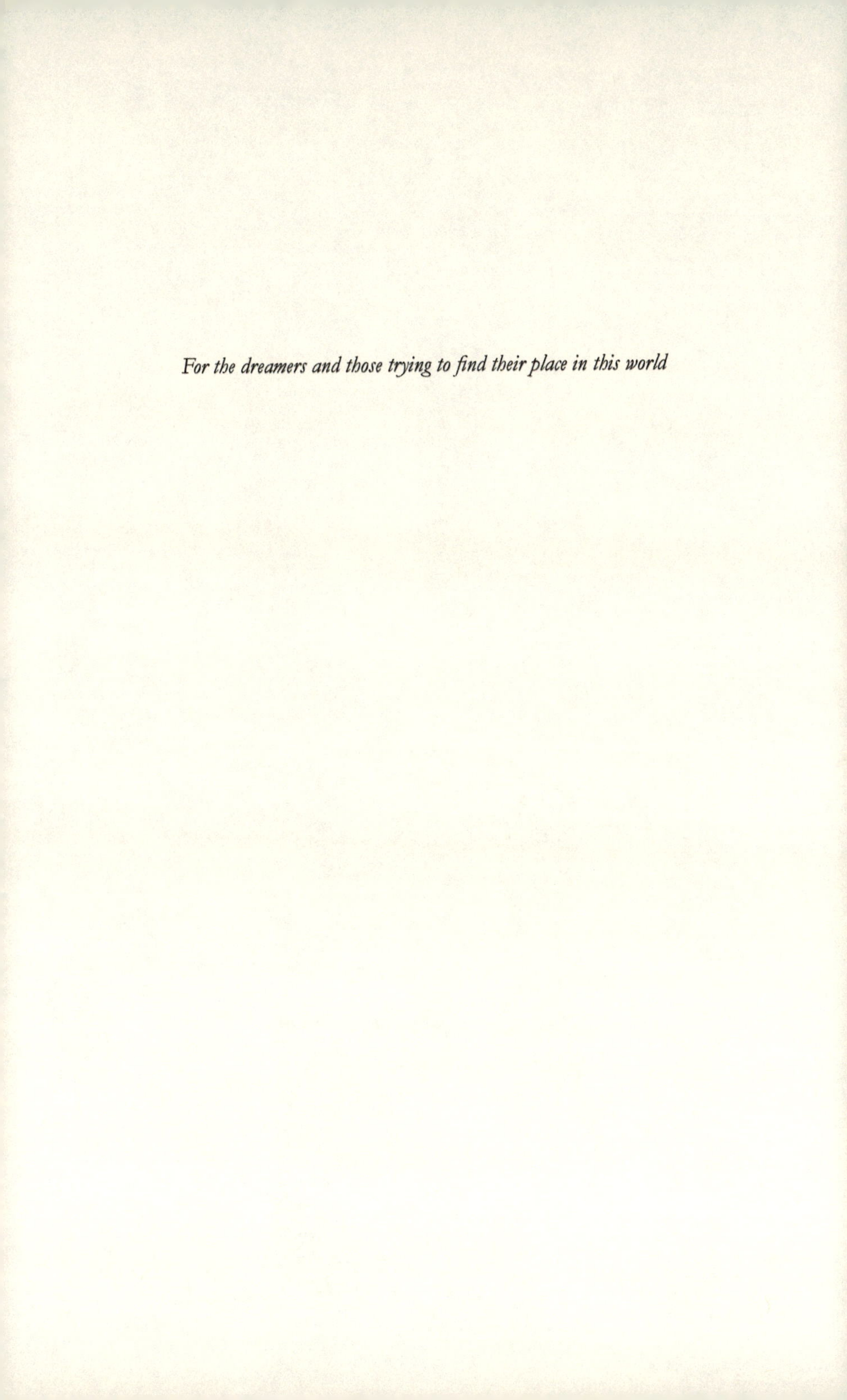

For the dreamers and those trying to find their place in this world

AUTHOR'S NOTE

Readers, some content in this book may make you want to quit your job, run away, and find your own Henry Cavill look-alike; I'm sorry. Blame Elle.

But seriously, there are some delicate topics within these pages related to mental health, grief and loss, and suicidal ideation.

The panic attacks experienced by one of the characters are representative of my own experience with panic attacks and severe anxiety. Please know that I am holding space for you and your personal experiences as they will likely differ from mine.

PROLOGUE

Six years ago

I knew death.

My silent companion in the darkest of moments. I, Elizabeth Watson, knew this mysterious presence that lingered in the shadows of my existence. She stole my family, she robbed me of my identity, and she devilishly whispered a sweet song of surrender while I sipped my glass of rosé. I didn't want to feel this sharp pain through my chest or the agonizing way my throat closed every time I remembered that I wasn't there for her, that I didn't know.

When my grandmother, the woman who raised me, died of cancer, cancer I wasn't aware of, I fell to my knees and screamed until my throat burned raw. Why didn't she tell me? I wouldn't have canceled my trip to visit her because of work. I would have been there. I would have taken care of her. I think.

Instead, I was here. Long hours and never-ending emails. I should have known. Even Jude said I was overworked, but I didn't care. I needed to work harder, to become better, to climb higher on the slippery corporate ladder.

Seated on my French Quarter balcony, three stories high, I scanned Bourbon Street, where crowds of tourists flowed in sync, and the smell of alcohol and cigars drifted through my fern-covered rails and around my heavy head. The music from a bar at the corner of Bourbon and Conti rumbled through the street and rattled the glass panes of my floor-to-ceiling windows. The humid October air was thick and uncomfortable; condensation slowly rolled down my chilled glass of rosé while I twirled it on the table.

What would happen if I did it? What would happen if I listened to this sweet song of surrender? I stopped twirling my glass, the stain of my bloodred lipstick still fresh on the side. Why did I feel so alone? My heart constantly ached, and all my emotions were void and empty. I was numb.

I slowly stood up and slipped my shoes off my swollen feet. I lined them up neatly next to my chair and lifted my chin as a slight breeze caressed my skin and brushed my hair away from my sweaty brow. I was aware of my body moving toward the edge of my balcony, and I felt my hips brush up against the iron railing. I leaned over, just to look, and my breath went shallow.

Memories rushed through my cloudy mind, glimpses of the life I'd thought was right. Now everything was wrong. Six years old and my grandparents officially adopting me. Fifteen years old and telling everyone I was going to be famous. Twenty years old and falling in love.

With blurry eyes, I pressed up on my tiptoes. My calves ached, my arches sore from my heels—stupid heels. Everyone was gone. I was alone.

My heart was beating through my lightweight linen dress. The orange one Grandma and I had picked together in Italy the last summer we had Grandpa.

My head spun and my vision tunneled as I gripped the cast-iron column with shaky, sweaty hands. My biceps began to quiver as I hoisted myself up, taller, higher.

I took a jagged breath and looked down one last time. A mother and her young daughter walked together hand in hand, the little girl taking two steps to her mother's one. The little girl looked up, and our eyes met. The mother stopped short and looked up to my balcony. Her face paled and her eyes went wide. I saw her pull out her phone, but I didn't care. My heart ached. I had to fix this feeling.

Would it hurt? How much longer could I keep pretending I was okay? No one would believe this. No one would think I was hurting. I never showed them.

A tear trickled down my cheek. No one would care. I closed my eyes and waited as a breeze, warm and muggy, tickled my face. I gave a small, delicate grin and leaned into the breeze. It would be okay. I leaned a little farther, and I heard a woman scream at the same time a man's voice boomed from behind me. All I could feel was darkness.

1

Now

My phone buzzed; the girls were going crazy on our group text. Sarah and Rachel had been texting nonstop about the idea of a girls' trip. I was pretty sure Rachel was eighty-five percent done planning one by the number of vibrations I was hearing.

The thread had started off with them wishing me luck on my presentation this morning on a major account, then about Rachel's pending promotion to PR director, and Sarah's oldest starting kindergarten. These days we kept in touch only with texting and the occasional phone call. It was minimal, but it worked. After college, Rach had moved to Saint Louis, and Sarah had settled down in Virginia. Our lives and schedules hardly lined up, so a group chat helped us still feel connected. Isn't that how it goes, though? Best friends who live in different states.

As I walked into my presentation, I thought about the ideas they were throwing around for a girls' trip. Did I have the time? What about the Calloway account, my big client? God, we hadn't been together in years, just the three of us. I closed my eyes and thought about what a trip with just the three of us would be like. Carefree? Relaxing? Refreshing?

A tap on my shoulder brought me back to reality: a cold corporate office and two men sitting around a conference room table waiting for me.

"Are you ready, Elle?" Anna was standing beside me looking into the conference room too. "I didn't know Chris Johnson was on this account with you," she said as her eyebrows arched up in surprise.

I rolled my eyes at the sight of Chris sitting arrogantly in the chair by the head of the table. His raven-colored hair was slicked back, and his long, narrow nose made him look like a weasel.

"That's because he's not." I sighed heavily as I rolled my shoulders back and prepared myself to walk into this presentation I knew like the back of my hand.

Neither man acknowledged my entrance until I took my seat on the other side of Mr. Landry, my boss, who was a short man with a constant scowl. He wore a pressed navy-blue suit, and his crimson tie was in bright contrast against his starched white shirt. As usual, his Rolex sparkled on his wrist, and he greeted me with a curt nod.

I readjusted my skirt and crossed my ankles in my chair. My formfitting Prada skirt suit was just as nice if not better than Chris's slim-fit Armani black suit. He wasn't wearing a tie, and his jacket was casually unbuttoned. My hands were clammy, which was never a good sign for me when Chris was around. When he first started, he tried to ask me out on a date, but Jude and I had just broken up and I was in no mood to date, let alone date anyone from work. Since then, he's called me "buddy" and likes to pat me on the shoulder as if to say, *Good girl.*

"Good morning, Mr. Landry." I ignored Chris. "Paul said that he and his boss, Mr. Guidry, are on their way."

Chris rolled his eyes, so I lifted my chin a little higher.

I hadn't met Mr. Guidry yet. He was the president of the Creekside Agency, and Paul, my contact, had told me he only attended the big presentations. No pressure, of course. No pressure at all.

When Mr. Guidry and Paul arrived, I shook everyone's hands firmly and walked to the front of the room for my presentation. Throughout the hour, I noticed Chris leaning in to speak with Mr. Landry while Mr. Guidry watched me emotionlessly. I was interrupted a few times for questions directed toward Mr. Landry and Chris. I didn't exist, yet Chris was front and center. *Where does he get this arrogance?* My anxiety started to flutter in my chest, and I shifted my weight from foot to foot. Mr. Landry looked at me and narrowed his eyes, but I smiled back and listened intently to Chris's explanation. I felt humiliated and small. Chris's nasal voice flowed through the room and made my skin crawl with disgust.

I tried to answer a question, but Mr. Guidry looked at me down his crooked nose and then back to the others. The second time I tried to answer a question about *my* proposal, Mr. Guidry snapped at me with a snarling growl and narrowed eyes. "Young lady, I appreciate your enthusiasm, but I'm not sure an assistant needs to be involved in the conversation." His lip was curled, and I noticed Chris smirking.

Mr. Landry glared at me, his expression daring me to speak again.

Anger boiled in my chest. Sweat gathered at the nape of my neck even though the room was frigid and sterile. This wasn't the first time in my career that men had assumed I was an assistant. Paul knew I was the one who'd put the entire proposal together, but he made no move to stand up for me. He sat there fiddling with his fingers, avoiding the plea in my eyes.

"Excuse me, sir." I glared at Mr. Guidry once he finished talking down to me. "I am not the assistant on this account. I am the broker. I put this entire thing together and have worked with Paul on it for months. If you have any other questions, I would be happy to answer them." I felt my legs start to shake. The adrenaline was coursing through my body, and I could feel every nerve tingling with anticipation of fight or flight.

Mr. Guidry's eyes widened in shock, completely gobsmacked, and Paul went white. Mr. Landry and Chris were silently glaring at me. I could feel the tension in the room, thick and heavy, as it became harder to breathe normally. All eyes were on me. I cleared my throat and finished the presentation without another interruption.

After the meeting concluded, Paul caught my eye before I could walk out and motioned for me to come over to him. He looked sideways to make sure everyone else was out of the room before speaking. "Elle, your proposal was fantastic. Truly, it was," he said with a broad smile.

I snorted and rolled my eyes. *Yeah, it went swimmingly.*

"I know Mr. Guidry loved the proposal. I . . ." He trailed off, thinking about what he wanted to say. "Look, I know Mr. Guidry ignored you a little bit. I guess he thought that the other fellow was the broker on the account, and—"

"He thought I was just the assistant. I know!"

Paul grimaced at my sharp tone. "He was obviously wrong. Elle, there's no one like you. Remember, I appreciate you. Please know that." His lips curved into a gentle smile as he touched my shoulder.

"Thank you, Paul." I sighed and picked up my papers from the conference table. "I'll see you later tonight for drinks."

He shook his head absentmindedly. "Yep, sounds good." He looked to the door. "I'll catch you later, Elle."

I followed Paul out the door and turned to shuffle back to my desk. Men were exhausting, and that proposal had gone about as well as trying to swim upstream in the Mississippi River.

"How'd it go?" Anna asked as she approached me in the hallway.

"Chris was there." I shivered at the mention of his name.

Before she could answer, we were interrupted by the man himself, Chris Johnson. "Hey, Elle, nice work on the presentation this morning." He said it with a sarcastic smile. His nose crinkled and his eyes narrowed while he stared at me.

"Thanks, Chris." My lips pressed into a forced smile, and a small throb began in my temple.

"C'mon, Elle. I'm serious. You do a good job making PowerPoints and stuff. It was good." He tilted his head with a sly grin and brushed off imaginary dust from his shoulder.

"Don't you have work to do or something?" My cheeks burned, and the throbbing continued.

He didn't miss a step. "You know that Calloway account is a big deal. Why don't we do it together? I could help you."

"Chris, what makes you think I need your help? I appreciate your offer, but no thank you."

He rolled his eyes and leaned in close to me as if he were going to whisper a secret in my ear. Anna made a little gasp, but he didn't back away.

"All right, your loss." His voice was calm and sent a chill down my spine. "Paul thought it'd be a good idea, considering—well, never mind." He took a step back and looked down at me with a predatory grin. "You look hot when you're mad, Elle. It's all over your face, and I like it."

I almost vomited. My iced coffee was making its way up my throat.

He stood back and snickered at me, ignoring Anna. "Oh, by the way, I'm going out for drinks with Paul later. Ya know, guy time." He winked and turned to walk away, leaving me with my mouth open and shock spread across my face.

After Chris walked away, Anna grabbed my arm and pulled me into the restroom. I'd always wondered why there was a couch in the women's restroom. Now I understood. She pulled me down next to her and grabbed my hands. I was still in shock. Why didn't I say anything to him? Why did my mouth forget how to move?

"Elle, are you okay? You don't look okay. Has he done that before?" Her eyes were soft but her gaze intent. Her concern felt like a hug I didn't realize I needed.

I shook my head and laughed half-heartedly. "I'm fine. No, he hasn't. I'm good, it's no big deal." *Um, it is a big deal, and my hatred for that man has no limits.*

She sat back and shook her head. "No, Elle, that's a huge deal. You need to report him. He got in your face, Elle!" Her wide eyes and firm grasp made me look away. The last thing I needed was a confrontation or a scene with Chris Johnson. I'd never win.

"Anna, seriously. I'm fine. I need to get back to my desk. I have a ton of things to get done today. I promise, I'm good." My heart was thundering in my chest, and each lie felt like a knot of anxiety twisting in my stomach.

She lifted an eyebrow and narrowed her eyes. "You promise?"

"I promise." I squeezed her hands and gave her a gentle smile.

She walked with me back to my desk, then left with one last concerned glance.

I plopped onto my chair and pulled out my phone. I had a blaring fifty-eight missed text messages. I groaned and rubbed my temples; the throbbing was worse.

I clicked on the icon to start reading what I had missed. There was no way I could let all those texts stay unread. Impossible.

I noticed most were from the girls, two from Paul, and a few spam messages. The most recent message was from Jude Ashford. My heart stopped mid-beat.

It had been years since I'd talked to Jude. My stomach knotted and my chest constricted. Was something wrong? Why was he texting me now? I clicked open his message.

> Hey, Elle, totally random, sorry. I was thinking about you today. Mom came to live with me in NY, and she asked me how you were doing. She forgets more now, and I don't have the heart to tell her again and again that we don't talk much. Hope you don't mind. Just wanted to say hi and hope all is well.

My mind went blank. Just thinking about me? Seriously? Five years later and he's just thinking about me? I tried not to overanalyze my reply. I didn't want to be mean, but literally, what the fuck was I supposed to say?

> Hey, Jude. Good to hear from you. Tell your mom I said hi and I'm all right. I hope you are doing well in New York.

I hit send and waited for his response. I still had butterflies even though I knew this was nothing, we were nothing. He was the past, and I couldn't go back. I reread my text at least five times, waiting for the little dots to appear. It was fine, it was professional and not too emotional. It was fine. I was fine.

My breath went shallow when three dots popped up on my screen.

> I knew you'd understand. Thank you. :)

And that was it. He didn't even use a genuine emoji. My mind was a whirlwind of confusion while my heart was in desperate need of CPR. I took a deep breath and finally opened Paul's message.

Paul: Elle, I talked to Mr. Guidry. Looking good! I told you.

Me: Awesome! Thanks, Paul. I heard you and Chris have plans tonight.

I could feel the anger start to flow through my veins. Why hadn't he told me when he saw me literally within the past hour? I kept glancing at my phone to see if he responded, and each minute that went by, I seriously questioned our friendship. Texting bubbles popped up five minutes later.

Um, yeah. He asked me before the meeting today. I know you don't like him, so I figured I'd see him alo   ne and spare you a night of hell.

I didn't know how to tell you . . .

I had a bad feeling. I couldn't explain it, but ever since Chris walked away, something had felt off.

No problem, we'll chat soon.

I had nothing else to say. This day had gone to hell in a handbasket, and it wasn't even noon yet. Okay, on to the one million missed messages from the girls.

Me: Meeting's over, sorry that took so long. Okay, Rach, spill.

Rach: Welcome back! We've been talking about Chris Pratt vs. Henry Cavill while you've been away. Even though we all know that HC is superior.

SARAH: Shut up, Rach. We've discussed this at length. We called a truce!

RACH: Yes, yes, well, I was only catching Elle up. OK, y'all ready for this idea?! I was watching one of those reality shows set at the beach, and this season was set in Puerto Vallarta. It looked amazing! So, of course I've already done some research, and I think it would be the perfect all-inclusive girls' trip!

SARAH: Like Mexico?

ME: Wow, Rach. I thought you hated the beach? In fact, I remember you specifically saying, "I hate the beach," when we all went to Gulf Shores for spring break freshman year.

To be fair, I'm not a beach girl either. I much prefer the mountains or a trip to Europe, but when Rach got an idea, she ran with it.

RACH: Well, don't everyone clap at once.

RACH: And yes, I do usually hate the beach, however, I saw a resort ad for a week-long all-inclusive vacation there, and it legit looked too good to pass up. Plus, it's super cheap split three ways So, Sarah, tell James this is mandatory self-care, and let's go! It's $500 each for the whole week.

SARAH: Ha, you knew my next question.

ME: When are you thinking of booking this trip, Rach?

All of the work I had to do was streaming across my mind, but then, I also thought of how nice guac on a beach would be with my two best friends. I hadn't been on a real vacation in forever, and I'd been burning myself out with the Calloway account. This could be a nice break once the account closed and I could put it behind me.

> RACH: The special pricing expires at the end of May, so I was thinking the week of May 5! I know it's a short window, but we have to book and get the ball rolling. You guys in?

My heart stopped. Shit, the Calloway account.

2

Twelve years ago

The humidity was relentless. My hair stuck to my face every time I moved, and my dress suctioned to me like skin. Our beers were covered in condensation, and the light buzz of the alcohol felt like a reprieve from reality. We were at a street concert in the middle of downtown Nashville—no complaining allowed, no matter how uncomfortable it was outside. The crowd was thick, bodies brushed bodies, and the music rolled through us like a drug. I couldn't get enough, and I moved and swayed without a second thought.

I was singing my heart out and dancing with my summer roommate when I accidentally bumped into something solid and warm. I swung around with a broad smile and carefree energy. My heart stuttered when I came face-to-face with a very pretty man's solid chest.

I stopped dancing and stepped back, caught off guard by the beauty before me. He was tall and athletic, wearing a white T-shirt that hugged his toned biceps and shoulders. The humidity wasn't sparing him either. My eyes trailed upward and took in his scruff along his lower jaw, sly grin, and amber-honey eyes. I had no idea that rich golden eyes like his existed until that moment, and his were peering down at me. Me, with the sweaty forehead, the wild wavy hair, and the audacity to bump into him.

"I'm so, so sorry! I didn't realize you were so close behind me." I spoke so quickly that his eyes widened in surprise. "Ah, oh my God, this is so embarrassing!" I clasped my hands to my cheeks and felt my face grow warmer.

"You're fine, you don't need to apologize. I think I bumped into you." His voice was silky smooth, and his eyes held me, warm and curious. Goose bumps rippled along my arms. *Oh my God, his voice*, I thought. Where was he from? What was his name? I felt my cheeks burn when he smiled with the most perfectly crooked grin.

"Sorry," I barely uttered. "I mean, thanks. I mean . . ."

He extended his hand to me. "Wanna dance, mystery girl?" A warm feeling radiated through my entire body as his voice overwhelmed me.

I couldn't resist him. I cautiously placed my hand in his, and he slowly pulled me into his warm, strong body. I attempted to concentrate on anything besides what was underneath my fingertips, underneath his light, thin shirt.

Our eyes held each other as the world fell away. It was just us. This mystery man couldn't be real. His wispy, sun-kissed brown hair fluttered across his glistening forehead every time I dipped. Hints of sandalwood and spice surrounded me with every twirl.

We danced as the band's music floated around us. We danced under the Nashville lights with hundreds of strangers. We danced as if no one was watching the silent conversation between our hearts. We danced, lost in the bliss of our own world.

As I lay in bed later, snug beneath my quilted blanket, I found myself replaying the events of the night in my mind. It dawned on me as my eyelids grew heavier that the mystery man who'd danced with me under the Nashville stars had never once asked me for my name.

3

Now

rolled over in my king-size bed, opened my eyes, and realized I wasn't in New Orleans anymore. A bird was standing on my porch staring at me, and the waves were thrashing against the shore. My body was completely calm, and for the first time in ages, I felt refreshed.

Puerto Vallarta.

While vacation had technically started, I still tried to work as much as I could to stay ahead. My cell service was extremely unreliable, and the Wi-Fi was painstakingly slow. I was having minor panic attacks every five minutes when my emails failed to load. I kept telling myself it was only one week. Just one week away from the office; it wasn't that big of a deal. I trusted Anna, and she was more than capable of handling things for me.

Mr. Landry was less than pleased about my spontaneous vacation. He was aware that I hadn't taken a vacation in the past decade, even after my grandmother's death. During our conversation about this vacation, he'd asked me one last time if I was sure about leaving the office for a week. When I said yes, when I told him the Calloway account was all but ours and Anna would handle any last-minute changes, he shook his head and looked at me like I'd given him the wrong answer. I felt a shift in the room, like something was wrong, but I couldn't quite place it. He hadn't mentioned the vacation again.

I rolled onto my back and shut my eyes. While I was enjoying the smell of the salty air, I randomly heard someone screaming.

"Yaaas! Girls' Trip 2022! Get up, bitch, no one is on the beach yet, and I saved us some spots!"

Sarah was standing on my porch with her hip out, dressed in her neon-pink mom-kini with a mimosa and flamingo sunglasses. It was six a.m., and the sun was just coming up from behind some wispy clouds to say good morning.

I stared at her with crust still in the corners of my eyes and what felt like a knife lodged in my temple.

"A mimosa already, Sarah? Can't we start with a coffee?" I asked, rubbing my eyes and pulling the covers back over my head.

I couldn't believe Sarah had a mimosa in her hand this early and had used *bitch* in a sentence. Mom Sarah would never drink so early or in front of her kids. College Sarah believed it was never too early for a mimosa.

"Yes, a mimosa." She emphasized the ending a little too much, and I could tell it probably wasn't her first. "Do you realize I haven't been able to do this in years? Like, actual years! Get up, grouch, we have the whole day in front of us." She walked over to my bed, threw off my blankets, and tossed a pillow at my head. I curled into the fetal position, cozy in my brand-new satin pajamas, and let the pillow hit my side.

"Just a few more minutes," I whined.

She didn't give in. "Get up! C'mon, Rach is already changing to meet us." Sarah turned toward my door, flipped the light on, and stumbled ever so slightly out of my room.

"I guess kids train you to wake up before civilization!" I yelled back at her through the glass as she walked onto the porch and slid the door closed behind her. I grabbed for my blankets again, but she'd thrown them on the floor—too smart. At this point, I was questioning why the heck I'd let them convince me we should all have adjoining rooms.

I admitted defeat and rolled lazily out of bed. A breeze drifted through my open window and brushed against my face like a soft kiss. The saltiness in the air rested on my tongue, and I swore I could taste vacation.

Rachel joined us on the beach within thirty minutes of Sarah's morning show. We spread our towels out side by side, just like we used to in college for spring break: Rachel, me, and Sarah. I missed those days every day.

Rachel and I had always been closest. She was my confidant, my first best friend away from New York. We both wanted to grow up to be journalists and rule the literary world, then life happened. Now she was a PR executive and I was a successful businesswoman, or so it would seem. I kept questioning the definition of *success* ever since Tina, my therapist, had asked me about it. I finally figured that after days of dwelling on it, I had absolutely no idea, and I needed to ask the girls what they thought.

Success isn't making the money; it's making the man while he makes the money, Grandpa told me over the phone one time shortly before he passed. I didn't realize at the time that it would be one of the few conversations we had left, and I still wasn't quite sure what he'd meant by that. Of course success was money, it had to be. Right?

It's weird how life works out; you believe in your audacious dreams, and then you end up ignoring them completely because you believe someone you love and admire knows better. I remember telling my grandparents I wanted to be a writer. I could see the sparkle in my grandmother's eyes, but just as quickly as it came, it disappeared. Not many knew that becoming a writer was her abandoned dream.

My grandparents were proud of me for getting dual degrees, including one in journalism, but at the end of the day, they'd told me to earn a secure job that paid well. Making a lot of money was success in their eyes, especially as the silent generation. More money meant more stability and less hardship. Being a writer was too risky, so I pursued a job with my business degree after graduation. I didn't want to disappoint my grandparents, but sometimes I wondered if I'd disappointed my grandmother regardless. And myself. My grandfather would remind me whenever he talked to me: *Go corporate, Elle. You need a nine-to-five career, Elle. Writers are poor, Elle. Be successful, Elle. You need to be successful.* No pressure at all. Rachel was told the same thing by her family, but public relations suited her. She really enjoyed the grind and the hustle.

Thirty minutes into tanning on the beach, I could feel sweat dripping down my chest and tried to convince myself to put away my phone and take a dip in the ocean for a second. Rachel flipped onto her back and looked over at me. I was still on my phone refreshing my email for the millionth time, looking for anything from Anna. You know, just in case she needed my help. But there was nothing. Anna really was qualified and hardworking enough to handle things while I was gone, but letting go was hard.

"Elle, what are you doing? We're on vacation, remember? If I can put it away for a few hours, I know you can, right?" She pulled her sunglasses down to stare at me.

"I know, I know. It's just this big account I've been trying to nail down for months. It comes up in July, and we are in the heart of getting it all together right now. But you're right, okay. I'm putting it down." I turned it off—seriously, all the way off—and showed her the proof.

She nodded in approval and rested back on her beach towel with her long tan arms by her side. Her black hair was pulled up into a high bun and her face was lathered in SPF 50. I readjusted my sunglasses and tapped Rach on the shoulder.

"Hey, can we share? I don't want to turn my phone back on." I smiled sheepishly, pointing to her headphones. "And I forgot to pack my Bluetooth speaker for us."

She smiled back and passed over her left headphone. Sarah was sleeping on her stomach on my other side, and it was impossible for me not to giggle every time she snored.

We sat side by side, just like the old days at the pool in college. Rachel's playlists were always the best, and while the sun warmed my body and the sand pressed between my toes, I let my eyes rest.

I had my eyes closed, but I couldn't keep my mind from racing. Work was work; life was life. I had everything I thought I wanted, but I was miserable. I knew I was missing something. Was I where I wanted to be at this point in my life? I really thought so, but I couldn't help but notice this trapped, anxious feeling when I thought about who I was meant to be. *Who the hell am I?*

I opened my eyes and pulled the headphone out of my ear. The music stopped and I looked over at Rachel. She looked back, confused.

"Rach, what does it mean to be successful? Have you ever really thought about it?" I asked while shuffling my feet in the sand. The sun felt magical and comforting. Sarah was still sleeping, and I'd have to wake her up soon so she didn't burn to a crisp.

"Girl, if I knew, I'd tell you." She sat up and took a sip of her margarita. "I think it's different for everyone, and it's a personal journey to see what it is for you. But I think if you're living your life how you want to, isn't that successful? I mean, money helps, though."

"Yeah, I guess." I took a deep breath and thought about what she'd said. I didn't feel like I was living my life how I wanted to, but I didn't know how to do that either.

"I also don't think it's one thing in particular, right?" she said. "Like, just because you have money doesn't always mean you're happy. And I heard once, if you don't have your health, do you really have anything at all?" She readjusted her bun and lay back down on her towel.

"Do you think you've found success?" I asked.

She was quiet for a moment, and I could see her thinking about it. "I think so," she finally said. "I really enjoy my job, the hustle, and of course, I'm comfortable with my income and my relationship with Josh. In fact, I'm hoping he'll propose soon." She smiled and wiggled her eyebrows. I chuckled and she continued. "But to answer your question, yeah, I do think I've found it. What about you?"

"Not really." My answer fell out of my mouth, and I felt startled by my lack of filter. Rachel went silent, and I felt embarrassed, so I backtracked. "I mean, I don't know. Maybe."

She nodded and gave me a small smile. Fuck, I didn't want pity—that was her pity look. "I know I'm not supposed to feel this way," I said after she stayed silent.

Her headphone was in her hand, and she sat up and crossed her legs to face me.

"Elle, you can feel however you want to feel. It's not crazy. If you're not happy, what are you thinking about doing?"

I shrugged and closed my eyes. "I don't know." It was barely over a whisper.

I felt Rachel's hand grab mine and squeeze. "It'll work out, Elle. You never give up. Remember, we're dreamers and we don't give up." She let go and I could hear her lying back down on the towel.

I opened my eyes. She had the headphone back in her ear. I put the other one back in mine and flipped onto my stomach like Sarah. Before lying down, I nudged Sarah to get her to flip over. "Sarah, you're burning."

Her eyes popped open wide. "Oh shit!" She shot up to a seated position, grabbed the SPF 50, and started rubbing it all over herself.

"Wait, wait, I'll do your back," I said as she struggled to reach.

I sat back up, took the sunscreen, and lathered it across her back. Sarah was a stay-at-home mom. I knew there were times when her kids drove her crazy, but she'd always wanted to be a mom. Even with her art degree, she'd known what her endgame would be. She adored children and James. As I rubbed in her sunscreen, I let my mind wander again to success. To happiness. To being content.

"You know, I haven't been away from the girls since they were born." Sarah was completely still and staring out at the ocean.

"Seriously?" I responded an octave higher than I meant to. "Sarah, that's years! Like, what, five?"

"Yeah, six. I can't believe it. I've been so busy momming, and James travels so often for work that I can never get away." She sighed and shrugged.

I poked Rachel and motioned for her to take her music out and listen. She sat up slowly, confused at first, then realized Sarah was talking.

Without moving her head, Sarah continued. "Thanks, Rach, for planning this trip. I didn't realize how badly I needed to get away and remember that I am my own person. I'm not just a mom."

Rach reached around me and grasped Sarah's forearm. "Of course, Sarah. I think we all needed it, huh?" She lifted her eyebrows and looked to me.

I moved to sit next to Sarah and reached for her hand. Then I grabbed Rach's hand and intertwined our fingers, sunscreen and all. "Same. I didn't realize how much I needed this, how much I needed both of you." I squeezed their hands again. "I already feel lighter. I guess the sun and guac will do that to you."

"Don't forget the mimosas!" Sarah laughed.

"Or the margs, thank you very much." Rach winked.

"I don't know what I'm doing." I let go of their hands, leaned back, and dug my fingers into the loose warm sand. "I don't know what I want. I feel so overwhelmed and confused. But I have absolutely no reason to feel the way I do. I've got everything I could ever want or need, and yet I feel so incredibly alone." A tear rolled down my cheek.

"I feel alone too sometimes," Sarah said. "Being alone with two kids and a dog can be isolating. I only get to talk to other moms or strangers in the grocery store. Even then, they aren't that exciting. I've become everything to everyone else, and me—Sarah—I'm just along for the ride."

"You're never alone, Elle." Rach's voice was low and soothing. "And neither are you, Sarah. You have me and my excellent problem-solving skills. I've been told I'm somewhat of a nurturer too, but I have cats, so I'm not sure how accurate that is."

I let that one tear fall and kept the rest back. It was too beautiful a day to cry. This trip was too beautiful. My friends were too beautiful.

I'm going to be fine, I told myself. Maybe all I needed was a week away from work. Some perspective. And maybe a shot of tequila.

4

Now

We were enjoying our final day in Puerto Vallarta, and as Rach's itinerary showed, we were posted up by the main pool for the swim-up bar. Sarah had hardly mentioned her kids since James had everything handled, and we were three girls again with zero responsibilities and a high alcohol tolerance. Well, except for Sarah. She tried. We made friends with the bartender, a dark charismatic man whose smile could do some major damage. He took a liking to our group, and I swear he poured double shots of tequila as protocol.

I left the girls in the pool and went to our poolside cabana. I was anxious to check my phone to see if any emails had come through. It was getting a little weird to see zero unread emails. I prayed that maybe the cell phone gods would grant me service since I had been so well behaved this entire trip. I hadn't stayed up working late at all—well, except for the first night—but I had to make sure nothing had come up since the account was going to be finalized very soon.

To my surprise, my work email loaded, and I had an unread message flagged as important and multiple missed calls from Anna. My heart skipped a beat. Maybe this was it. Maybe this was the final application and signed paperwork needed from the Calloway account. This could be the big news we were all waiting for! At a second glance, I noticed it was from my boss, Mr. Landry, which seemed odd, but maybe he was just forwarding it on to me. Yes, I was going to get it, the big break!

Good afternoon, Elizabeth,

I hope you are enjoying yourself on vacation. As you know, the Calloway account comes up on July 1, and we need to get everything bound as soon as possible.

Even though you have been the contact for the Calloway account, Mr. Guidry, the owner of the Creekside Agency, has changed his mind about whom to work with in our company. He has developed a trust with Chris Johnson, who, might I add, has been available to him all week, and would like him to handle the Calloway account moving forward through completion. Therefore, Elizabeth, Chris will be taking over the account from here.

I hope you can understand that this is a team effort, and I truly appreciate all the work you have done to help our office win this account. Chris will be in touch with you shortly and would appreciate it if you could share your information with him so this can be bound seamlessly and as soon as possible.

We do not want to upset or delay Mr. Guidry, Mr. Calloway, or his business operations.

Best,

Don Landry

Branch Manager, McKinney and Smith Inc.

I shot up to a seated position in the cabana and felt the tequila start to rise in my throat. I couldn't breathe and my chest was getting tighter. My heart was pounding and my mind went blank. There was no way I'd read that correctly. There was no fucking way I'd lost the account to Chris Johnson.

I reread the email just to be certain. No, I'd read it correctly. My account was being stolen from me. Given to that son of a bitch who hadn't known a single detail of the account in our meeting. Everything went blurry, and rage consumed me. Fire and fury pulsed through my body. A shrill shriek escaped from my lungs, and everyone at the pool turned to stare.

"What the fuck just happened? Can they even do this?" I yelled at my phone with tears streaming down my hot face.

The short answer was yes, they could. And they had. Ethically, though? Probably not. I'd never seen this happen before, but if a customer wanted to work with a different broker, they did have that right. They would fill out a form and then move their business.

I couldn't help myself. I started bawling. Shamelessly, helplessly crying. My shrieks scared the couple next to me, and a manager was walking toward me. Somewhere deep down, I'd known things were too good to be true. How could I be on vacation and taking time off when I had things to take care of at work? I shouldn't have come. I shouldn't be here.

Rachel and Sarah heard me scream, because the next thing I knew, my two best friends were right next to me, hugging my shoulders and rubbing my back. I could feel the pool water dripping from them onto my arms and legs, but I couldn't care less. I was starting to go numb, and my breaths were becoming rapid and uncontrollable.

"Elle, oh my God, Elle, what happened?" Rach had a tight grip on my arms now, and she was trying to get me to speak. My voice was momentarily caught, trapped, just like me.

I snapped out of my rage-filled trance and felt the anger radiate down my arm to my fingers holding on to my phone. One more tight squeeze, and before I could change my mind, I slammed my iPhone onto the ground by their feet. I felt my shoulder start to throb the second I released it. I'm not certain, but it sounded like my screen had shattered upon impact. I didn't care.

Sarah picked it up and stood next to Rachel so they could both read the email through the cracked glass.

"That bastard!" Rach growled and hugged me tight to her.

I think I was in shock. Nothing made sense. I knew Rachel was holding me, but I hardly felt her. I could only feel my heart hammering against my rib cage. I could only hear each rapid beat keeping tempo with my chaotic thoughts. How did this happen?

"Can they do this, Elle?" Sarah was trying to analyze it, to make sense of it all. Typical Sarah.

All I could squeak out was a weak, "Yes." As the realization truly took root, I collapsed against Rachel's shoulder and convulsed in wrenching sobs.

Sarah went into mommy mode and rubbed my back again, murmuring soft, encouraging words. "It's all right, honey. It's going to be okay, Ellz. We're here," she hummed over and over.

Rachel stood up, face flushed with anger. She knew corporate America; she knew corporate politics. "What can I do? What do you need? Who do you need me to call?" She was pacing along the edge of the pool holding her elbows, knowing that there wasn't really anything to do. "I can call a lawyer. Elle, do you want a lawyer?" She held up her phone and scrolled. "I have the perfect guy, Elle. Just tell me and I'll make the call."

I stared at her, devastated, and let my tears fall.

5

Twelve years ago

never expected to see him again—my mystery dance partner. Nashville had thousands of people, and I was subletting an apartment in Murfreesboro, about an hour away on a good day. I despised myself for not getting his number or even his name. *Way to go, Elle.* I felt like there was a connection, some kind of spark, but maybe he was only meant to be my dance partner for one night and one night only. It wasn't love or anything—you don't fall in love with a stranger dancing in the middle of the street. That doesn't happen in real life.

My neighbor for the summer, Katie, was a student at Middle Tennessee State University, and her boyfriend, Harrison, was throwing a house party for the Fourth of July at his parents' house. I was excited to leave the office behind and have some fun. Katie and I arrived early with our overnight bags and trays of Chick-fil-A, because there's nothing drunk people love more than fried chicken. Harrison specifically requested the nugget trays and, in his words, "a shit ton of Chick-fil-A sauce."

Eventually, the front yard was full of lifted trucks, Solo cups, and college kids celebrating America. I knew Harrison's family was wealthy, but the house left me speechless. It was all that was left of a historic plantation estate—a grand white-brick mansion with Greek columns and oversized moldings on the inside *and* outside. The home radiated grandeur from the second you laid eyes on it. His parents were out of town, so the house was fair game for a celebration. Since we were staying the night, Katie placed her things in Harrison's room, and I was given a guest room upstairs past the grand staircase.

In a matter of hours, I had to squeeze by crowds of people to get anywhere. I knew before coming that a ton of people would be at the party because Harrison was in a fraternity. But what I didn't know was that on July 4, 2010, I'd find the other half to my heart.

The noise started to overwhelm me, and my throat began to tighten. Bodies were packed throughout the house, and sweat trickled down my chest thanks to the intense heat radiating throughout the rooms, as well as the humid Tennessee summer night. At this point, I was thankful for only wearing a bikini top and cutoff denim shorts. My American flag bandana was damp against my forehead, and the little hairs that fell out of my messy bun were stuck to the back of my neck. I looked for Katie, but she was nowhere to be seen among the ocean of people. I saw Harrison and hoped Katie was nearby. I pushed through the crowd and spotted an empty lounge chair by the pool. Some people I didn't recognize were playing chicken in the water, and a few others had a pool float holding a cooler full of ice and beer. After a deep breath of warm air tinged with a hint of firework smoke, I relaxed back into the chair's cushion. Finally, a little bit of space to myself. I opened my fresh beer and slowly lifted it to my lips, anticipating the refreshing liquid rolling down my throat. Before

I shut my eyes to savor my beer, I noticed him. My eyes widened and my hand froze before the can could touch my lips.

He stood across the pool in front of a row of loungers. A girl with a short red skirt and a white bikini top was kneeling on the chair with a strong hold on his arm. Was she flirting with him? Were they together? He lifted his beer to his lips and took a quick sip. I squeezed my thighs together as I watched his throat bob. I would never forget this man. His smile once made my knees shake. His voice once made my soul vibrate with need. God, I still had dreams of that night.

I knew that smile. He didn't see me at first, but I'd like to think he felt my stare, because after only a few moments he looked over and his eyes found mine. There they were, those amber eyes I dreamt about.

I noticed him excuse himself from the girl and peel her hands from his body. She sat back with her girlfriends, and as he walked away, another boy sat at the end of her chair. *Popular lady*, I thought. The corner of his mouth lifted. He knew who I was, and he didn't break my gaze as he walked over to my lounge chair. My heart squeezed tighter, and my brain left the building entirely. I didn't think I'd ever see him again. The butterflies in my stomach forced me to catch my breath. My pulse quickened and warmth spread throughout my lower body. I watched his every step. His every breath. I noticed the dimple on his left cheek and the way the American flag T-shirt stuck to his broad chest. As he got closer, I felt a subtle electricity in the air.

"Look who it is." His voice dipped low and sultry as he stopped in front of my chair. I lifted my head slightly to meet his sparkling gaze. "It's my mystery girl."

Um, excuse me, he said, "my mystery girl." Oh my God, I'm going to pass out. I held his stare and leaned up in the chair one slow vertebra at a time. I brought my legs onto the chair, crossed them, and angled my body toward him, neck arched delicately. His eyes dipped to my exposed throat—and possibly a little lower. Inside, I was freaking out, but on the outside, I kept my expression trained and coy.

"Why hello, mystery boy."

I saw his throat contract when he heard my voice, and his eyes darkened. He motioned me back with a wave of his hand, and when he had enough room, he sat on my chair, one leg tucked under, the other firmly on the ground. He extended one arm and leaned into it casually, looking sexy as hell. My eyes were drawn to his bare muscular arms. He noticed.

"What brings you to the party, mystery girl?" His words hummed through my thoughts.

"Free booze, of course." I shrugged and leaned back into the chair, away from his radiating electricity.

"Ah, yes. Very good reason." He scooted a little closer and turned to the side so that both of his legs hung off the chair. He reached across our pretend boundary, and while his hands moved for my legs, he looked at me, eyes questioning and silently asking for permission. With my nod, he took my legs and placed them across his thighs. *Thank God I shaved, thank God I shaved.*

"You know Harrison, then?" he asked casually, as if my legs across his lap was a normal occurrence. I wasn't sure how much more of this flirting my sanity could handle. His voice was going to make me do questionable things. It wasn't quite a drawl, but I swear there was a hint of New York in it. But he didn't look like a New Yorker, so his mysterious accent intrigued me.

"I met him today, actually," I said. His eyebrows lifted slightly in surprise. "I'm Katie's summer neighbor."

He nodded in understanding. "Oh, okay, Katie."

"You know her?" I asked quickly. Why did my body feel like it was on fire?

"Not really, no. He's just talked a lot about her. I know they're on-again, off-again"—he paused and took a breath—"and on-again, off-again . . ."

"I get it," I laughed. "I only met her this summer, and I know they broke up momentarily right after I arrived in town, but then by that Sunday they were back together. So I totally get it. I'm rooting for them, though." My cheeks were sore, but I couldn't stop smiling around him. His presence made my world lighter and my heart beat with real joy. The kind that makes your toes tingle and your eyes sparkle. The joy every woman deserves to feel at least once in her life. The joy of knowing that someone chose you in a roomful of maybes because you're not a maybe—you're the one.

Someone had set up a bonfire in the yard, and most of the crowd made their way from the house over to the gathering. I closed my eyes as his hands gently massaged my legs. I didn't know for sure, but I thought I could sense his eyes on me. *He's on my chair. He's holding my legs—no, massaging my legs. Stay cool, stay cool. Oh my God, this is heaven.*

"So, you said you're Katie's neighbor. Is this permanent?"

I opened my eyes and placed my hands behind my head, elbows wide. He shifted in his seat, and his eyes dipped again, noticing my tanned stomach with the bonfire's flames throwing shadows over my body. I'm sure he noticed every curve, every breath I took.

I knew what I was doing, and I loved teasing him. "I'm only here for the summer." He squeezed my calf, and a moan escaped my lips. *God, this man.* "I'm not from here. I'm interning in Brentwood and then heading back to Duke in a few weeks."

His eyebrows lifted. "Duke? Interesting, and you ended up in Brentwood?" His flirtatious voice made me ache.

"Well, technically, I'm in Murfreesboro by Katie, but I commute during the week. I'll tell you, though, traffic here is nothing like it is in New York. That's a living hell."

"Wait, I thought you were from North Carolina." He stopped massaging my calf and I actually whimpered. His warm hand rested on my shins.

"No, I'm going to school there, but I'm from New York. My grandparents raised me in Brooklyn, and I have a deep, probably unhealthy, love for visiting Central Park and pretending to live in one of the brownstones."

His laughter made my heart stutter. "Nice, I'd love to move to the Northeast one day. Who knows, maybe I'll get a brownstone." He winked as I chuckled. "I'm not from here either, though I'm sure my accent makes that hard to believe."

Now my eyebrows shot up. "You're not from here? I mean, I figured not Tennessee, honestly, because you're not as twangy."

His forehead crinkled and his smile spread across his face, reaching both eyes. "Twangy?"

I felt my cheeks get warm. "Yeah, you know. That Southern twang that most guys have here? You don't have it." He continued to stare at me with amusement glistening in his eyes. "Now, this sounds crazy as hell, but your accent reminds me of a New York accent. But, like, I know you aren't from New York."

"Yeah?" He chuckled. "What makes you think I'm not from New York?"

"Oh, you might not have a drawl, but you have something, and it's different. It's . . . I can't place it." My nose scrunched and my lips pursed together as I tried to think where he could be from.

"Well, you're right. I'm from a land far, far away. I prefer my cities surrounded by water." He used spirit fingers as he quoted a fairy tale, causing me to almost cackle.

I bit my tongue to hold it together and pretended to take a guess. I threw out the first city surrounded by water that I could think of. "Miami?"

His laughter echoed around the pool, and the girl from earlier glanced our way. I pretended to ignore her glare, and he never turned around to notice.

"I'll take that as a no?" His laughter was contagious.

"No, a little more west. You ever been to New Orleans?"

Oh my gosh, a NOLA boy.

"No, can't say that I have. What are you doing here, so far away from home?" I teased.

"I'm clerking for a judge in Nashville. That's how I know Harrison. He's clerking too. And NOLA is a fun time. You'd like it."

"You don't know me." I stuck my tongue out, and a giggle escaped my lips as he reached for my sides and tickled me.

"You're right." He released me and placed his hands back on my legs. "But I'd like to."

A bashful smile spread across my face. I couldn't believe this was happening; this was what happened in fairy tales. You randomly meet Prince Charming, then later he finds you and usually saves you. But I didn't need saving. Not today. Today, I needed to kiss this man. My body would revolt if I didn't feel his lips brush mine or his hand caress my skin. It might have been the alcohol talking, but I felt an invisible force, an invisible string pulling me toward him. I wanted to be closer.

Fireworks exploded in the sky and created a glow behind him. He turned his body, my legs still on his, and placed a hand on either side of me. He leaned in until his nose brushed mine. "May I?" he whispered in a husky voice.

I nudged his nose and smiled slightly, taking in the sandalwood and spice that surrounded me. "Yes," I whispered.

My lips barely brushed his. His right hand lifted to my face, cupped my cheek, and slowly pulled me in toward his sly smile. My eyes closed, my lips parted slightly, and then he was kissing me. It was slow at first, exploratory, but he pulled away. I ached for more. The absence of his lips on mine felt wrong. They felt cold even though it was a hot summer night. Our kiss had lasted only a few moments, but I noticed the hunger in his eyes as he sat back, breath deep and ragged.

Panting, I opened my eyes. "That was hot," I rasped.

He sat back, his wicked grin making me shake. I was certainly tipsy, but not drunk. I felt good, and that kiss, that kiss . . .

"If I do that again, if I touch you again out here, I won't be able to stop." He brushed his hand through his hair and looked down at the ground, shaking his head. When he lifted his eyes back to me, they were desperate and hungry.

Instead of talking, I stood and held out my hand. With an eyebrow quirked up, he placed his warm hand in mine. My fingers curled around his as he pressed himself up to stand in front of me.

"What are you doing?" he asked with his eyebrows pinched together.

"I want to get another beer, and I want to watch the fireworks. Will you join me?"

6

Now

Three days had gone by since the email that changed everything. Thank the universe I'd received it on the last day of vacation, because vacation ended the second I opened the message. From that point on, everything felt like it was over. Everything I'd worked so hard to achieve, everything I thought I wanted was gone. I had failed.

My years-long work addiction meant I had accumulated quite the gold mine of vacation hours, so I decided to cash some more in and postpone my return to work. I was still trying to process what had happened, what had been taken, and how I was supposed to move forward from here. For the past few days, I'd watched the ebb and flow of people on Bourbon Street, considered listening to a true crime podcast, and obsessively replayed all my life's decisions that led to this point on my couch, watching reruns of *The Office*. No matter how I looked at it, I had done everything right. I'd followed the formula that society and my grandparents had given me to become successful: exceptional grades, a college education, a big corporate job, and plenty of money. Where was my error? In this whole process, had I wronged somebody? God or gods? The universe? I guess, who's to say.

I was technically using my vacation hours to watch Michael Scott terrorize his Scranton branch, but also, I was preparing myself to see my boss, Mr. Landry, and my forever enemy, Chris Johnson. This wasn't a vacation by any stretch of the imagination; it was more like a torturous amount of time between the sun rising and setting that was filled with self-loathing, crying, a stuffy nose, and unadulterated rage taken out on a box of Oreos.

I tried to relax and prop my feet up on the wall by my kitchen. That's what yoga says you're supposed to do to calm down, right? Elevate your legs on a wall or something? I sat like that for a few minutes and tried to clear my head. The email kept sneaking into my thoughts, causing my head to throb. Every time I thought about the email, I'd get a migraine and a queasy stomach. The worst part was the betrayal and disrespect. I knew I was worth more than this. I didn't deserve to be treated like I could be replaced so easily or dismissed. That was what made me so upset—I was just another cog in the wheel, when this whole time I thought I was more. It only took one email and one man's decision to change everything. I was never in control.

Not for the first time since everything went sideways, I reached for my phone to call Grandma Di. I yearned for her comfort, for her reassurance and calm voice. As usual, I got as far as going to my favorites, tapping the home phone, and listening until the second ring before I remembered. I couldn't call her. She was gone. Gone, just like the life I had so meticulously planned out.

I let my arm fall to the side of my body, my old shattered cell phone still clutched in my hand because I didn't want to buy a new one yet. Slowly, I rolled myself up and let my back rest against the wall with my knees curled to my chest. The floor was unforgiving, and goose bumps covered my arms and legs, but I didn't try to move.

I let the grief and the rage wash over me. I don't know how long I cried, but my lungs ached from screaming, and my face was swollen with tear tracks staining my cheeks. I managed to shuffle to my bathroom and glance at myself in the mirror above my vanity. My eyes were a bright vivid green, and my unruly brown curls clung to my skin.

I could hear Jude's voice whisper in my ear from somewhere in my past: *Did anyone ever tell you that your eyes are the same color as emeralds? Especially when you cry, they're radiant.*

I closed my eyes, cupped cold water in my hands, and splashed my face. *Get yourself together. Get yourself together.* I was already annoyed with myself for crying, again. Crying meant a clogged nose, which meant difficulty breathing and an inevitable physical anxiety response. I could already feel my chest getting tight from not being able to take a deep breath. *You're okay. You're safe. You're okay.* That's what Tina, my godsend, my therapist, had taught me to say. She recommended affirmations and use of my senses to calm myself down. Breath work was useful most of the time too, but when you can't breathe to begin with—well, yeah.

I dried my face and walked slowly back to my bedroom. Against my better judgment, I made one more phone call. I knew I shouldn't have done it. I knew nothing good would come of this call. Future me was going to be very disappointed. I scrolled for his number, let my finger hover for only a second, and then hit dial. The phone rang once, twice, three times . . .

"Hello? Elle, is that you?" His voice was soft and husky, making my heart squeeze and my stomach tighten. I tried to articulate my thoughts, even a few words, but nothing came out other than a few muffled sobs. I heard the blankets shuffling.

"Elle, it's almost midnight by you. Are you okay?" His voice was becoming more alert, worried.

Shit. What am I doing?

Before I could apologize or make up an excuse and tell him I accidentally butt-dialed him, I heard someone else's light, groggy voice in the background.

"Jude, baby, who's Elle?"

7

As the flames of the bonfire smoldered and the crowds thinned, we lay together on a blanket we found and watched the stars. Most people were asleep throughout the house, some were still drinking by the pool, and others had called Ubers. While my head rested on his arm, he told me about his life in New Orleans. He wanted to be a lawyer, and it was just him and his mom. His dad died when he was younger, and he'd always wanted to travel. I told him about my grandparents and how I never really knew my parents because they'd left. He didn't feel like a stranger; he wasn't a stranger. He became something more that night. He listened to me and wanted to know me. He cared. My eyelids grew heavy, and the night went from humid and clammy to chilly and damp. He gently moved my head from his shoulder, stood up, and reached for my hand. Once it was nestled in his firm grip, he lifted me to my feet and pulled me into his body.

No one would understand. They'd think it was a one-night stand, some drunk girl fucking a boy she met at a summer party. But that wasn't true. Every decision was my own—every kiss, every touch. I allowed it because I wanted it. I led him into the house, tiptoed around the sleeping bodies that blocked our way, and guided him up the grand staircase. The stairs creaked with every step, but no one stirred. I opened the door to my guest bedroom, which thankfully wasn't occupied, and walked toward my bed. He let my hand fall and stood on the other side of the door.

"Are you sure?" He didn't move. His eyes were searching my face, telling me he wouldn't move unless I asked him to.

I stepped back into the hall, lifted onto my toes, and kissed the tip of his nose. "Yes."

He walked over the threshold, and before he came farther into the room, I turned at the bed and put my hand up. He jerked to a stop, not moving another inch.

"The door, we need to lock it. You never know," I said, and his shoulders relaxed and his lips curled up. He turned around to lock the door, and when he faced me again, I saw—no, felt—the hunger in his eyes. My body was fully awake, it called to his, and neither of us could ignore this pull. This magic.

He walked up until I was pressed against his firm, hard chest. He leaned down and brushed my lips with a light, delicate kiss. Before I opened my eyes, he lifted me into his arms and gently laid me down on the comforter. Eyes wide with delight, I ached for him. Heat continued to build within my core, and I wanted his body on mine. He slowly crawled onto the bed, the mattress sinking with every move of his hands, every shift of his knees. He stopped once, hovering over me. His warm golden eyes searched my face. I smiled and let a moan escape between my lips.

He leaned down so that his lips were by my ear. His hot breath sent tingles through my body. "I want you so fucking bad." His whisper caused goose bumps down my arms.

I whimpered; the tension felt torturous. He nibbled on the tip of my earlobe for only a second before moving his head down to kiss the side of my neck. My hips shifted in smooth circles, desperate for his touch. I wrapped my arms around his torso and lightly brushed my nails along his spine. He shivered and released a guttural groan. He worked his way back up to my ear, nibbled one more time.

"Tell me your name. Tell me so I can scream it as I come," he whispered.

"Fuck," I rasped.

He chuckled as his hands moved from my hips, up my ribs, all the way to my breasts. His fingers slid under my bikini top and gently teased my nipples.

"Elle. My name is Elle," I moaned.

His hands stopped and pulled away. He sat up on the bed and straddled my body between his powerful thighs.

"Jude." He smirked down at my flushed body. Then he grabbed the bottom of his shirt and lifted it over his head and threw it on the floor. Oh my God, this beautiful man. He leaned over to my other ear, and his breath made my spine arch as he whispered, "I want to hear you scream my name as I do unspeakable things to you, Elle."

My eyes closed and breath heavy, his name escaped my lips, barely a whisper. "Jude."

He moaned and moved his hands to push my bikini top over my chest. His kisses brushed my skin, slowly down my stomach, and then his fingers touched the button on my shorts.

"You're sure?" He gazed into my eyes, asking for permission one last time.

I reached down between our hands and undid the button myself. The hunger in his eyes was back, and my shorts were on the floor in a matter of seconds.

"But your shorts. You're still dressed," I said as he undid the side ties of my bikini bottoms with delicacy and focus.

"Ladies first, Elle Belle." I swear that his eyes were molten as my bikini bottoms ended up next to my shorts. He pulled me to the edge of the bed, and I couldn't help but laugh with giddy excitement as he left a trail of kisses up my left inner thigh and then my right. And then my mind went blank.

8

Now

Reality could only be avoided for so long, and I knew I had to get back to mine. I'd reached that part of the grief process where I was nothing but pure rage, and my anger hangover was having a disastrous effect on my well-being. The headaches were nonstop and all I could eat—when I remembered—were a few tortilla chips with cashew queso. There was no energy to cook, no energy to move my body, and no energy to be a human being. Most of the time, it felt much easier to exist than to live.

This was my last day before going back to work. It had been easy enough to take a few extra days after the vacation, but I couldn't sit on this resignation any longer. I didn't want to go back, but I didn't want to entertain this anxiety and darkness any longer. I needed to finish my resignation letter. Tonight.

I'd felt this way before. I'd been lost in darkness, angry and sad, confused and hopeless. I'd lost myself in a cycle of despair and anxiety right after Grandma Di passed. I remembered how that darkness had felt like an escape, how the world was too much, and every decision I made had felt like the wrong one. It almost killed me. It took a lot of time with my therapist and medication to get me through that season of my life. *I can't let that happen again. This ends now.*

♥

A few hours later, I texted Rachel and she agreed to video-chat with me while I read her my two weeks' notice. I thought about taking two weeks of vacation time, but I decided I'd rather have my vacation time cashed in on my last paycheck.

"You know," Rachel said as she finished the letter, "I really love the part about 'exploring new opportunities.' Even though I know you're super pissed, I wouldn't know it by the letter. Way to stay classy, Elle." She lifted her wineglass to the screen and gave me a virtual cheers. Turned out, even with my sizzling rage and copious amounts of red wine, I had written a solid two weeks' notice—professional and straight to the point.

"Tomorrow I'm going to turn it in to Mr. Landry. I just want to get it over with. I can't eat or sleep, and I feel like pure shit," I said after swirling my malbec. "Do you think he'll make me work the next two weeks?"

"I don't know. I mean, you're not going to work for the competition, are you?" she asked.

"No, I don't plan to stay in corporate, let alone insurance." I watched Rachel's wineglass stop halfway to her lips.

"Wait, what? I didn't realize you were leaving corporate entirely. Elle, it was just one bad company." Her eyebrows were pinched together and her tone was sharper, as if she was trying to understand something that made no sense at all. After another slow sip, she continued. "Well, to answer your question, I'm not sure. In my company, if someone is going to a competitor, they have to leave the office that day." The corner of her mouth tilted in an apologetic frown. "I wish I could tell you definitively what to expect, but I've never quit before."

Oof, that felt great. Does leaving make me a quitter?

"What are you going to do? Corporate is what you've always done. It's what you planned to do. What could you possibly want to do that isn't within corporate America? Even journalism jobs can be corporate. I mean, I'm sure I can get you a job here with the PR team. Why don't you try that? We could live so close to each other, finally!"

I let Rachel go on about all the people she could talk to, what positions I could apply for. She'd make sure it was a done deal, and I'd have a new job before I even quit my old one. I let the rich, fruity flavor of the malbec sit on my tongue.

How did I explain to someone who loved her corporate career that I just knew it wasn't the right path for me anymore? I think I'd known for a while. My body had known, and I hadn't listened.

The depression. The anxiety. The abhorrent mental health. It was all real. I was never taught there was another way to be successful. But I felt it. There had to be. Corporate wasn't for everyone, and I was confident that I was one of the unconventional ones.

The world might say, *Okay, they took an account away from you, big deal.* But that's just it, it was a huge deal. I was crushed. Corporate may be perceived differently depending on the person, but to me, I no longer wanted to sit at a desk from the strict hours of nine to five. I'd never been cutthroat or competitive. I didn't want to have a career that drained me or trapped me in a certain location. I wanted to be free. I wanted to be creative. I wanted to be unconventional.

9

Twelve years ago

He was still here. I glanced over my shoulder just to check that this was real and noticed his relaxed face and steady, soft breathing. His long eyelashes touched the top of his sculpted cheekbone, and I fought the urge to brush a tiny piece of hair off his smooth forehead.

I tried to get out of the creaky full-size bed, but his arm was draped heavily across my waist. Instead, I slowly turned over to face him, all the while trying not to wake him up. I slid my top leg between his powerful thighs and drew my hands up under my chin. Our noses barely touched as I leaned in toward his forehead. I smiled to myself and released a controlled exhale. His amber eyes softly fluttered open and found my peaceful gaze. A slow, drowsy grin spread across his face as he pulled me closer to his warm body and kissed the tip of my nose. He smelled of last night's bonfire and pine; my heart stammered with my next large inhale.

"Good morning, mystery girl." His raspy voice hummed through my chest.

"Hi," I whispered as I leaned in to kiss the tip of his nose.

"What time is it?" He twisted in the bed to stretch his back and reach for his phone. "Damn, it's eleven thirty." He brushed his hand down his face and yawned.

"Have somewhere to be? Big plans?" I teased and reached for his arm to wrap it back around my waist.

He dropped the phone on the nightstand and obliged.

A glimpse of his smile made my stomach flutter, and before I could say another word, he twisted and rolled on top of me, his strong arms framing my face. His smile was replaced with a smug grin, and my raucous laughter echoed in the large room.

"I do have big plans." He leaned down slowly and hovered right above my lips. I could feel my breath getting faster, my chest rising higher.

"Big plans?" Our lips brushed and I knew I was in trouble.

10

Now

The day I quit my job was the day I finally listened to myself. Not society, not my grandparents—me. I hadn't slept much in the days since my embarrassing call to Jude, and last night the hours had melted away until daylight bled through my curtains. Curled up in my down comforter, I rubbed my palms over my face and groaned. I couldn't believe I was about to quit my job. I slowly rolled out of bed and made my way to my closet. My body was sore and sluggish, but Rach and I had planned the perfect outfit to give me confidence and power. I stepped inside the closet and gazed upon my grandmother's bright white pantsuit. High-waisted with a wide leg, the pants were timeless and still on the dry-cleaning hanger from when my grandmother wore them last. I knew they would fit even though I'd never tried them on. My grandmother and I were the same size, and most of her clothes were home in my closet now. I never had to worry about a capsule wardrobe because my grandmother had given hers to me, and classic never went out of style.

Once I was ready to get dressed, I put the outfit on and stood in front of the mirror. I could have sworn Grandma stood right next to me, beaming. Her fitted blazer accentuated every contour of my body, and the trousers elongated my slender legs. To the side of my mirror were my shoes, every heel, boot, and flat. I knew which ones I wanted, though. Alone on the top shelf and safe in their dust bag sat my most prized pair of heels, my blue satin Manolos.

While driving to the office, I got a text from the girls. They asked me to text them after I left the office to fill them in on all the details. I planned on giving my two-weeks to Mr. Landry first thing. Then I assumed I'd pack my desk and leave. I wasn't really sure what happened after you quit a job; I'd never done it before.

Thankfully, I worked in downtown New Orleans, a quick trip from my French Quarter apartment. At eight a.m., I walked outside and was immediately smothered by the humidity of a Louisiana spring, almost summer. My feet began to swell in my heels, and my hair went from zero to frizzy in no more than three seconds. Instead of walking in the devastating humidity, I drove to our office and parked in our company's garage within the Poydras Center—a sleek angular building at the corner of Poydras and St. Charles. It used to be known as the Exxon Building, but by the time I started working with Mr. Landry, its name had changed.

Now, theoretically, I could have walked to work. However, I learned my lesson my first year when I tried to walk in heels with swollen feet. It was an absolute failure, and the blisters lasted for weeks. Before I opened my car door, I flipped down my mirror and pulled my Chanel red lipstick out of my purse. Once I applied the last piece of my outfit, my Taylor Swift–inspired bold red lip, I stepped out of my Jetta and tossed my keys in my purse.

You've got this, you've got this.

My stomach gurgled with anxiety, and I rubbed it gently. Quitting a job was definitely worse than test anxiety. I walked toward the elevator in the parking garage and kept repeating my mantra. *You've got this, you've got this.*

I stepped onto the elevator and hit the button for floor twelve. I held my elbows tightly as I tried not to bump into anyone else. I was surrounded by men and women playing the game of the daily hustle. My stomach turned when a woman in a blue blouse sprayed her citrusy perfume three times before getting on the elevator on floor three. She smiled and took a tight spot next to me and the doors. Behind me, a young guy with headphones was tapping his fingers on his leather portfolio. On the opposite side, next to the other set of buttons, was Chris Johnson. I wasn't sure if he noticed me when I walked on, but I didn't plan on bringing any attention to myself. He might be the last person I wanted to have a conversation with, though Mr. Landry was a close second.

The elevator went slowly, letting people off as it hit each floor. Blue blouse lady finally exited on the ninth floor, and headphones guy left on floor eleven.

Each ding was a reminder that I was getting closer and closer to releasing the tightness in my chest. It was going to be over soon. Chris never looked over at me, though the tension was thick and stuffy. By now, it was only us, so he had to have noticed it was me standing on the other side. He kept his eyes down, but his shoulders were rigid with a tense stance.

Ding. Floor twelve. Chris scurried off the elevator and turned in the direction of his office. He never looked back. I stepped out of the elevator in my blue satin Manolos, and even though I felt like Carrie Bradshaw, I channeled my inner Samantha Jones.

Chin lifted and shoulders back, I donned a smile and greeted my coworkers like normal. Anna, who'd been checking my emails while I was gone, looked up as I walked by and mouthed, *Are you okay?*

I gave her a quick wink and continued to my desk. I was repeating my resignation speech to myself as I walked past Mr. Landry's office and noticed he wasn't in yet. I smiled devilishly to myself, picturing his face as I gave him my resignation letter. He wouldn't be expecting me to quit. I had allowed him to treat me poorly over the years with no consequences. Sometimes he held my arm a little too long or talked down to me and said I was a good girl whenever I consented to take on more responsibilities that belonged to others in the office. I never wanted to notice it. I only ever wanted to keep climbing the ladder. Now, I wanted to burn it all down.

About an hour later, I walked up to Mr. Landry's office to check and see if he had arrived. Mr. Landry liked to arrive after everyone else, typically around nine a.m., so he was still settling into his office when I knocked on the heavy glass door. He furrowed his brow and rolled his eyes as he sighed and waved me into his office.

I took a quick breath and stepped over the threshold. "Excuse me, Mr. Landry. Do you have a minute?" I kept my tone calm and even, but I could feel my anxiety tingling throughout my body. The back of my neck was starting to sweat.

"Sure, Elle. But make it quick, I have a call with Mr. Calloway in fifteen minutes." He pulled his chair out from his desk and fell into it with an audible thud. He scratched his nose, took a deep breath, and leaned forward to listen.

I was standing right in front of his desk, trying not to shift my weight from one foot to the other like I usually did when I was nervous. My legs felt heavy and my tongue was momentarily paralyzed. Mr. Landry impatiently motioned for me to continue.

I clenched my teeth and tried to ignore the headache that was emerging with a fury. The letter was in my hand, burning to be submitted. Before he realized what I was doing and why I'd asked to meet with him, I handed him my letter of resignation. I almost forgot to breathe as his eyes scanned each carefully crafted line. I folded my hands neatly in front of my waist and forced my face to remain neutral. I was right about his reaction. I knew when he got to the part where I officially quit because his mouth dropped slightly and his nose crinkled in disgust. His shock was delicious.

"This is outrageous! You can't leave this office, Elle. You know this will put us behind next month—hell, the rest of the year—and with the Calloway account bound, who will help manage it?" Spit dripped from the corner of his mouth, and the vein on his forehead was pulsing.

In all my time at the office, I'd never seen him this angry. The one time our summer intern accidentally erased six months of files was a contender, but this took the cake. We'd been able to recover the deleted files, but Mr. Landry wouldn't be able to recover me. His anger was radiating in the room; my heart was pounding against my ribs, and my palms were getting sweaty. Confrontation usually sets off my fight-or-flight, and typically I prefer flight. I couldn't get away, though. I had to follow this through and stay composed.

"Sir, you said that the Calloway account is Chris's now. I hope that his team can manage the organization and daily tasks associated with it efficiently enough. Even if I stayed, I wouldn't pull my team aside to handle another person's book of business." I stood up a little taller and lifted my chin. My adrenaline was pulsing, and I waited as Mr. Landry grasped for any form of logic, anything to guilt me into staying.

He waved his hands and backpedaled. "Yes, yes, well, we were hoping you would be able to handle the organization and day-to-day once it was bound. You are so organized, Elle. We need your help keeping the others organized and on track. We need you. Remember how you helped everyone organize their emails and work more efficiently?" He looked up hopefully. His eyes were sliding back and forth, watching for any flicker of weakness on my face.

"Mr. Landry, with all due respect, I am not an assistant, and helping other people organize their accounts is not my responsibility." My voice echoed in my ears. I felt far away, floating, watching myself stand up to the man who'd made me question my very self-worth.

"Please accept my two weeks' notice." I gave him a stern look of finality.

He was still scanning me, thinking. He absentmindedly brushed his chin and then lifted his other hand. "Wait, wait. Elle, what if we gave you more money? We can promote you. How about vice president? How does that sound? Whatever it takes to make you stay, just write down a number and show me."

I wasn't sure if I should laugh or scream. He wasn't listening and I was getting annoyed. I was done with not being taken seriously.

"No, thank you, Mr. Landry." I gave him a fake grin and changed my voice to a lower, calmer pitch. "I appreciate your offer but will not be staying."

He sat back in his leather chair and folded his hands on his chest. "In that case, Elle, I need to know if you will be staying in the industry. What are your plans once you leave us?" His eyes had gone dark, his tone hard and cruel. A shiver went down my spine as he glared at me.

"I'm not sure, Mr. Landry." I smiled again, knowing it agitated him. He couldn't read me.

His mustache twitched and he sat up taller with authority. "Well, even so. I'm afraid we will not be able to keep you on for the two weeks. As a matter of company policy, we must protect our proprietary information in case you were to stay in the industry."

"I understand, sir." I nodded in agreement.

"We will pay you for your two weeks, but you must leave. Now. Please pack up your things." He pointed to the door and then quickly turned his chair to face his computer screen and began jabbing the keys on his keyboard.

When he looked away, I let my mask slip, and my lip curled in annoyance. The fact of the matter was that I had nothing to be annoyed about anymore. This man had just given me freedom, and paid freedom at that.

Don't let anyone know what you're thinking. Grandpa's advice drifted through my mind like a ghost haunting my memories.

I replaced my mask and took a calm breath. Lips pressed thin, I gazed directly at the side of Mr. Landry's balding head. "Absolutely, Mr. Landry. I completely understand."

11

Twelve years ago

Jude's love was raw and passionate. I could never get enough of his kisses, and he could never get enough of mine. I knew it was going to end; my internship was going to end. My gut told me this was too good to be true, and long distance never worked. But my heart told me the present with Jude was worth every tear that would inevitably come.

I stole kisses when he took me kayaking in the Cumberland River. He stole my heart when we danced in his driveway under the moonlight.

Jude drove me to the airport in his roommate's truck the week after my internship ended. I had to get back to Duke to prepare for my senior year. The drive was silent, my heart breaking while my mind tried to find a solution. When we arrived at the terminal, he noticed the tears rolling down my cheek and reached for my hand.

"I know you don't believe in it, but we can do long distance, Elle. I can do it with you."

I took his hand and rested my cheek in his open palm. I looked at him with sad eyes, my tears silently flowing while I memorized his strong jaw and every inch of his face.

"Elle, seriously, I know we didn't talk much about this—us, our future—but I believe we can do it. We can make this work." The desperation in his voice made my stomach clench.

I closed my eyes and leaned more into his palm. "Jude, you're about to start at that firm in New Orleans. I don't want to distract you; I don't want you to feel trapped waiting." He pulled his hand away and put it back on the steering wheel.

"I won't feel trapped!" His voice grew louder.

"You don't know that. I'm still in college, Jude. This summer, it was fun, but you don't want to be with a college girl." I tried to stay calm and wiped my tears with the Duke sweatshirt I was wearing.

"You don't get to tell me what I want, Elle. Because what I really want is to be with you." He pinched the bridge of his nose, and his voice cracked as he tried to continue. "This is something, Elle. You know it. I know you do." His eyes were pleading for me to agree.

"Jude, it's not fair to make you wait for me."

"You're not making me do anything."

"Don't give up your freedom and the chance for love with someone else because you think we have something. Jude, I can't wait. I don't even know where I'll be after graduation. Long distance isn't a long-term solution. I don't want to do long distance and restrict my career options after graduation."

"So it's not me you're concerned about, it's you. You, Elle Watson, don't want to wait for me." His eyes were glazed with hurt, and tears streamed down his face.

"Elle, I want to come to your graduation in May and cheer as my girl walks across the stage. I want to be the one you call with the news of your first job offer. I want to help you move into your first apartment after college. I want to wait. For you."

I looked away and out the window. I didn't want to say goodbye. I didn't want to walk away. I didn't want to miss out on the possibility of a life with him. But I had to.

"It was just a fling. You'll forget me." My words were flat and unemotional. I had to end this. Bile rose in my throat as the words echoed in my head.

His body flinched and hurt clouded his eyes. "A fling?" he rasped.

The lie felt acidic in my mouth. Two weeks with him felt like we'd known each other for years. I'd shared my most intimate stories with him while we lay under the stars in the bed of his roommate's truck, and he'd told me about his over mimosas and pancakes. He took care of me when I got stung by a wasp, and I constantly reminded him to wear sunscreen. My favorite memories, the ones that made me smile and giggle to myself, were the ones where we'd danced in the kitchen while cooking dinner or in the living room just because.

"We only just met, Jude. Two weeks is nothing." I was horrible. "If I was done with school, if we both had our careers situated, this might have worked. This just isn't the right time." I wanted to smack myself in the mouth.

He stared at me, his expression dumbfounded. "Elle, no. I—"

I cut him off before he could finish his sentence. I knew I was close to breaking him, but he was closer to convincing me of this dream of *us*. "Jude, I . . . I can't." I unbuckled my seat belt and grabbed my purse. "Goodbye, Jude." My heart hammered in my chest, and my throat tightened. Everything felt wrong as I opened the car door.

He jumped out of the car and ran to the trunk.

"I have to go," I whispered, staring into his eyes. I turned away to open the trunk, but he grabbed my wrist and twirled me into him. I felt his heart pounding, fast and rhythmic. He leaned his forehead against mine. So intimate. So perfect. His hands held mine to his face, cupping his cheeks.

"Please," he whispered back.

Eyes closed, I breathed in the sandalwood and spice from his cologne. When I opened my eyes, his glassy amber eyes held my stare. I leaned in slow and deliberate. He closed the distance. Our teeth clicked as he kissed me deep and hard. This was goodbye. Breathless, I pulled back and licked the tears from the side of my mouth before biting down on my bottom lip. I didn't want to go. I pulled his head a little closer and whispered into his ear, "Goodbye, Jude."

I discovered my first love that summer but didn't realize it, no. I didn't admit it until it was all over.

12

Now

went straight home after leaving Mr. Landry's office. I called the girls as promised, and after our three-hour conversation, Rachel texted me.

Rach: I'm coming.

Me: WTF, when?

Rach: Tonight

Me: Shit, okay, you're sure? I think I'm okay. I can't really explain it, but I feel free, ya know?

Rach: I know you're okay. You're strong as hell, Ellz. I'm just a little worried about you, you just changed your life in a matter of minutes this morning. I want to be there for you and support you, even if it's watching Sex and the City from episode one or Gilmore Girls after

Rory goes back to Yale. I guess what I'm saying is you don't have to be alone.

ME: Fiiiine. But my house is a mess, and you'll see everything is totally and completely fine. Pizza or Chinese??

RACH: Is that even a question? Shrimp fried rice, spring rolls, gyoza. Get the goods.

ME: You got it! Keep me posted on your flight info so I can come get you, k? xo

RACH: Definitely. I'll book in the next few minutes and send you the itinerary. xo

Rach booked the next flight out on Southwest. Ever since the pandemic started, her boss had been more lenient with her working remotely, so I wasn't surprised she grabbed her laptop and found a last-minute flight to New Orleans.

In college, if one of us had a shit show of a situation, the other was there. One time, a guy and I broke up the day before Valentine's Day, so she showed up with the *Sex and the City* DVD collection and a pint of ice cream. Sarah joined us later, around episode five, because of an art project she had to turn in to her professor. I knew I wasn't alone, but when my best friends lived states away, loneliness crept into my mind more often than I'd like to admit. I didn't expect either of them to come to New Orleans after I quit, but when Rach sent me her itinerary, I felt a glimmer of hope that everything would be okay. Sarah couldn't leave the kids since James was on a work trip, but she'd be with us in spirit.

♥

Rachel's flight came into New Orleans around seven thirty, and I was waiting at arrivals in joggers and my favorite oversized Taylor Swift T-shirt.

As soon as she walked out of the airport and saw me waiting by the car, she jumped and squealed in delight. She ran over to me, dropped her backpack, and threw her arms around my neck.

"Holy shit, you look like hell." She squeezed a little tighter, then let go.

"What? It's comfortable." I saw her exaggerated eye roll as I reached for her bag. She was right, though. This outfit wasn't my usual business casual and might have qualified for a midlife crisis.

The ride home was quick and easy on I-10. We pulled into my building's secured parking only twenty minutes later, doing our best not to hit any wandering Bourbon Street pedestrians. The music was already echoing through the French Quarter, and obnoxious yelling irked my overstimulated mind.

Rach followed me through my front door and dropped her bag in the entryway as she lifted her chin to gaze at my fourteen-foot ceilings and oversized crown molding. The living room was separated from my bedroom with enormous double doors, and my kitchen was tucked neatly in a corner, next to my back porch.

"Elle, I know for years you've talked about leaving this place, but damn, I love your apartment. It's a Monday night, and look how packed Bourbon was as we drove up."

I glanced at my floor-to-ceiling windows, which opened onto my balcony overlooking Conti and Bourbon Streets. "Yeah, I guess." I shrugged nonchalantly. "I do love my high ceilings."

"You live in the French Quarter, and all you can say is I love my high ceilings? Jesus, Elle." She shook her head as she picked up her bag and walked through the doorway to my bedroom suite. She tossed her bag onto the left side of the bed and kicked off her shoes.

"You know, I . . ." She trailed off as she turned around and noticed I was silently sobbing in the living room, staring outside at the empty balcony. Only my ferns were enjoying the view the French Quarter had to offer.

"Whoa, Elle. Wait, what's happened?" She scurried over to my side and lightly put her hand on my forearm. "Well, I mean other than the obvious, of course." She chuckled and squeezed my arm gently.

I looked up, trying not to cry, but I couldn't stop the tears from falling. Frustrated, I used my fist to wipe my face and snuffled. "I just hate this place, Rach. I just fucking hate it here." I opened my arms and sobbed. "The humidity, the memories, everything." I stopped to wipe my cheeks again, this time with my sleeve. "I'm suffocating here, Rach. And I don't know what I'm doing. I was so confident—I mean, I am confident that quitting was the best thing."

She grasped my hands and held them firmly. "No, it definitely was, I promise."

"Then why do I feel so empty? I was fine. Everything was fine after I left. And now, it's like the realization is hitting me and I can't breathe." I gasped for air, and Rach guided me to the couch to sit down with my head between my knees.

"Deep breaths, Elle. Deep breaths." She placed a hand on my back and rubbed in slow circles.

"I . . . I don't know. I just feel so many things right now. I can't process. I failed, Rach. I fucking failed." I was being crushed with emotion, and I began to breathe faster and heavier.

"Elle, you did not fail. Listen to me. Breathe. You need to breathe. I'm right here. You did not fail, you hear me? Elle, tell me you hear me." She shook my arm until I looked up at her.

"I hear you," I rasped through sobs. Embarrassed, I tried to pull myself together. "Okay, okay, I'm okay." I sat up slowly so as not to get dizzy and lifted my T-shirt to wipe my face. I closed my eyes and took a deep, full breath. When I opened my eyes, Rach was still next to me, holding my hand.

Her eyes scanned my face, and she released a soft sigh.

"Sorry, that was dramatic." I laughed half-heartedly as I kept wiping my face with my damp shirt.

Even if Rach didn't see it, I still believed I'd failed. The feeling would probably ebb and flow, but I knew I'd have to work extra hard with Tina to resolve this feeling of inadequacy.

"You know," I said as Rach crossed her legs on the couch, "my therapist asked me to explore what I thought success was at our last session. Deep, right?"

Rach raised her eyebrows and tilted her head. "Hmm, so that's where the question came from on the trip. Have you figured out what you think it is?"

My breathing was starting to normalize. I'd given the idea of success some thought since my session with Tina. The corners of my mouth lifted into a modest smile.

"Freedom," I whispered softly with my eyes closed.

Rach nodded slowly, but before she could reply, a knock echoed throughout the apartment. My eyes shot open. I wiped my face one more time and hopped off the couch.

"Chinese food. You know, the goods." I winked at Rach, whose confused stare transformed into excited beaming.

"Gyoza and fried rice, here we come!" She launched herself off the couch and beat me to the door.

13

Twelve years ago

Jude and I tried to keep in touch, but life got in the way. A text every day turned into every few days into once a week into *I'm not sure when I'll hear from him again.* Sarah and I studied abroad together in Oxford during the fall semester of our senior year. I was working on writing courses, and she was studying in Oxford's fine arts program.

I'd always had a strong desire to go to the United Kingdom, and this was my first opportunity. It was probably all those Harry Potter and Jane Austen books I read as a child. My first day in an Oxford classroom was like living in a fantasy world. The high ceilings and ornate architecture embodied the history that lived within the walls and reminded me of Hogwarts. The atmosphere was full of academic tradition, as well as the faint aroma of aged wood. Bookshelves lined the back wall of my classroom, and footsteps echoed off the ancient stone floor.

After class, I emailed Jude a picture of the building and typed "Oxford."

I should have left him alone. I just couldn't resist; I wanted to share the beauty with him.

He never responded.

14

Now

After some more fried rice, two episodes of *Sex and the City*, and one episode of *Gilmore Girls*, Rachel turned to me.

"So, I was thinking about what you said before. You know, about freedom?"

I nodded but kept one eye on the television.

"Right, well, I know that you're unhappy here, but sidenote, can we agree you have an amazing apartment? That's totally a positive, right?"

I moved my head from side to side and hummed my agreement.

"Okay, so on the bright side, then, what does your freedom look like? What's next?"

I pursed my lips and threw my head back onto the couch, looking at the ceiling. "Hmm, well, I don't know entirely." I sat back up and smirked at her. "But I do know that my lease ends soon."

"Hey, I said positives," she teased.

"That is a positive!" I argued, then grinned behind my wineglass.

"Well, if it's ending, why don't you leave? Think about it—you can go anywhere, be anything, do anything. Positives. What do you want to do? Who do you want to be?"

I thought about what she said, and it was true. Getting out of here had always been my end goal, but I'd never had enough courage to leave my job before. I knew money wasn't going to be an issue for a little while. I was a conscious saver, my grandparents had left me a healthy inheritance, and though I never took advantage of it, they'd also left me a condo in Boston. It was a historic brownstone and our little piece of Back Bay.

"You think?" I asked. "Like, Eat, Pray, Love kinda shit? Leave, start over, and figure out what makes me happy?" I laughed into my wineglass.

She rolled her eyes. "Not quite. I don't see you making it very long in India."

"Me either." I grinned. "It's too crowded and I enjoy a hamburger every now and then."

"Elle, where is your happy place? Did you ever have one?" she asked.

I immediately thought of the Boston condo and of Jude. Jude was my happy place, my safe place.

"I think this is your moment. You don't have children; you don't have a boyfriend." She wiggled her eyebrows and bumped her shoulder into mine.

"Whoa, whoa, watch the wine, lady." I moved my glass out of the way. "It's kinda hard to find a boyfriend when you never leave the office." I rolled my eyes and exhaled loudly as I flopped back onto the couch.

"True, true. But now you're done with the office. No more corporate, isn't that what you said? You aren't tied to Louisiana. Where are we going?" Her cheeks were flushed and her words slightly slurred.

Jude was gone. He'd left to follow his career and was in New York City with a new woman who called him *baby*. I didn't have authentic friends here. They were all coworkers, and many of us were in different parts of our lives. Most of the women had young children, and it was difficult to find common ground or respect with the men. For the rest of the evening, Rach and I envisioned what my new life could look like.

"Okay, okay, how about I'm an influencer in Los Angeles?" I pursed my lips and made a duck face. "I would love to go to all of those red-carpet events. Maybe I'll meet Henry Cavill and live happily ever after!" I threw my arms open and flung myself into the back of my couch, making kissy noises.

Rach cackled. "Stop! Wait, how about you're a dog walker in Miami?"

I snorted my wine through my nose. "Fuck!" I laughed as the wine dribbled down my chin. "No. I want to be a Gilmore Girl, not a Golden Girl!"

"How about a small-town newspaper reporter? Maybe we can find you a real-life Stars Hollow!"

Now this conversation was getting ridiculous. "Find me a Logan Huntzberger and I'm there."

She tilted her head and quirked her lips. "No Jess? I always thought you'd be team Jess since you love writing so much."

I shook my head and let a mischievous grin spread across my face. "Nope, always team Logan. I felt bad that he was pressured to work in the family business and how his dad was so controlling of his future. He never really had a say in his life, and it was sad. I'm a sucker for emotionally damaged men."

"Because of course you are." She lifted her glass to mine, and a soft clink filled our silence.

"You know, I've always wanted to live somewhere with four seasons again. I miss that about New York City."

"Why don't you go back to New York, then?"

"You know why." I lifted an eyebrow and stared at her.

"No, seriously, I don't. Oh. Oh, wait." Realization dawned on her face, and she nodded in understanding. "That's right. Jude went to New York. Have you talked to him lately? Is he still there?"

I hadn't told the girls about my embarrassing call to him over the weekend and planned to keep it that way. "No, not too recently. He texted me about his mother a few weeks ago before that meeting, but that's it." I shrugged and looked away, back to the TV. Rory was having dinner with her grandparents, and Logan was with her.

"I've been thinking about a condo my grandparents left me in Boston."

Rach stopped her wineglass halfway to her lips. "Oh, Boston? I didn't know your family had a condo there."

"Yeah, Grandma left it to me in her will. It's the top unit in an old brownstone on Commonwealth. We used to stay there for holidays when I was a kid."

"Shut up. Your family owns a condo in Boston? What the hell are you still doing here? Why did you never mention it?"

"Trust me, I've asked myself that same question. And I don't know, I guess I never really thought about it. It's been occupied by a tenant for years. I never considered using it myself, but I got a letter last month from the tenant, an adorable elderly lady, and she's moving in with her daughter, so it's going to be available."

"So, wait." Rachel readjusted in her seat and took a quick sip of her wine. "Are you telling me that you have a rental property in Boston and you were still working your ass off here?"

I shrugged. "You remember when I got the call about Grandma Di?" I asked with an ache in my heart.

"Yeah, I remember." Rach furrowed her brow, and her sympathetic expression made me look away.

We were both remembering how well I'd handled that phone call. The center of my world was taken away, and Jude had already left for NYC.

"Well, only a few days before, she had been talking to me about visiting the condo again and spending a weekend in Boston together. I thought it was odd, because of course we were renting it out, but I still told her I was too busy and couldn't take off from work. Maybe it was some weird memory trick or death premonition for her to want to go back to Boston. She used to tell me how much she loved it there."

"Oh, Elle, I'm so sorry." She placed her hand on my forearm and squeezed.

"Yeah, so the Boston condo wasn't something I wanted to remember . . . yet. Those holidays and trips were full of great memories, but I don't know, it still hurts. And to know it was one of the last things we talked about and then I was too busy to even visit her at home, I still feel guilty."

She nodded in understanding and picked up her wineglass. "To Grandma Di and Grandpa Will."

I looked up with watery eyes. Then I lifted my glass to hers. With a shaky voice, I toasted, "To Grandma Di and Grandpa Will."

I closed my eyes and took a long, deep breath. "I want to remember now. I want to feel snowflakes land on my tongue." I opened my eyes and smiled to myself as memories floated to the surface. "I want to go to Revere Beach again and feel summer waves crash on my thighs. I want to smell spring flowers blooming in a garden and feel the crisp fall air tinged with pumpkin and spice." I looked over and met Rachel's warm gaze. "Am I crazy?"

Her eyes were gentle. "No. Not at all. That all sounds absolutely dreamy."

"I think so too." I smiled and brought my glass back to my lips.

15

Twelve years ago

Of all the places Sarah and I traveled to that semester, London became my favorite memory. We were in a queue for a popular Indian restaurant in Shoreditch, but after waiting in line for more than two hours, we decided to try our luck elsewhere. We swiped our Oyster cards and got on a tube to Piccadilly Circus.

"Please mind the gap," the operator echoed as we disembarked.

It was chilly, and even though Sarah and I had on matching tan overcoats, the brisk wind gave me a shiver. Sarah had adventure in her eyes as she grabbed my hand and jogged up the stairs with me in tow.

It was a clear, cold night once we exited the tube station. We couldn't see the stars because of all the light, but the city was alive. We were alive. It felt like Times Square except better—it was British.

An advertisement popped on a screen in the area. *Wicked* was playing at the Apollo Victoria Theatre.

"Oh my God, I've always wanted to see that on Broadway!" Sarah squeezed my arm and pointed to the advertisement.

"You know, I read that you can get discount tickets for shows. There's like a booth or something." I looked around to see if I could find the mysterious booth.

"Seriously? That's perfect, because judging by that sign, we may be a little short on cash for the regular price." She laughed. I glanced up and noticed the price the next time the advertisement flashed by. We couldn't afford seventy-five pounds per ticket.

After talking to a handful of passersby, we found out that the booth we were looking for was in Leicester Square. Once we had our tickets, we rushed to the Apollo Victoria Theatre for the beginning of the show. With fifteen minutes left to spare, we stood outside the theater for a moment to take in the night. Sarah grabbed my hand and held it firmly in hers. Then she placed her head on my shoulder.

"Isn't this incredible, Elle? Can you believe we are in London together and get to do this?"

I leaned my head against hers. "I mean, I should believe it. We are here. But yeah, it's unreal. I wish Rach was here with us."

"Me too." Sarah pulled out her digital camera from her tan overcoat and told me to get into the frame. She held the camera up in front of our faces and blindly snapped the picture. "There, now we can show her and always be able to look back on this with a smile." She grinned at me and put the camera back into her pocket.

We made it to our seats just in time for the play to begin.

16

Now

Thirty hours in the car and an excessive amount of Starbucks later, I made it to Boston in the heat of summer. I'd had a few months to process all of the changes in my life, and I could honestly say September in Boston beats September in New Orleans. I hadn't been to the condo since my grandmother's death, and the first step over the threshold felt like a punch to the stomach. I cried for most of the first day and managed to eat some popcorn while watching Disney+ on my iPhone. On my second day in the city, I picked myself up and began moving my furniture around the condo. I ordered pizza, hung artwork, and scrolled through the Pottery Barn website for an unspeakable number of hours. I told myself it was worth it, though, when my new bookshelves arrived, along with my muted gold curtains and oversized wool area rug. Yep, totally worth it.

While cleaning out the closet, I found a metal box on the very top shelf pushed all the way against the wall. My tenant had been a shorter woman, so there was no way she would have noticed this. I pulled the box down and stepped off the stool to see what was inside. I never could have imagined the treasure I found—a box of letters!

> *My Dearest Willie,*
>
> *I miss you. I hope the floor was exhilarating this week. You'll be away from the stock exchange and back here in just three weeks, my love. I can't wait any longer to tell you, I'm writing because I have the most fantastic news.*
>
> *Remember that writing competition I entered for fun? The Literary Times Challenge? I heard back! My dear, I won! They told me that I won $1,000 and an opportunity to work with a publisher. The very one that works with Margaret Atwood. Oh, Willie, I'm so excited!*
>
> *I talked to my parents, and they weren't altogether thrilled.*
>
> *They still believe my writing is a waste of time. A woman's job is in the kitchen or with her husband, they said. My goodness, you know how that angers me.*
>
> *I hope you will be proud, Willie. I love you and can't wait to be in your arms again.*
>
> *Love,*
>
> *Your Sweet D*

There was one other letter behind the first. The rest of the stack was tied together. I shuffled the pages with tears in my eyes and read some more.

My Sweetest D,

I am extraordinarily proud of you. I never doubted your talent. The floor is busy, as always. In fact, my love, I have some news of my own. They are promoting me! We can finally live together here now that we can afford it. Dearest, come live with me here in New York. I already have a realtor looking for our new home, my bonus was very generous, and I promise that our lives are going to change for the best. Say you'll come live with me here?

In fact, we can finally start a family, and you'll never have to work, I swear it. No need to write your books and worry about your next paycheck or whether you can afford that fur coat I've seen you ogling at Bloomingdale's. I'll have it all taken care of.

Diana, I'm so thrilled to live my life with you. No more letters back and forth. We will finally truly begin our married life together, no more living apart. I'll be up this weekend, in fact, to help make arrangements.

All my love,

Willie

My eyes traced every loop and curve of their handwriting. She gave it all up. For him. I knew the ending. I was part of the story. But to hold the letter that had changed my grandmother's life—it was surreal. I took the letters with me to the living room, where I still had boxes to unpack. I opened the one labeled *Pic Frames* and found an empty eight-by-ten I'd packed from T.J. Maxx. I put my grandmother's letter in first and my grandfather's behind it. I don't know why, but I felt like this was important, and I wanted to keep this part of Grandma Di with me.

♥

One morning I was sitting in my favorite part of the condo, my balcony. Well, that and the exposed brick wall in the living room. I closed my eyes and inhaled the fresh morning air. Still nervous it wasn't real, I slowly opened my eyes and sighed with relief when Comm Ave was still four stories below me. I held my coffee up to my lips and enjoyed a long, sinful sip while bright leaves fluttered to the ground.

I was about to go back inside with my coffee and get ready for a yoga class, but before I looked away, I noticed the mailman park and head toward my building. Always excited for mail, I placed my coffee on the counter, put on my sandals, and went downstairs to greet him. He noticed me walking up and turned to face me with a bright smile. He gave me a wink and held out a small square package.

"This one's for you, Ms. Watson. Looks like someone likes to doodle." He chuckled as I took the parcel from his ink-stained hands. I smiled back and flipped the package around. It had *Fragile* written on it in permanent marker and then a few scribbly scenes of suns, rainbows, and a bird—I think—maybe a dog. *Sarah*.

"Thanks for this," I said, hugging it tightly to my chest. "You always bring the best mail."

He blushed.

"Have a great rest of your day. I really appreciate you."

He smiled gently and gave me a nod. Then he was back to sorting the mail and humming to himself.

I took the stairs back up, and once I shut the door, I sat on the couch with Sarah's present. The package was light and covered in *Priority* tape. It took me a whole three minutes to rip through the tape and bubble wrap and pull out a square framed canvas. My heart skipped the tiniest beat as I stared at the beautiful small painting Sarah had created for me. A card fell on the couch next to me, so I picked it up and read.

Dear Elle,

For your new home. I'm so proud of you, and I think your walls should be filled with happiness. Here's a happy memory that I cherish every single day.

Love you!

—S

I brushed my finger across the canvas. Two girls were holding hands. They wore long tan overcoats, and the blonde had her head resting on the brunette's shoulder. They—we—were standing in front of the Apollo Victoria Theatre in London. She'd even remembered it was *Wicked*.

♥

After yoga, I grabbed a quick bite from a nearby sushi restaurant for lunch, but as I stood in front of my refrigerator hours later, I realized how pathetic it looked. One shelf had a carton of eggs, old almond milk, and ketchup. Without a doubt, my grandmother would have given me so much grief had she seen it.

Back on the couch with my computer heating up my lap, I decided to go on a mission to the grocery store. I scanned over some recipes from accounts on social media and made a quick grocery list on my phone. I went into my room and grabbed the closest T-shirt and a pair of leggings because there was no need to look cute. Nothing exciting ever happened at the grocery store. Next, I reached for my headphones, slipped on some white sneakers, and hurried out of the condo.

When I arrived, the produce section was packed. Granted it was five p.m., and my fault for coming at such a busy time, but damn, I couldn't even see the romaine lettuce. Apparently, everyone in Boston needed lettuce this evening.

Out of the corner of my eye, I noticed someone standing to the right of me, and when I turned my head, I saw piercing blue eyes staring back. A flush of heat rose to my cheeks, and I quickly decided to look at the avocados on my left.

I looked back up when the stranger walked past me to pick out a bunch of kale. As he walked away, the smell of clean cotton and Christmas lingered in the air. This man, this stranger, was the epitome of gorgeous. His five-o'clock shadow lined his firm jaw, and his thick espresso-brown hair was well styled with a slight wave. My knees betrayed me just by looking at him. Those eyes, oh my God—I'd never seen such a crystal-blue color. A small shopping basket hung on his muscular forearm while he picked out his kale and some arugula. As if he knew I was looking, he glanced back at me with a playful grin on his face. Embarrassed that I had been caught staring (again), I grabbed an avocado and turned around to rush—but not too obviously—into the closest aisle.

Once I found sanctuary by the cereal, I brought my hands to my cheeks and tried to cool them down. *Idiot*, I thought. *Why did you have to stare at him?* Officially mortified, my attention went to my clothes. Holy shit, I forgot I was dressed like a college freshman, and to top it off, my bra was at home on the back of my desk chair. "Oh God." I groaned and rolled my eyes.

The most excitement I had expected at the store was a sale on avocados. A few minutes later, I snuck around the aisle and scanned the produce section. He was gone. I rushed to grab the lettuce and other vegetables I needed and walked with motivation to self-checkout. On the way, I grabbed a bag of quinoa off of an endcap, along with some Oreos. Thankfully, I didn't see Kale Guy again.

On the drive home, I was unable to shake the stranger from my thoughts—Kale Guy, as I had officially nicknamed him. He was gorgeous, sure, but I think what was really bothering me was that I hadn't noticed anyone that way since Jude.

17

Now

My days blurred together since I didn't have to go into an office anymore, but on therapy days, I found structure, if only temporarily. Before I moved to Boston, I'd cried to my longtime therapist, Tina, in our last NOLA session that I'd have to find another person, but she assured me I didn't have to worry about it because she would be able to get a license in Massachusetts.

"I made a friend today at my yoga studio." I fiddled with my fingernails as I waited for Tina to continue.

"Elle, that's fabulous news. What are they like?" Her eyes were bright with enthusiasm.

"Well, her name is Emma, and she reminds me of someone I've met, but I'm not sure who. I really don't know why, but she looks familiar for some reason. Anyways, she's sweet and was set up next to my mat after I got back from the restroom in class the other day. After class, she asked my name and we got to talking." I pushed my hair behind my ear and crossed my legs to get comfortable on my oversized couch, sinking into it, letting it cradle me in my anxiety.

"She sounds friendly. I'm so happy to hear you're finding new environments you enjoy and meeting new people. Does she seem like someone you would be interested in getting to know better?"

"Yeah, definitely! And, so like, okay, here's the thing. She works for a local magazine, *Boston Social.* I told her that I just moved here from New Orleans and was changing careers and that I'm a writer." It still felt odd to say I was a writer out loud. "Tina, she didn't even bat an eye! She accepted that as if it was totally normal."

Tina smiled and I continued, the excitement bubbling over into my words. "How could that be normal to her? It's still not even normal to me, ya know? She was literally like, 'Oh, that's so cool, you're so lucky.' I kid you not, I stared at her, waiting for the sarcastic remark."

"Did it come?" Tina asked.

"No, it didn't!" I raised my arms in a confused shrug. "In fact, she asked if I'd had any luck with my freelancing, and I told her a little. So she said to email her some of my work and she'd show her boss. Can you believe that?"

"That sounds incredibly kind and serendipitous. Why does it seem so hard for you to believe that a stranger wants to help you? This all sounds really good, doesn't it? She's showing a magazine editor your work—or I assume that's it, right?" Tina's calm voice echoed from my laptop's speakers. Even hundreds of miles away, she centered my thoughts and grounded my anxiety.

"Yes, that's right. The editor in chief, and then from what I understand, if she likes my writing style and the articles I've written, then she may offer me the opportunity to freelance for them."

"Elle, that's incredible. I'm so excited for you!" Tina's smile was contagious. I couldn't help but smile back.

"I don't . . . I guess I just didn't expect it. It's insane. Like, why? Seriously, why of all people did I run into her, and why is she so nice?" I stared past Tina's face and let my mind get lost in the nonsense of it all.

"Elle? Elle?" Tina was talking and I was completely zoned out.

"Sorry, sorry, yes?" I shook my head and looked back at my laptop.

"It looks like you got lost in thought. Where did your mind go just now?"

"Just how crazy this all is. What if the editor likes my stuff? What if I get this opportunity? Did I ever tell you what my real dream is?" I asked.

"No, tell me. What's your real dream?"

"I want to write a book. I don't want to freelance and report. I want to be an author and write stories and let my imagination go wild. I want my writing to impact my future readers and hold them, challenge them, but also make them feel safe." I closed my eyes and thought about all the books I'd read as a child that held me and kept me safe. Books were there when my parents weren't. Stories allowed me to believe in hope and love and magic.

I opened my eyes and looked back at Tina. "So I guess this isn't wrong, this is a step in the right direction. But if I'm risking financial stability, social validation, and job security, how do I say yes or no to the right opportunities? My mind is so jumbled and disorganized, and I'm getting lost in it." I held my head between my hands and squeezed my eyes together. The conflicting thoughts were confusing and felt like too much.

"Elle, sometimes we don't know what the right choices are for us until we dive in and experience them. If it feels right or beneficial to you, trust yourself and go for it. You have made choices that are allowing you to create a life that is right for you. Every choice you make is an opportunity to learn more about yourself and a step in carving the path to your goals and dreams. The ability to have choices and explore opportunities such as this one was a driving force behind establishing this new life you are currently living, right?"

I nodded slowly in understanding. "This isn't easy," I murmured.

She tilted her head and gave me a reassuring smile. "No one said it would be."

18

Now

It was a morning-run kind of day. Jogging through the Comm Ave Mall was my favorite way to think—or not think, for that matter. The fall leaves were vibrant and stunning, and it was a cool fifty-eight degrees as I jogged into the Boston Common. I felt my wrist vibrate and glanced down at my smartwatch to check the notification. An email.

I'd seen Emma again in class, but she hadn't mentioned anything about her boss or the magazine. In fact, she was complaining about her older brother, who'd missed family dinner again on Friday night. Apparently, he and their father didn't quite see eye to eye. Curious who was emailing me at seven a.m., I slowed down to read the entire message and hoped it was Emma.

"No fucking way!" I yelled and immediately covered my mouth.

A mother pushing her baby in a stroller glared at me when I looked up. *Oops, definitely didn't mean to say that out loud.*

From: Emma J. Henry <ejhenry@bostonsocial.com>

To: Elizabeth Watson <ewatson@gmail.com>

Dear Elle,

I forgot to mention in class yesterday that I spoke with my editor in chief, Olivia Hughes. I read the samples you sent, and she agrees with me that your writing is special! She'd love to set up a meeting with you and even discuss a piece she's been hoping to get into our next issue. Are you available to meet next Tuesday at our office at 10 am? Please let me know at your earliest.

Best regards,

Emma Henry for Olivia Hughes

♥

Tuesday parking was usually scarce on Newbury Street, but my stars were aligned, and a car pulled out of a spot right in front of the magazine building as I was driving up. Across the street was Align, the yoga and Pilates studio where I'd met Emma. I glanced inside and saw Finn, my favorite instructor and the studio's owner, behind the desk. He looked up as if he could sense my stare and gave me a crooked grin. I waved and walked to the crosswalk on the corner. I'd fill him in on the interview at the coffee shop afterward. I was counting down the minutes until I had a lavender latte with oat milk in my hands.

Emma Henry stopped me right as I stepped off the elevator. Her crystal-blue eyes caught me by surprise, and I had the weirdest sense of déjà vu.

"Elle, oh Elle, so glad you could make it." She came right over to me and gave me a warm hug, no professional handshake, no pitiful ass-out hug—a delightful, authentic hug just like she did when she saw me at Align.

"Of course. You said ten o'clock, and I wouldn't miss this opportunity if I had to run a marathon to get here," I joked.

"Oh please, we have enough of those around here." She laughed back. "Okay, Olivia is on the phone right now with a photographer about a shoot for tomorrow, so you can come with me to my desk, and we'll just wait for her to call you in for the meeting. She knows you're here; Audrey downstairs rang up already. Isn't she the nicest little thing you've ever met?" She shook her head and beckoned for me to follow.

I zigzagged with her between cubicles, all low so that the roomful of creatives could talk to each other whenever they needed to. I saw a group of people gathered around a large table with pictures and fonts spread out before them. A gorgeous petite woman with straight red hair and cat-eye black glasses was in the middle talking to a blonde on her left.

Emma noticed me staring and stopped in front of me. "Ah, I see you've discovered our design and layout team. They are fantastic." Then she pointed to the redheaded woman I'd seen before. "And the woman in the middle, that's Margaret Thompson. She's our art director." Margaret looked our way, and Emma quickly pulled her finger back. Margaret tilted her head down and pulled her frames to the center of her nose. Nervous, I smiled weakly and offered a quick wave. She continued to stare, pushed her glasses back up, and turned away.

"She seems nice," I muttered.

Emma rolled her eyes. "Don't worry about her; you won't have to meet her officially today anyways. Her office is between mine and Olivia's." I nodded slowly and continued to follow Emma.

"Here we are!" Emma opened her arms to display her cozy office. Walking through the glass door, I felt like I was in her personal library. She didn't have a cubicle like the others; she had two walls covered in bookish quotes and magazine covers, and the back wall was a large window overlooking Newbury Street. Her brown oak desk was centered with the view behind her, and two bookshelves full of hardcovers and plants lined the wall on the right with the door.

"Wow . . ." was all I could muster as I took in her space. "I didn't realize you had a corner office here. Are you sure *you* can't hire me?" I said with an awestruck chuckle.

Her espresso-brown curls bounced as she walked over to her desk and sat down in her chair complete with lumbar support.

"Elle, go ahead and sit down." She motioned to a pink velvet barrel chair in front of her desk.

I took a seat and looked around. "Yale undergrad, that's awesome. I didn't know that." I didn't realize the words had come out of my mouth until she replied.

"My whole family went to Yale. My brother, parents—all of us." She sat up straighter and crisscrossed her legs on the chair.

"Oh, cool, I didn't know you had a brother. Oh, wait, yes I did. You mentioned him in class."

"Yep, he's here too. Well, not at the magazine. I mean he's here in Boston." She laughed. "He comes around sometimes. I'm sure you'll meet him if you decide to freelance with us."

"Wait, I'm still new to this. Will I have to come into the office if I freelance with you guys?" I hadn't thought about going into an office, and it made my chest itch.

She shook her head and leaned back in her chair. "Oh, no, no. That's not what I meant. Of course you can work wherever you want, but we leave two spaces open for any freelancers who want to come into the office and work. Especially if they want to chat with design or Olivia about something they are working on." Emma gestured in the direction of the cubicles we'd passed. "Where did you say you went to school again?" she asked.

"Oh, I went to Duke. But I'm an NYC girl at heart."

"Oh yeah, I remember you telling me about the city in class. So how did you end up here in Boston?"

"That's a very long story, actually, but in a nutshell, I'm taking a chance and hoping I don't crash and burn."

"Fair enough," she said, and then the phone rang. She picked it up, gave a quick "Mm-hmm," and hung up. "That was Olivia, she's ready for you. Let's go!"

I followed Emma into Olivia's office and was pleasantly surprised that my *Devil Wears Prada* expectation was the furthest thing from reality. Olivia wore a classic 1950s green pantsuit with dangling gold earrings. Her wispy short blond hair was perfectly styled, and her gray eyes revealed neither her thoughts nor her emotions. Yet despite her professional demeanor, she had a warmth about her. She could have been my mother's age, mid-fifties, and I felt myself wanting to trust her. I wanted to know her.

"Olivia, this is Elizabeth Watson," Emma said as we walked through the door.

"Hi, Ms. Hughes. Elle." I extended my hand to shake hers.

"Oh, no, don't call me that. Please, I'd rather not sound like I'm reading my obituary." She laughed, so I laughed as well, albeit nervously.

"Call me Olivia, please. And, Elle, I'm so pleased to meet you. Emma told me all about you and showed me some of your work." She motioned for me to take a seat, and Emma too.

"Oh, that's great! Thank you for taking the time to review it. What did you think?" Nervous excitement was bubbling in my chest.

Olivia smiled at me with a tiny glint in her eyes. "Well, Elle, I must say, you have natural talent. I was committed after the first sentence, and that's a tough feat when I'm reading a blog on skincare and another on pool maintenance." She pressed her lips together, suppressing a laugh. "Emma tells me you are looking to freelance, correct?" She rested her chin on her fist and tilted her head to the side.

"Yes, that's correct." I looked over at Emma, who sat beside me in a leather chair. "Emma mentioned that your publication hires freelancers and that I might be able to submit work for you, as well." I smiled confidently and Olivia smiled back in response.

"Of course, my dear, we are always open to freelancers who are interested in submitting their work. Whether or not their work is satisfactory is always to be seen." Olivia lifted an eyebrow and tilted her head toward me. "After reviewing the blogs you sent over, I certainly see potential with your writing. It's got emotion, and it draws the reader in despite the subject matter. Your voice is strong and unique. That can't be taught."

My cheeks heated; I hadn't had a compliment on my writing since my grandmother passed away.

"I have a proposition for you, Elle." Olivia picked up a small black book and opened it. She scanned the page, then looked up at me. "Cirque du Soleil is coming to town next week, and I need a writer to cover the event, and even further, write a piece about the significance circus fashion has had on street fashion." She stopped, and I felt the butterflies fluttering in my stomach.

For the record, I knew nothing about fashion, let alone the circus or cirque.

She looked back at her book and continued. "I'll need the first draft within forty-eight hours of the show, then you'll get edits within another twenty-four hours. We are fast-paced and have strict deadlines since we are a monthly publication. Would you like this assignment?" Olivia's tone was firm yet kind. Sure, I was nervous, but this was my shot. And I wasn't going to waste it. I beamed with enthusiasm and lifted my chin, making eye contact with Olivia's misty gray eyes.

"I'll do it."

♥

Finn Bennett was my unexpected new best friend. I'd walked into Align Studio to sign up for a yoga class, and he was behind the desk talking to an instructor. His kind eyes met mine, and after an hour-long conversation that felt like five minutes, I knew he was going to be my person. Then he asked if I liked coffee, and the rest was history. He shared his favorite coffee shop with me, and our friendship was born.

> ME: Meet you at the coffee shop?

> FINN: 10 minutes. Save our table?

> ME: You got it. ♥

I got to the coffee shop, ordered my lavender latte with oat milk, and pulled out my laptop. Research started now. Finn walked in with his yoga mat strapped over his shoulder and sunglasses in his hand. He was a strong man with an athletic build, and oh my God did he love his short shorts. When I met him, I told him his doppelgänger was Tiger Woods, minus the short shorts. They both had a rich, deep brown skin tone and confident demeanor.

He got his usual cold brew with almond milk and came to sit with me.

"Hello, my love," I teased as he took his seat.

"Yeah, yeah. What's up, Ellz? How did the interview go?" He hung his yoga mat on the chair and turned to face me.

"Well, what are you doing next Thursday?" I asked with a sly grin.

He shrugged. "I have a feeling something with you, but as of now, Jackson and I don't have anything planned. Why, what's up?"

Jackson was Finn's partner. He worked in the Red Sox office and was a former professional baseball player in his twenties. Finn told me he'd made it to Triple-A, but after a torn ACL, he'd had to retire. Jackson still had a slender build, but I knew without a doubt how he'd caught Finn's attention. They met before Jackson's injury, so Finn saw him in his uniform more than once. If there's one thing we have in common, Finn and I both appreciate a nice derriere.

"Ding ding, you are correct. So the editor in chief thinks I have promise and gave me an assignment to cover Cirque du Soleil next week. I have two tickets. Wanna go with me?" I gave him the best puppy eyes I possibly could.

"Um, abso-fucking-lutely I do. I love Cirque. I saw it in Vegas and it's incredible." He closed his eyes and shuddered. "Those costumes."

I rolled my eyes playfully and continued. "Great! Okay, awesome, I'm glad I don't have to go ogle these tight costumes alone." His side-eye was devilish. "Speaking of costumes, my assignment is to see how circus fashion affects street fashion, so I really do have to evaluate them. It's my job, after all." I winked and his eyes sparkled with mischief.

"So how was it up there, other than the trial piece?" Finn asked. "Even though that building is right across the street, I've never been inside."

"Oh my gosh, the floors are white marble, and the lobby feels fancy." I shut my laptop and leaned in toward him. "You know Emma Henry, right? The girl I usually set up next to in yoga?"

He furrowed his brow and set his drink on the table. "Yeah, what about her?" he said.

I ignored his change in tone and continued with my thought. "Well, she is the one who helped me get the interview, and I think she must be someone important there, because she has a corner office. It was really cool up there, overall."

He sighed deeply and crossed his arms over his chest. "Oh, Elle, you *would* find the Henrys already. You're such a friendly person, it's like people are drawn to your magnetism." Finn took another sip of his drink and then smacked his lips. "Okay, so here is your Boston 101 lesson for the day. Ready?"

Confused, I nodded slowly and rested my chin on my hand.

"Emma Henry's family is super rich and well connected. Her dad owns a mega real estate and investment company, and her brother works with him."

"Oh, really?" I said. "I mean, she didn't mention much about her family, just that she and her brother both went to Yale."

"Ha, yeah. Of course they did. The Henrys are huge donors to Yale."

"Shit, wait, Finn. How do you know all this?" I asked, cocking my head.

"Oh, I went to school with Emma as kids, and then she went to a feeder school. You kind of hear things. Also, it's common knowledge among locals that her family owns the studio building, and I'm pretty sure the building across the street with Boston Social." I stared at him with an open mouth. "Remember, her dad is a big real estate guy. It's not surprising."

"Wow, I had no idea. That's crazy as hell that they own all of this real estate." The disbelief left me breathless.

"Oh yeah, the Henrys are a big deal around here. Definitely don't go pissing one of them off. But if you're friends with Emma, that's cool. She's one of the sane ones. I hear the brother is nice too, but I don't see him around that often, and he's older than us, so I never saw him in school."

"She mentioned her brother today. She said I may see him around if I'm at the office."

"Well, you can't miss him. He and Emma look pretty similar. They both have the same espresso-brown hair and blue eyes. Did you notice how fucking beautiful her eyes are?" He shook his head. "It's actually disgustingly unfair to be that beautiful and rich."

I would have laughed along, but I was too focused on his words. *They both have the same blue eyes.*

I went home right after our coffee and looked up Emma's Instagram profile, which was private.

Damn it. Facebook? She didn't have one. Next, I googled her.

Bingo.

Emma Henry: Boston's Junior League. Of course. Emma Henry, recent Yale graduates. Already knew that. Oh, there we go: Barrett Henry Named Boston Spotlight Honoree with Sister Emma Henry. I'd know that smirk and crystal-blue stare anywhere. Kale Guy was Barrett Henry, and I finally knew his name.

19

Ten days after graduation, I moved into my studio apartment in the New Orleans Warehouse District. A little more than six months later, I walked into the Roosevelt Hotel for a young professionals' cocktail hour.

I stepped through the hotel doors and was whisked away to a winter wonderland in the middle of the Deep South. Towering Christmas trees with twinkling warm lights lined the lobby, and the scent of pine filled my every inhale. Wreaths and mistletoe adorned the spacious entryway, and strings of lights sparkled with magic.

My coworker Anna had begged me to go with her to this event, and I'd reluctantly agreed. Since I moved to NOLA, it'd been tough to make friends. For me, work always stayed at the front of my mind, and by the time I could socialize, I was exhausted.

Nervous, I sat with Anna in an elegant corner booth of the Sazerac Bar inside the hotel. We gossiped about office drama and watched as the other young professionals mingled throughout the bar.

"We need more champagne," Anna announced when she looked at my empty flute. "C'mon, let's go grab a seat at the bar. We're just wallflowers over here in this booth."

Before I could refuse, she grabbed my hand and pulled me toward the bar. She saw her opening when two spots vacated, and we hurried over to claim our new seats. I wasn't fully aware of the man next to me on my right, but I noticed he was twirling the cherry in his old-fashioned. I tried to look at him through my peripheral and saw that his head was turned away. I couldn't pinpoint why I had a nagging sense of recognition for this man. Anna tapped my shoulder on the left and snapped me back to the present.

"You okay, Elle?" Her brow was slightly furrowed, and she glanced around me to the man on my right.

At the mention of my name, the man at the bar turned to look at us. His amber eyes met mine, and every ounce of breath left my body. My lips started trembling and my eyes went wide in recognition.

"Oh, hey, Jude," Anna said in a teasing tone. "I see you're staring at my friend Elle." Her eyes sparkled with mischief.

He was here. He was in front of me literally at this very moment. I'd always hoped to run into him if he still lived here, but I'd lost hope after a few months of disappointment. I'd dreamed of this moment since we'd lost touch. I'd missed him.

Ignoring Anna, his eyes never left mine as he took my hand in his and slowly lifted it to his lips. I had to figure out how to breathe; my brain was short-circuiting.

"Hello, Elle." He gently kissed my hand and pierced through my soul with his stare.

The bartender interrupted. "Can I get the lady something to drink?"

Before I could answer, Jude replied, "Tequila, water, three limes."

He remembered. Throughout the whole introduction, Anna stared at us with her mouth open.

"Wait a minute, what in the actual fuck is going on here? Jude, you know Elle?" Her wide eyes and puzzled expression were completely valid.

He finally let go of my hand and turned to Anna. "It's a small world, isn't it, Anna?" His voice was silky and warm. His sexy accent still made my knees weak, and I was sitting, so that was saying something.

"Actually, champagne, please," I called to the bartender.

He looked up and acknowledged my outburst.

"For both of us." I pointed to Anna, and he nodded in understanding.

"No more tequila?" Jude asked as I took out my credit card.

He lifted his old-fashioned to his lips.

"I still drink tequila, but tonight is a champagne night." I gave him a devilish smile.

The right side of his mouth lifted, and I knew he was holding back.

"So, wait, Anna, how do you know Jude?" I asked, trying to piece it all together.

Oh God, what if she's an ex-girlfriend?

After all this time, I still felt electricity pulsing through my body at his warm amber stare. The bartender brought our flutes of champagne and put it on my tab, but before Anna could respond, Jude's words shot through my heart like a poisoned arrow.

"It's been over a year, Elle." He watched my every move.

I felt a panic attack starting to rise. I knew exactly how long it'd been. I knew every time I'd looked at my phone, hoping he'd respond. I knew how fucking long it'd been since he'd moved on.

"I texted you!" I snapped.

His body tensed and his eyes narrowed. "No, you didn't."

I cut him off before he could say another word. "We have to go." I looked at Anna, who seemed entirely confused and still hadn't answered my question about how she knew Jude. I was holding it together, but to say I didn't text him, no. No, absolutely not. I can't do this right now.

"Elle, wait!" he shouted over the crowd and tried to weave through to get to us.

I grasped Anna's hand and navigated us to the women's restroom. Before we went through the door, I looked back and didn't see Jude. Once we were inside the restroom and in the fancy seating area by an antique couch, Anna whipped around and stared at me. Her lips were a thin line, and I could tell by the way her eyebrows almost hit her hairline that she wanted the story.

"Okay, okay, just one more second, okay?" I took another sip of my champagne. "I need to get my thoughts together."

"Oh, do you now? Elle, cut the shit. What the heck was that?" She crossed her arms over her chest and cocked her hip to the side.

I took a deep breath, and within that one inhale, that one exhale, my memories flashed back to that summer in Nashville. Jude's smile. Jude's hand holding mine. Jude's body warm against my back. His kisses. His hugs. His breath tickling my ear as he leaned in to say, *I love you*, at the airport.

"So, yeah, we kind of know each other."

"Obviously." She rolled her eyes.

"We, um, we were kind of together one summer. The summer before last."

"You used to date Jude!" Forget her eyebrows, her eyes were wide as saucers. "What happened? As far as I know, Jude has never had a serious girlfriend. He doesn't date."

"Well, wait, how do you know Jude?" I turned the conversation around to take the attention off me and because I was dying to know how she knew him. "You never answered me in the bar."

She shook her head, obviously knowing I was changing the subject. "We grew up together. He was friends with my older brother and went to Newman with us. Then after graduation, he and my brother went to law school together."

I nodded slowly and imagined a young Jude in high school.

"I'm telling you," Anna continued, "in high school, I never saw that boy date. He was a closed book."

"It was a summer fling, that's all. We met at a friend's party in Nashville." I shrugged nonchalantly.

"You're not getting off the hook that easily, Elle Watson." She placed her hands on her hips and gave me a sassy glare. "Did you notice the way he stared at you back there? It was like you were the center of his world. I couldn't believe it."

"Oh my God, shut up." I laughed into my flute, feeling embarrassed. My cheeks were burning, and my heart was thudding against my ribs.

"Well, maybe you'll see him around," she said casually. "New Orleans is the smallest big city you'll ever visit."

20

Now

The Cirque du Soleil performance with Finn was exhilarating. He was with me while I interviewed performers, the show director, and most importantly, the costume designer. I felt confident my piece was going to blow Olivia away and was honestly shocked by how much circus fashion affects the fashion industry in general.

Finn and I stayed out after the performance and went to the Ritz for cocktails.

"Espresso martini." Finn glanced at me and noticed my cheeky stare. "Actually, make that two." The bartender smiled and walked away to make our drinks.

"They're good here?" I asked as we took two seats at the bar.

"Oh, the Ritz has the best in town. I hate to say that with so many killer local spots, but there's just something about the bartenders here." He winked.

"Oh yes, his butt, right?" I chided. "I mean, it is rather perfect." I smiled and chuckled behind my glass.

"Elle, I'm an ass man till the day I die, but while he does have a perfect ass, Jackson's is even better." He tipped his head and smirked.

We were both laughing when the bartender came back with our drinks. I tried to give him my credit card, but Finn dramatically took it from my hand and threw it on the floor.

"Absolutely not, Ellz. My treat for my favorite writer."

"Thanks, best friend." I leaned over and kissed him on his stubbly cheek. I raised my martini and gave him a nod to raise his. I started the toast that Jude and I had created in New Orleans an entire lifetime ago. "Here's to a long life and a happy one, best friends and hearts won, an espresso martini . . . and another one."

♥

Two days later, I sat with Finn again at our coffee shop table.

"You turn it in?" Finn asked as I tossed my bag into the booth next to him.

"Yep, I had to have my first draft to Olivia within forty-eight hours." I leaned back into our oversized booth in the corner. "It's done, Finn. I really did it."

"I'm so proud of you, Elle. Ya know, off topic but not really, I heard a group talking over by the couches about a writing contest going on right now." He looked at me and then continued. "Apparently, it's been a bit of a tradition in the Boston literary community, and they have a knack of getting debut authors published."

My ears perked up. "Wait, what? You caught all of that just walking by?"

He shrugged. "Okay, well I eavesdropped a little, but yes, I got the gist of the conversation."

Sitting up, I remembered my grandmother's note hanging on my wall. "What's the name of the competition?"

"Oh, um, let me think." He pinched his brows and shook his head. "Literary Times something or other." He pulled out his phone. "Okay, yes. It's the—"

"Literary Times Challenge," I finished for him.

Finn raised his eyebrows and gave me a sideways smile. "You've heard about it, I presume?"

"It's the competition my grandmother won in the seventies. Remember? I showed you that note hanging in the living room. This is *that* competition." I shook my head in disbelief. "I didn't know it was still going on."

"Ohhhh, no way! Yeah, like I said, it's a bit of a literary tradition, apparently." He gave me his phone, and I scrolled through the rules and regulations.

Over eighteen? Sure.

Unpublished? Definitely.

Write a full novel by December 31, 2022, at 11:59 p.m. EST? *Fuck!*

"Oh my God, write an entire novel in a few months, that's insane." My eyes were wide as I kept scrolling, my chest tightening.

"I think you can do it," Finn said with absolute certainty.

I looked up at him in disbelief.

"Please, seriously?" I quirked an eyebrow.

"Definitely. Why not?" he responded with a shrug.

I kept scrolling and reading. The winner would be chosen in March, and the grand prize included five thousand dollars and the opportunity to speak with acquiring agents and editors.

"Holy shit," I muttered.

"I mean, your Grandma Di won it. Why can't you, Elle? I feel like it's a sign I heard about this. It's the same competition. C'mon, you *have* to enter now." He put his hand on my arm and squeezed. "I think you should try."

"I don't know. If I don't win, wouldn't that prove I'm not author material? God, and my grandma. I feel like I have to win because she did. If I don't, I . . . I don't know."

"Ellz, I think Grandma Di would be so proud of you for just trying." His voice was soft and comforting.

"I know she won, right? But even after winning, she still didn't truly believe that writing was a career." I kept staring at the web page with the rules.

"From what you've told me, your grandmother was an extraordinary writer, and she only stopped because she was not quite encouraged but *told* it wasn't her path. She had kids and had a family; you aren't in the same place as her. You have more freedoms and choices than she did." He sat back and crossed his arms over his chest.

"You're right, I do have more freedoms than she did. They married young." I looked away from the computer and into Finn's chocolate-brown eyes. "You really think I should go for it?"

He nodded encouragingly.

"Elle, you know I wouldn't lie to you. I think you need to take your shot. Make Grandma Di proud."

I bit my lip and tried to make sense of the chaos in my brain. Five thousand dollars would be nice and would certainly help keep me afloat until I had a few more freelancing sources. But I'd never written a book. I wondered if Grandma Di had ever written a book before the competition. She never elaborated. I wish she could have published. I wish she could have followed her dreams. But like Finn said, I had the chance to follow mine and do it for myself and for Grandma Di.

I licked my lips and took a deep breath. "Okay."

"Okay?" he said.

"Okay, I'm going to enter." A huge smile spread across my face. "But first, I'm gonna text Rach and Sarah to let them know!" I pulled out my phone and started typing wildly.

♥

When I'd texted the girls about the competition earlier that week, they were ecstatic for me. Rach even offered to help me edit and proofread, but I had to remind her that exactly zero words were written so far. I smiled when I saw Tina wave on the screen as she entered our session. I was bursting at the seams to tell her my news.

"Tina! I'm entering a writing competition!" It felt weird to say it out loud—up until then I'd only texted it. I crossed my legs on my couch with a huge grin on my face.

"Elle, that's wonderful! That will be a great way for you to explore your writing on a bigger level," Tina said with authentic joy in her voice.

"Yeah, I'm excited. I've already started outlining." I slowly twirled a lock of hair around my finger.

"What's on your mind, Elle?" Tina asked through my computer screen.

"I don't know. I just . . . I'm just nervous, I guess." I took another sip. "The grand prize is a huge deal, and it would help out, ya know?"

"Financially? Yes, I can see that if it's a large sum."

"It's five thousand dollars."

She paused for a minute. "Wow, that is certainly substantial. But remember, if you don't win, it's not the end. You still have your freelancing and you're a hard worker." She adjusted her thin navy-blue glasses on her nose and continued. "Elle, I'm wondering, what encouraged you to sign up for this writing contest?"

"My friend Finn." I laughed and wrapped my arms around my middle. "But also, my grandmother."

Her eyebrows rose. "Your grandmother? How so? I know you adored her."

"Oh, you know what? I don't think I mentioned it really, but my Grandma Di was a writer too."

Tina tilted her head to the side and furrowed her brow. "No, we haven't talked about that. Elle, that's incredible. What an inspiration!"

"Yeah, she did it after she and my grandpa married, before they had children. But she quit." I took a deep breath. My grandmother's forgotten dream had never sat right with me. "She quit because my grandpa asked her to move to NYC and wanted to start a family."

"You seem upset by her choice." Tina was sitting cross-legged on her sofa as well. She leaned forward and rested her chin on her fist.

"I don't get it. I mean, I do, but I don't. She won this competition, Tina. The exact one."

Her eyes widened and her lips formed a small O.

"I feel like I need to win. I know it's not the end of the world if I don't, but I want to win for both of us. I want to live my dream so she can have hers too."

"Elle, that's truly beautiful. I know she would be so proud of you," she responded softly.

"I know, but also, I need to prove to myself that my writing is good enough. That I can really write, just like she did. She gave it all up for a man. I won't do that. I didn't do that before; I won't do it now." I rolled my eyes. "Not that there is a man to speak of at the moment, but yeah. I think that's my big problem with her decision. She gave it all up for a man."

"It sounds like you have a deep need to validate your talents and abilities. Elle, this is completely understandable. I hear that you have conflicting feelings about your grandmother's choices, feeling admiration for her but also frustration for her choice to stop writing. Her path is not necessarily your path. You get to have a unique writing journey all your own."

My sight became blurry as my eyes watered. How could my body contain happiness, grief, fear, and excitement all at once?

"Elle, you are a fantastic writer. I know that to be true."

Tears trickled down my cheeks. "I don't even really know why I'm crying right now." I grabbed a tissue from my coffee table and wiped my eyes.

"Because you're being validated, Elle. You are overcoming old ideologies of success and forging your way. That's not easy," she replied softly.

"My friend Sarah, she's a stay-at-home mom. She loves it." I cleared my throat, holding back a sniffle. "I'd never want that, but she did. We used to joke we'd travel the world together, but then she got pregnant unexpectedly, quit teaching art at the local college, and says she can't imagine doing anything else."

"How did her decision make you feel? It's similar to your grandmother's choice, isn't it?"

I gave a shaky laugh. "Yeah, I guess. I never thought about it. I never understood how Sarah could have a plan, and then it just disappears. Suddenly, she's okay with a life that is completely opposite of what she thought her dream was. But now I do. I think." I stared tearfully at Tina on my screen.

"You do." She understood.

"I know I want to write. I want to be a published author. I want to be the one in control of my life and, in a way, live the life my grandmother didn't get to. She gave in to expectations of her life. I don't want to let society dictate mine anymore." My face was hot with frustration and pent-up anger. A headache was forming at my temples. "That is the complete opposite of who I was supposed to be, who I used to be." My tears were flowing now, and I frantically rubbed my eyes to make them stop.

"It's okay to cry, there are a lot of emotions and a lot of barriers coming down. You are working through a lot of learned behaviors and teaching yourself to live in a different way that is very much out of your comfort zone. It's okay to feel these emotions. No one is judging you here, Elle. Cry."

I needed to get out of the house after therapy. I felt raw with intense emotions that kept overloading my brain, and I craved a change of scenery. I was sitting in the Boston Public Library in Copley Square working on my outline when my phone buzzed.

Finn: Hey, wanna go to the Pats game with me tonight?

Me: Jackson isn't going? He loves football.

Finn: No, he has to work, I have his ticket. Is that a yes?

Me: Sure, sounds fun. I'm at the BPL outlining right now.

Finn: Oh, sounds fancy. OK, I'll come get you around four and we can get a quick bite before the game.

I stopped outlining and looked at the schedule to see who the Pats were playing tonight. My eyes went wide when I saw they were playing the New Orleans Saints. I would definitely be a Patriots fan tonight. I was not a Saints fan, much to Jude's dismay when we dated. I hadn't texted or called him since that embarrassing night in New Orleans after Mr. Landry's email. But I felt like even if he had a girlfriend, this would be a friendly chat, nothing serious. He was a huge Saints fan, so he'd appreciate that I was going to a game, even if I wasn't rooting for his team. I couldn't explain it, I just wanted to talk to him and tell him the news—pride be damned.

ME: Guess who's going to the Pats vs Saints game tonight?

He replied two hours later. I was about to hop in the shower when I heard the notification.

JUDE: No shit.

JUDE: How've you been? It's been a while.

ME: Doing all right, big changes and such. Ya know, unconventional Elle and all.

This felt easy. This was us, though. Even if we had a fight when we were together, we'd pick back up like nothing ever happened. Thinking back, that probably wasn't the healthiest communication, and here we are . . .

JUDE: You're anything but unconventional. How are you going to the game, isn't it in Boston?

I'm anything but unconventional? He had no idea.

ME: Oh yeah. I moved to Boston a few months ago

He didn't waste any time in responding.

JUDE: Damn, Elle. Boston? We're basically neighbors! Well, I'm glad you're doing okay. You're okay?

ME: yeah

JUDE: Elle?

ME: yep

JUDE: Elle . . .

ME: Jude, I'm fine. Long story. Anyways, just wanted to say hi and let you know that I will not be cheering for the Saints this evening.

JUDE: Okay, if you say so. Go Saints.

ME: Never.

21

Ten years ago

Jude and I were magnetic. I tried to stay away; I swear I did. I was running in City Park, passing the horse barns, when I noticed another runner coming toward me. As he got closer, my heart rate shot up.

He slowed down and walked the rest of the way to me.

"Beautiful day for a run, wouldn't you say?" Jude asked as sweat glistened over his toned body. I'd always loved his broad shoulders.

I'd run three miles already and had no plans on stopping. My head told me to ignore him, but some imaginary string pulled me to him.

"Elle?" His voice was deep and assertive.

I couldn't keep going. I stopped running and turned my iPod off. "Hey, Jude." He noticed my forced grin.

"Elle, what's wrong? It's me." His eyebrows drew together, and his mouth formed a tight line.

"I . . . I'm sorry," I stammered. "I just don't know what to say," I said nervously, scratching my forearm and looking down at my sneakers. "You're really here. You're here, I'm here, and it seems too good to be true. I can't wrap my head around this." My lungs were barely allowing me to breathe.

"You're right. I'm here. Elle, let me explain about the messages."

I looked up at him and saw the plea in his warm eyes. "Okay, what happened?" I crossed my arms over my chest defensively, holding myself.

"Elle, I swear I didn't want to stop talking to you. I know you left Nashville saying we wouldn't work, but I wanted us to work." He brushed his hand through his chestnut waves and continued. "I got a new number a few months after I came home. I left my phone at the bar in the airport on a trip. It was stupid, and I didn't have your number saved."

"But what about the emails I sent?" I responded defiantly.

"I never got any emails." His features twisted in confusion.

"Look." I pulled out my phone and scrolled to my sent messages. "Here, see? I sent you photos and all from the UK."

He pulled out his phone and began to swipe toward the date I sent the messages. He turned his phone. "Elle, nothing."

"That doesn't make sense." Confused, I looked at the messages I'd sent. Then it dawned on me. "Fuck, Jude, I'm so sorry." A sheepish grin spread on my face.

"What is it?" he asked cautiously.

"I misspelled your email address." My cheeks were burning, and I felt like crying. This was so stupid it was funny.

"How do you know?" he asked, looking over the top of my phone.

"Well, I assume your name isn't spelled J-u-e-d." I looked up with a sarcastic twinkle in my eyes.

"Elle." He chuckled. "That's . . . something." He rubbed his jaw and shrugged. "Why don't we start over?"

I squinted and pursed my lips. "Not all the way over, I hope?"

"Well, I sure hope not." He winked.

"Wait, one more question. What about Facebook? Did you try to find me on there?"

"Elle, you hadn't reached out, or so I thought, so I didn't want to annoy you or scare you with how much I thought about you. How much I wanted and needed you in my life." He started bumping his fist against his thigh mindlessly. "I've been a wreck for the past year, seriously."

A dull ache spread through my chest. "So you wanted to hear from me?" I playfully pushed his shoulder and soaked up his beautiful wide smile and delicious dimples.

"Elle, I dreamed of hearing your voice." He stepped forward and cupped my face in his warm hand. "I dreamed of touching you and holding you. If I'd seen those texts, I would have . . ."

"You would have what?" I felt breathless and wanted to melt into his touch.

"I missed you."

My throat was tight, and tears were clouding my vision. "I missed you more."

He brought his other hand to my face and pulled me in gently to his lips. I pulled back to say something, and that's when I noticed that Jude, beautiful Jude, was crying.

22

Now

We were seated right off the fifty-yard line in Gillette Stadium. The seats were similar in location to the ones Jude and his family had in New Orleans, except outside. "I've never been to an outside stadium before," I admitted to Finn while rubbing my arms. It was a frosty forty degrees, and my nose was turning red.

"Really?" He feigned shock. "Well then, bundle up, buttercup, you're about to freeze your ass off." He laughed, showing his perfectly straight white teeth, and wrapped his arms around me. "Good thing you wore this puffer jacket. It's perfect—maybe the wrong color, but perfect."

The teams came out to warm up.

I was wearing my long black Lululemon jacket from years ago when my grandparents took me skiing. I never had to wear it living in New Orleans.

"We can just pretend it's navy blue. Deal?" I pulled my houndstooth scarf tighter around my neck. I truly forgot the team colors for the Saints were black and gold, and I didn't own another heavy-ish jacket.

Finn rolled his eyes playfully and put his arm back around me. "I've got you, Ellz. We'll make you a Bostonian yet." He wore a navy puffer with a fashionable red men's scarf. His warm skin held few imperfections, and with each exhale, a puff of fog escaped his lips.

"Yeah, yeah. I'm so glad you're my person, Finn." I rested my head on his shoulder and inhaled his cologne. God, it was good. "Finn, what are you wearing."

"It's Mind Games," he said.

Confused, I lifted my head. "No, I'm not playing games. I just want to know the name."

He furrowed his brow and looked down at me. "Right, Elle, it's called Mind Games. I get it at Neiman Marcus."

"Well, I don't feel dumb or anything." I laughed and put my head back on his shoulder. "Fuck, it's cold." I snuggled deeper into my scarf and his arm.

"Seriously, though," he said, "I'm glad you moved here. I didn't know I was missing my person until you showed up at my studio. Of course I have Jackson, but he's my partner." He squeezed my arm a little tighter. "You're you, and we're us."

"God, Finn. Stop. I'm gonna cry like a baby." I sat back up and wiped my eyes. "I love Rach and Sarah, and they are my best friends, but with you, it's soulmate, best friend, person—all of the things." His eyes glistened in the lights of the stadium, and then as if in slow motion, I saw his face change. His eyes widened and he looked at me, then back up behind me.

"Elle, oh my God, Finn! Finn, I didn't think Elle was your type!" Emma winked with a playful smirk.

Finn rolled his eyes, then said loudly, "If it isn't the Henry siblings! How the hell are ya, Emma?"

Laughing, Emma walked through the row above us and leaned over the seats to hug Finn. He glanced down at me and gave me an apologetic smile.

Oh shit. He said siblings. I stood up and turned to hug Emma. "What a surprise!" I opened my arms, and that's when I noticed Barrett standing quietly behind her. He was looking at me with a vivid blue stare that mirrored his sister's. "Barrett," I gasped.

At the sound of his name, his eyes narrowed as he tried to place me. He cleared his throat. "I'm sorry, have we met?" he asked, still looking me over.

But I remembered him, and I was mortified. No longer cold, I burned with humiliation. Why did I just say his name out loud? I heard Finn giggle behind me.

"I, um, uh, mm, no. Uh, no, we haven't," I managed to stutter while he kept his gaze fixed on my face.

"Oh, Barrett, stop." Emma lightly smacked her brother's arm and said enthusiastically, "This is Elle Watson. She works with me now. I probably told her about you at the office. Right, Elle?" Emma said, looking at me with raised eyebrows and a twinkle in her eyes.

I regained my composure and played along. "Yeah, when I came into the office the other day, you mentioned your family and your brother, Barrett." I cleared my throat and forced a smile. He remained impassive but nodded slowly and then looked away down toward the field.

"Exactly. Anyways, Elle, officially"—she winked—"this is my brother, Barrett Henry." He looked back at us and gave a curt nod. "Quite the talker, obviously." She rolled her eyes. "Well, it looks like we're seat neighbors. How exciting!" She clapped her hands together and motioned for Barrett to follow her around the row of seats and next to us. She sent Barrett in first.

I leaned over to Finn, who was sitting back down, watching all of this with intense amusement. "Kale Guy" was all I managed to whisper before leaning back and readjusting my scarf. Finn understood immediately and again started giggling to himself.

Barrett took his seat next to me, then Emma at the end. "Emma, you don't want to sit next to your friend?" he asked.

I felt unsure. Did he not want to sit next to me? Did I smell? I tried to smell myself but as casually as possible.

Finn elbowed me. "Elle, you're fine." He gave me a quick wink and turned to Barrett. "Barrett, what's wrong? Her Saints colors embarrass you?"

"Oh, I promise I'm not a Saints fan." I gave Finn major side-eye, then wildly motioned my hand to show that I indeed was not a Saints fan.

They both looked at me, Emma with a raised eyebrow and a sly grin, Barrett with brows pinched and confused.

"So where's Jackson tonight?" Emma leaned over her brother to talk to Finn.

"Jackson's got a prior engagement, so I brought Elle to her first Pats game." Finn smiled bright.

"Please tell Jackson I said hi, then. I haven't seen him in class lately," Emma pouted.

"Work, work, work. You know the drill when you're a cog in the wheel," Finn replied.

"Don't we all," Barrett said, chiming in.

We all looked over at him. I felt my cheeks warm up again.

"He talks?" Emma elbowed her brother, and he instinctively smirked.

"So you work at the magazine now?" he asked, turning to look at me.

"I think so?" I looked over at Emma for verification.

"Yep, I saw Olivia today. Your article was incredible! Fuck, Elle. You can write really well," Emma said as a roar erupted from the crowd.

The teams were lining up, and an electric energy vibrated through the stadium.

"So then, yes, I freelance for *Boston Social*," I yelled over the screams to Barrett.

He smiled and gave me a nod, but his mind had gone to the game now. The kicker ran up to the ball and sent it into the other end zone.

"Let's go!" Barrett jumped out of his seat and brushed my arm as his body slid past mine. My skin tingled even under all my layers—a jacket, two sweatshirts, and an athletic long-sleeve.

I was still staring at his body when Finn kicked my shoe.

"You're staring, Ellz."

♥

When I got home from the game, I went straight to my room and flopped onto my bed, letting my king-size duvet swallow me. I pulled my phone out of my pocket and frantically opened the group chat with Sarah and Rach.

ME: You guys, I officially met Kale Guy!

RACH: OMFG, you have a name?

RACH: Details, details! And wait, it's late as hell. Why are you up so late?

ME: His name is Barrett Henry, and he is the BROTHER of a girl I work with at the magazine. I mentioned Emma, I think?

SARAH: Wait, what's going on? Sorry, I saw my phone blinking but was getting in my late-night cycle sesh.

RACH: Elle met a boy.

SARAH: Elle, that's fantastic! Share all the details please.

SARAH: But wait, are you finally over Jude? You haven't talked about anyone since y'all broke up.

ME: I hope so, but are we ever really over our first love? I mean, we still talk and stuff. And remember I told you guys he texted me about his mom being sick and living with him in NYC. So, I mean, I've talked to him a few times since then.

SARAH: ?

ME: It's nothing, I swear. I think we're just kind of friends who text now.

RACH: What?! Elle.

SARAH: Be careful, Elle. You never really seem to get over that one.

RACH: Seriously, he's like your fucking Prince Charming or Achilles' heel or something. I really can't decide. But this new guy, back to him. We like him, right?

Sᴀʀᴀʜ: To be fair, she literally fell into his arms. *Jude's arms* I mean.

Mᴇ: You're a comic, Sarah, seriously.

Mᴇ: But omg, Rach, I melted when I heard Barrett's voice tonight. He didn't say too much, but he sat next to me, and when his body brushed my arm, I felt things I haven't felt in a very long time.

Rᴀᴄʜ: Uh-oh.

Sᴀʀᴀʜ: She's a goner.

23

Ten years ago

Nine months of Jude. Nine months of continuing what we'd started at that Fourth of July party more than two years ago. We hardly spent a night apart, so a month ago, we'd decided to rent an apartment on Royal Street together. Yes, together.

Our cozy little apartment was close to Frenchman Street, where we'd listen to local musicians play on the streets, as well as our favorite late-night spot, the Verti Marte. Jude Ashford introduced me to the bacon-egg-and-cheese po'boy at two a.m. on a random Wednesday night, and my life has never been the same.

"You're something else, Elle Watson." He held my hand while we walked up the ramp to our seats in the Superdome. The Saints were playing, and he had season tickets.

"You do realize this is a Saints game?" He smirked. "And you are wearing the other team's colors rather proudly?"

"What can I say, I like to be different." I squeezed his hand and pulled down my bright blue Titans jersey.

"Oh, of that I have absolutely no doubts." He laughed and ran his other hand through his wavy chestnut hair. "You're certainly spicy. That's a brave thing to do in New Orleans." He wrapped his arm around my waist and leaned down to kiss the top of my head.

"Good thing you like spicy." I looked up at him and grinned mischievously. "Let's go, Titans!" I yelled into the open atrium.

Hundreds of people stared, their eyes narrowing in disgust. A few whoops and yeahs echoed, but nothing compared to the glares sent my way.

Jude held me a little tighter and whispered into my ear, "Go Saints."

"Never." I lifted my chin to kiss that shit-eating grin off of his face.

24

Now

I sent over my final draft about Cirque to Olivia this morning. I'd been going back and forth with the editors for more than a week, and we'd all come to the agreement that we had the article ready to go to print. I was thrilled it was turned in, because Margaret, the art director, was starting to make me nervous. She needed to have the final layout in today, and she was adamant about my article fitting on a certain page. Crisis averted.

I was sitting on the couch with some leftover Mexican food when I heard a knock. I did a double take and looked at the TV, thinking it was from *Schitt's Creek*, but then I heard it again.

It was definitely my door.

"Hello?" A man's voice carried through my wooden door. I knew that voice, even if I'd only heard it say three sentences during the whole Patriots game.

I'd rolled out of bed that morning in a pair of Jude's old boxers I'd stolen and an oversized Duke T-shirt—no bra. I didn't have plans today, so I never changed clothes.

"Shit," I muttered to myself as I ran to my bedroom to throw on a sports bra under my tee. I heard his voice again and another knock.

"Elle? Elle, are you home? Emma said you were home." His voice was sheepish.

I could pretend I was dead, or I could be bold and answer the damn door. Spoiler, I answered the damn door.

"Hey!" I opened the door slightly and leaned into the frame with my hand on my hip. "What's up, Barrett?" Yeah. Super smooth.

Barrett's blue eyes sparkled. "Hey yourself." He had a shy grin on his face, and I noticed his ears were red. "So, I'm sorry about randomly coming over, but Emma said she'd talked to you and you'd be home today. I was gonna catch you at the magazine office first, I swear." His words were rushed, and I noticed he was embarrassed.

I rolled my eyes playfully. "Your sister, huh? I'll have to remind her not to give my address to random men."

He relaxed at my playful tone. "Yeah, they could be really weird and come over unannounced."

"Heaven forbid, they're the worst." A sly grin spread across my face.

He shivered, and I noticed that we were still standing in the hallway. *Shit, I forgot to invite him in!*

"Oh God, you're not even wearing a jacket. You know it's cold out, right? Come on in." I motioned him inside and shut the door. The smell of his cologne made something stir in my belly.

"Go ahead and make yourself at home. Do you want coffee? Water? That's about all I have right now."

"Coffee sounds great, actually. I'll have it how you do," he said casually while his eyes lowered down my body, then quickly back up.

"You sure? I add in almond milk." I shifted my weight, fully aware that I was standing in front of Barrett Henry in Jude's boxers and a T-shirt.

"Yeah, that's fine. Emma's lactose intolerant, so we never had real milk at home anyways. We either did almond or soy."

"No sugar? I don't do sugar," I said.

"Just like you do it, promise," he repeated.

"Okay, you asked for it. Coming right up." I smiled to myself and turned to go into the kitchen. *Schitt's Creek* was still playing in the living room, and I watched him take a seat on the couch and pull out his phone. Before he could turn around, I quickly ran my fingers through my wavy, unruly hair to make it look somewhat more presentable. I hadn't been expecting guests today.

"You know, I'm sorry if I was a little standoffish at the game the other night." His remark startled me while I was pouring some almond milk into his mug. He was facing the kitchen now, his phone gone and his left leg pulled up onto the couch as he leaned into the sturdy back.

Still staring at the mugs, I raised my voice over the Nespresso machine. "Oh, it's no big deal. I could tell you were really into the game." *And not into me*, I thought.

I brought him his coffee and sat down on the other side of the couch with my coffee in my favorite Disney mug. I wasn't sure what to make of this. Why did he ask Emma if I was home? What was his angle? I smiled at him. "So, to what do I owe the pleasure, Barrett?" I kept my voice casual and curled up on the couch, like nothing out of the ordinary was happening right now.

He shifted in his seat, then placed his mug on the coffee table. When he lifted his gaze to mine—well, those goddamn eyes.

"Well, Elle"—he smiled—"after the Pats game the other night, I realized I was a total ass."

I chuckled into my mug.

He continued. "But I also realized . . ." He paused, and I looked up at him with narrowed, playful eyes. "I realized I couldn't stop thinking about you." He shrugged as if he hadn't just dropped a bomb in my living room.

"What?" The words flew out of my mouth. No thought, no filter. "You hardly said two words to me. Did you even notice I was sitting next to you?"

"Oh, I definitely noticed you were sitting next to me." He held my stare with a mischievous smile. "Truth is I couldn't talk to you. I had no idea what to say or even ask."

"Stop fucking around. You're lying." I rolled my eyes and lightly slapped the foot closest to me. Was I flirting with Barrett Henry?

"I'm not. I swear. You're enchanting, Elle Watson." He continued to stare at me as if he was studying me. His gaze made my breath hitch, and I could feel the sweat slowly rolling down my chest. "So, after the game, I asked Emma if she could help me talk to you. Lucky me, she said yes."

He scooted closer to me. "Is this, okay?" he asked cautiously when he noticed me watching him intently.

"Yeah, yeah, you're fine." *Note to self, do not—I repeat—do not lift your arms!* This was a bad day to forget deodorant.

"Okay." He smiled reassuringly. "Please let me make up for my rude behavior. How about a date?" he asked with a glint in his eyes. I could feel his foot touching mine.

I gave him a sideways grin. "Seriously?"

"Seriously." He waited patiently for my reply.

"All right, but no more football, okay? As much as I love the cold, that was a little brutal."

"Deal." His smile reached both of his eyes. "Are you free next Friday? Say around sixish?"

I pretended to think about it and shifted my gaze skyward. "Hmm," I mumbled. After a few seconds, I looked back into his hypnotic stare. "Yeah, that should be good. I'm about to start writing a novel, so that will be a much-needed break."

"You're writing a book? That's pretty cool. What's it about?" He leaned sideways onto the back of the couch, comfortable and relaxed. Foot still touching mine.

"It's a romance novel inspired by my grandparents. My grandmother was born in NYC, and my grandpa was an immigrant from Palermo, Italy. They both happened to be at the Belmont Stakes at the same time, and my grandfather noticed her sitting next to his assigned seat when he walked up. The rest is history."

"Sounds like quite the story." He smiled.

I took a small, satisfying sip and then held my mug in my lap. "I hope so." My voice was soft and wishful.

"Oh, by the way"—he brushed his free hand through his styled espresso-brown hair—"remember how I asked you if we'd ever met before, at the game?"

"Yeah, I remember." I tilted my head to the side, wondering where this was going.

"Well, I want you to know I remember." His voice went soft and velvety. "You were in a band T-shirt and wearing leggings. Tight leggings." He winked, and I felt a blush bloom along my cheeks. "You were standing next to me at the grocery store, and I remember thinking, *Oh my God, who is this beautiful woman?*"

I tapped my mug nervously with my nails and tried to breathe like normal.

"I remember like it was yesterday." He paused. "And you know what?" His voice was low, intimate.

"What?" I whispered.

"You're even more beautiful today, especially in an old pair of blue-striped boxers."

25

Now

Me: You guys, I feel like a high school girl with a crush!

Sarah: So, you're like dating already?

Me: Well, not officially or anything. We have our date tonight.

Rach: Nice, Elle. When's the wedding?

Me: Shut up. A million years from now, if ever. Oh, by the way, I have some other news . . .

Sarah: Your article was published?

Rach: You're done outlining?

Me: Okay, well, yes, my article will be published, Sarah. My favorite optimist. And Rach, YES! I'm about 15,000 words into it!

Rach: Get it, Elle! So proud. Can I buy your first book? It has to be signed, though.

Sarah: How are you feeling about the competition in general? I know you have until the end of the year, but this is a huge feat. Like, I'd be freaking out.

Sarah: p.s. I'm proud of you too.

Me: So, like, I have all the feelings, right? Nervous I won't really fulfill Grandma's legacy. Ya know, the one she could have had.

Rach: Wait, what? Oh shit, I forgot you told us your grandma won this competition. How weird (but in a good way) that you are entering the same one.

Sarah: Omg. It's fate. You're going to win.

Rach: You're creating your own legacy, girl. We believe in you.

Me: Thanks, guys.

Rach: But question, what happens if they don't pick you? What's your plan?

ME: It'll be a blow, that's for sure. If I don't win, then am I really good enough to have a career as an author and not just a writer? I haven't told you guys, but my savings could use a boost. If I win, that's $5K!

SARAH: I believe in you, Elle. I think you following this path is worth it, and you'll discover just how good of a writer you actually are. I may have been an art major, but I remember those killer articles you wrote in the Duke newspaper. Your gossip column was completely Carrie Bradshaw-esque.

RACH: Elle, why didn't you tell us about your savings? You know Sarah and I are here for you. The offer still stands, I can help you get a job, and instead of the financial sector, you can try publishing. You never know, you might like it.

ME: Yeah? I don't know. I don't want to discount myself yet. I'm going to see this competition through and pick up projects with the magazine as often as they'll let me. This is so hard, but--and I don't know if this will make sense--it's not as hard as being miserable. I'm having fun.

SARAH: Totally makes sense. You're finding your happiness.

RACH: We're in your corner, let us know how we can support you throughout this process. We love you, Elle.

ME: You guys are the best. Idk what I did to deserve you.

RACH: So, one more question . . .

ME: Uh-oh

RACH: I'm not trying to be mean or to tell you what to do, but Sarah and I have seen you lower than low when it comes to Jude and being half in, half out with him. If you're seriously interested in Kale Guy, I think you need to give him 100% of you and let Jude go.

SARAH: Rach, not now. Let her be happy, she's going on a date tonight.

RACH: No, no, I just want to say that whenever Jude was (or is) kind of in your life, it doesn't typically end well. You get hurt. We don't want you hurt again, we don't want that darkness to come back into your life . . .

I studied Rachel's text message. I knew she was right, but also, I didn't want to care. I was going on a date with Barrett, not Jude. I was allowed to text Jude and be friends; it was mature. I got help with that darkness; I had Tina now. Back then, I didn't have the resources, I didn't have a therapist who cared, and I didn't know I could make it out.

SARAH: I think she's right, Elle. Either he's in or he's out. You were never able to balance both with Jude.

I stared at my phone and felt the familiar tightening in my chest and anger rising in my throat.

ME: Jude has a girlfriend. It's fine, guys. It's all fine.

RACH: Famous last words.

♥

"Finn, I don't know what to wear!" I was standing in my closet pulling out outfits for my date with Barrett in a few hours. Most of them ended up on the floor.

"Elle, he already saw you in boxers and a ragged old T-shirt—oh wait—twice." Finn winked. "I think you'll be fine in anything you want to wear. He didn't ask you on a date because of your outfit choice." He smirked, so I threw the next dress at his face.

"Violence! Abuse!" he yelled playfully as I threw another dress at him, laughing.

"Finnnnn, seriously. Which do you like better? I think I've narrowed it down." I held up a navy-blue dress with a scalloped neckline in my right hand and a dark emerald-green dress with an open back in my left.

"Ohhh, I love, I love," he said as he evaluated both dresses. "I'm really in love with the green dress, though. It's sexy but not trashy. You'd look like a model in that dress."

My mouth curved slightly to one side, and the wheels in my mind were spinning. "Okay, I agree. This will work, then. Let me put it on so you can see the full effect."

Before Finn could respond, I shut my closet door and changed. I stepped out in the green dress and my neutral Prada heels.

"Wow! Holy shit, Elle." Finn's mouth was open, and surprise lined his face. "You are stunning. Absolutely gorgeous!" He raised his hands and clapped. "This is the one, absolutely this is the one."

I felt my cheeks get hot. It had been a long time since someone told me I was stunning.

Barrett arrived for our date five minutes before six o'clock. I watched from my bay window as he parked his Porsche, then walked up the steps to the main door. I took a deep breath to calm the butterflies in my stomach and anxiously waited to hear his knock on the door.

Within minutes, I heard a steady, confident *thump thump thump*.

My hand was shaking as I put my shoulders back and prayed I didn't mess up the night. I was nervous, considering I hadn't been on a date since Jude and I were together. Dating around was off the table when he left for New York; I didn't have the heart or the energy for it. For some reason, Barrett intrigued me. Plus, I was starting a new life here, a new me.

I slowly turned the handle, and when he saw me standing before him, he gaped and stared right into my vibrant green eyes.

A few awkward seconds later, he cleared his throat. "Elle, you're . . . you're"—he rubbed his jaw and ran his fingers down to the tip of his chin—"you are absolutely gorgeous. Your green eyes are breathtaking in that dress."

I tilted my head down and noticed my body getting warm. I looked back up with a bashful grin on my face. "Thank you," I replied softly. I couldn't say another word. I was too lost in the sea of blue looking back at me.

We pulled up to a chic high-rise building in Seaport, a part of town I hadn't been to yet, but Finn told me it was very posh. The building was modern and sleek, with floor-to-ceiling windows and lush greenery around the entrance.

"So, the restaurant is new," he said when we stopped at the valet. "They just opened last month, and it's had rave reviews on Yelp. They are on the top floor and have the most incredible rooftop bar and dining." He paused and looked over at me. "I think you're really going to love this." Then he gave me another million-dollar smile and got out of the car.

The valet opened my door and offered me his hand.

Barrett walked around the car and, once I was standing, offered me his arm. "May I?" he asked.

"You're such a gentleman," I teased.

"I'd like to think so," he said with a crooked grin.

Our table was in an exclusive corner with a view of the river all around us. It was simply stunning as the city lights twinkled along the river and the stars lightly dotted the sky.

"I can't get over this!" I gawked. "It's gorgeous up here."

"I love the view too," he said, his gaze fixed on mine.

Before I could respond, the server came to our table, introduced himself, and asked if we wanted anything to drink other than water.

"May I have a dirty martini—Tito's, please—and three blue cheese–stuffed olives?" I said.

"Of course, madam. And you, sir?"

"I'll have a Johnnie Walker Blue, neat."

"Of course, I'll get those right away."

Smiling at Barrett, I took my napkin and folded it onto my lap. "So, tell me, I'm thoroughly impressed, but wouldn't most guys go for Italian on the first date?"

"Well, Elle"—he put enough emphasis on the end of my name to make my heart skip a beat—"my sister told me she'd disown me if I took her friend to an Italian restaurant on our first date."

The boisterous laugh that escaped my lips startled me, and I quickly slapped my hands over my mouth. Eyes wide, I noticed Barrett was turning red trying to hold in his laugh and there was a brilliant sparkle in his eyes.

"Yeah, so I knew I didn't want to take you out for Italian." He smiled largely and unfolded his napkin on his lap, then leaned his chin on his fist, his grin slight and warm. "Please tell me you like steak and seafood. Otherwise, we need to go to plan B."

"Or the rooftop bar." I tried to drink some water but ended up snorting into the glass. What was wrong with me? I'd never been this unhinged on a date.

"Seriously, that's not a bad backup plan. You saw all the firepits out there when we walked in, right?" His voice got lighter and excited.

"Oh my God, my favorite thing. Firepits and espresso martinis."

"But you ordered a Tito's, correct?" he asked with a raised eyebrow.

"Barrett, you don't start with an espresso martini." I rolled my eyes flirtatiously.

"Fair point. Fair point, Elle Watson." He was nodding in approval.

Out of the corner of my eye, I noticed the waiter come toward our table with our drink order.

"Have you had a chance to look over the menu?" he asked professionally as he placed our cocktails on the table. Barrett looked at me with another slight head tilt and a soft curve of his lips. I nodded and looked to the server.

"I'd like your scallops dish, please." I smiled and handed him my menu.

"Of course," he replied. "And you, sir?" he asked, his pen ready to write down Barrett's order.

"The rib eye, medium rare." Barrett handed him his menu as well.

I savored my smooth, briny martini as the server walked away. As I was about to speak, Barrett started to ask me a question.

"Oh, sorry. You first." He smiled and gestured for me to continue.

"Oh, it's nothing. I was just gonna say, I don't know much about you, Barrett Henry."

"There's not much to tell." He chuckled. "Born and raised in Boston. My family has been here since the revolution, and . . ."

"Oh my God, wait. Were they here for the Tea Party?" I asked, overexcited.

He rolled his eyes playfully. "Yes, the Henrys were here when the tea was thrown into the harbor."

My eyes went wide and my lips curved into an enormous smile. "That is the coolest thing I've ever heard. Please tell me that's your interesting fact whenever you meet people?"

He laughed again and then shrugged. "Sometimes."

"Okay, so your family is Boston royalty. Any other fun facts?"

He quirked his mouth. "How about you tell me a fun fact first? Emma told me you moved here from New Orleans . . ."

I sighed and then took a quick drink of my cocktail. "Well, if you must know, I'm originally from New York."

His eyebrows lifted as he nursed his scotch. "A New York girl, huh? Interesting."

"Yep. My grandparents raised me, so I lived with them in New York. We actually used to come to Boston quite often when I was young. The condo I have now is the condo they left me in their wills."

I saw understanding dawn on him. His mouth parted slightly, but he stayed silent as I continued with my story.

"Here's my fun fact. My grandmother was also a writer, Grandma Di. And she won the exact same writing competition that I am trying to win."

"No way!" He leaned closer with his drink in his hand. "That's some family legacy stuff right there. Your grandma was Boston literary royalty, then." He winked.

I shrugged. "Eh, I don't know about that. She won, but she never went through with the publishing. She decided to live in New York City with my grandfather and become a mother and housewife. She left her writing dreams behind in Boston."

"I'm sorry, I didn't mean to bring up an unpleasant memory," he said softly.

"No, no. It's fine," I lied. "It was her choice, not mine. I can't be mad at her for her decisions. Hell, if she didn't do that, I wouldn't be here, right?" I winked at him this time. "But yeah, okay, New Orleans. I was there for about ten years working in the financial sector. I quit in May."

"You quit? After ten years? What happened?" He leaned forward in his chair and crossed his arms on the table, mindlessly swirling his scotch.

"There was a situation with my boss, and he didn't appreciate or respect me very much even though I'd dedicated so much of my life and efforts to the company. I don't know, I just kind of broke, ya know? I realized I was miserable and that maybe I could be happy somewhere else." I looked at Barrett from under my eyelashes, waiting to hear his response. I wasn't disappointed.

"Actually, I get that. Good for you on leaving, and fuck them for treating you like shit." His passion charmed me, and a thin smile spread on my face. "So, you asked for another fun fact, but this isn't so fun." He brought his scotch to his lips again. "I don't know if you've heard, but my dad is quite the mogul in this area." Sitting up straight now, he scratched the back of his head with his other hand.

"Really? I hadn't noticed."

"Yeah?"

"Well, Finn told me your family owns a bunch of real estate and not to piss you guys off." I shrugged nonchalantly and sat back in my chair, smiling at him.

"Finn happens to be right. Except it's not me and Emma you have to worry about—it's my father." He gave his head a small shake, as if clearing his thoughts. "Anyways, in my family, the sons work with their father and eventually take over the company. Our business has been in the family for decades, and it's expected that I take over the company after my dad."

"That sounds good though, right?" I asked.

"I know I should say yes. I know that's the right answer and what most people would say, but"—he hesitated before finding my gaze—"I don't want to work for him. I don't want to be a part of the Henry corporation."

Sympathy flooded my system. I reached across the table and placed my hand on top of his. "I get it. It's hard when you want to do something for yourself when others expect you to do or want something else." He was staring at our hands, and I felt a tingle radiate through my fingers. He carefully flipped his palm over, curled his fingers, and held mine gently in his. "So what do you want to do?"

He chuckled lightly and then looked up from our hands. "I want to teach people how to sail." His ears were turning red, and he looked back down at the table.

"Teach people to sail?" I asked. Then, noticing his tense shoulders, I continued. "That sounds like an amazing dream job if I've ever heard one."

His head whipped up and he studied my face with inquisitive eyes. Maybe he thought I was being sarcastic. But I wasn't. I was all in for Barrett Henry, the dreamer. "You mean that, huh?" he asked with a furrowed brow and the slightest grin.

"I think you know the answer." I smiled radiantly at him and lifted my glass. "To the dreamers who dream and the ones who never give up."

He lifted his glass to mine and responded with an enthusiastic grin, "To the dreamers."

26

Now

Our first kiss was on November 4. My key was in the lock, but I didn't turn it, and my shoulders were facing him as if I wasn't ready for him to leave. "Well, thank you for an amazing night, I—"

Before I could finish my sentence, his hand slid to my cheek and his eyes locked on mine. He leaned forward, slowly, intentionally, and I closed my eyes and met him the rest of the way.

Our first coffee date was November 6. He was there when I walked into the Bean Shop, and he'd picked the corner booth, my favorite. The night before on the phone, I'd let it slip where I liked to do most of my writing and who I thought had the best coffee and corner booth views.

"You've scored quite the table, sir," I said as I walked up with my honey lavender latte. He was looking down, and at the sound of my voice, he startled upright. "Whoops, sorry about that." I chuckled. "Waiting on someone?"

"Only the prettiest girl in the city," he said, running his hand through his dark wavy hair and grinning. "Please, take a seat, she just arrived." He motioned for me to sit next to him on the teal cushioned bench.

"You're something else, Barrett Henry." I felt my cheeks lift with joy, and each step felt like I was floating toward him. When I sat down, he leaned over and kissed my cheek with a light, delicate peck.

And later after we finally had our first night together, that's when I knew I was in trouble.

♥

Barrett picked me up and we went to a basketball game together. He assured me that I would enjoy an indoor sport better than outside in November. But also, they had barbecue pork nachos, and he knew by now that I was a sucker for tasty bites. I wasn't expecting basketball to be fun because, well, sports, but it was exciting being seated on the court with Barrett. Especially when he would put his arm around me or kiss me on my cheek just because. I felt light. I felt . . . happy?

After the game, Barrett and I left the TD Garden and drove south.

"I thought we were staying at my house tonight?" I asked when I noticed we weren't going toward Back Bay.

"Actually, I wanted to show you my place. I think it's time you met the most important person in my life." His flirtatious side-eye made my stomach flutter.

"I'm right here, aren't I?" I gave him a wicked smile and reached for his hand. We intertwined our fingers, and he gave my hand a gentle squeeze.

"My other special person, smart-ass." He sighed playfully. "Are you okay with coming by?" This time he looked over at me and I saw the excitement in his eyes.

"I don't know, B. I do like sitting on *my* balcony with you in the mornings." I loved teasing him. "Plus, I have a comfy bed, you said so yourself." I lifted my chin in fake triumph.

"Oh, don't worry about your balcony, sweetheart. I've got a surprise for you." The corner of his mouth lifted. "And you're right, your bed is very comfortable."

Barrett parked his Porsche and let the valet take his keys. I knew Barrett was a luxurious guy, but his building took my breath away.

"They just finished building this a few months ago," he said as he saw me staring at the high-rise and its peculiar shape.

"Is this . . . a sail?" My forehead creased as I turned my head sideways and tried to understand the architectural design. Barrett laughed and reached for my hand, his fingers locked with mine.

"Actually, you're right. It's supposed to resemble a sailboat." He leaned down and kissed the top of my head.

My jaw hit the floor the second we stepped through the towering glass doors of the lobby. Magnificent crystal chandeliers sparkled overhead, and exquisite artwork adorned the walls. We strolled across the pristine marble floors so I could take in the opulence. Once inside the mirrored elevator, Barrett pressed the button for the top floor.

"Shut up, the penthouse?" I shrieked.

He flinched at my high tone but gave me a shy smile.

"Sorry, sorry, that was louder than I meant. But holy shit, Barrett."

He stayed quiet with pressed lips and took my hand in his as we ascended twenty-two floors.

"Are you ready for it, Elle?" he asked as we stepped off the elevator and walked to his door.

I glanced at him and tugged his arm. "I'm dying to see. Show me already."

As the door opened, I felt the breath leave my body. The immaculate beauty of his panoramic harbor view, floor-to-ceiling windows, marble, and—oh my God—his balcony.

"What do you think?" he asked nervously.

I gathered what was left of my thoughts and turned to look at him at my side. "I don't think I *can* think." I rubbed my eyes and opened them wide again. "Barrett, I have no words. Your condo is absolutely stunning. I . . ." As I was about to tell him I didn't need to go home tonight, or ever, something ran up from behind me and jumped onto the back of my right leg. Caught by surprise, I toppled forward, but Barrett caught my arm before I could truly fall.

Confused, I stood up straight and looked down at my feet.

"And this," Barrett announced with a grand gesture of his hand toward the bright white ball of fur, "is Louie. The number one, most important being in my life." His teasing grin could kill.

"Your most important . . . is a dog?" I couldn't help but smile. Barrett Henry was a dog dad to the cutest Frenchie I'd ever seen.

"Excuse me, miss." He knelt to Louie's level and picked up the playful pup. "He is purebred and only yells at me sometimes, okay?"

My laugh echoed throughout the condo, and Louie tilted his head to stare at me.

"Now, Louie, this is Elle. Okay?"

The dog just stared at Barrett with his tongue hanging out of his mouth.

"Right, well, she's going to be visiting us, and we have to be a good boy, yeah? Who's the goodest boy? Who's Daddy's baby boy?"

The dog began to pant and wagged his tail like a maniac.

Barrett snuggled him close and gave him kisses all over his head.

"Do you need a minute?" I said as he gave all the snuggles to Louie.

"Okay, buddy, go play. Go get your toy." Barrett put the dog back on the floor and pointed to the corner, where a small toy basket was overflowing with stuffed animals.

"You might be obsessed." I crossed my arms over my chest and stared at him. I felt warmth radiate from my stomach down to my—oh boy. I didn't know I had a thing for men who adored their little dogs and spoke to them in baby talk. "You're also a pretty sexy dog dad."

"Yeah?" he answered in a low and husky voice. "Tell me what else is sexy." He stepped closer, his presence stealing my air.

I changed the subject even though my entire being wanted nothing more than for him to pick me up over his shoulder and throw me into his bed. "So, can I get the grand tour?" I broke eye contact and gestured around, stepping back slightly.

"Sure," he said. The condo had an open floor plan. He walked behind me, leaned down to rest his chin on my shoulder, and wrapped his arms around my waist.

A giggle escaped my lips before I could think to stop it.

Pointing, he continued. "This is the living room, kitchen's over there, and down the hallway"—he turned his head and whispered into my ear—"is one of my favorite rooms."

"Hmm, would that be your bedroom?" I teased, turning my face slightly, allowing my cheek to rest on his nose.

"No, of course it's the library, you dirty girl." He nudged me with his nose and our lips brushed against each other. "Mm, Elle, I love your kisses."

I turned my body in his arms and let my tongue brush against his.

He broke away, slightly panting, his gaze fierce. "Follow me." His smoky voice made my toes tingle.

I followed him down the hallway and into a room right before the library. His bedroom. Every wall was a floor-to-ceiling window, and the harbor sparkled in the moonlight. He picked me up in the doorway and kissed me desperately before placing me down on his soft black comforter. It smelled of him, it all smelled of him. Oak and white musk. My body was pulsing, I wanted him. Jude and I used to be something, but Barrett . . . Barrett was here. Barrett was now. That night, in his bed, I entirely forgot about Jude Ashford.

After sleeping over at Barrett's multiple nights in a row, I went home to my cozy little condo with its exposed brick and uneven wooden floors. As much as I loved his place—seriously loved it—it felt too . . . sterile. We were supposed to work together at the coffee shop this morning, but in true writer form, I was procrastinating. I started cleaning the kitchen, which led to the bathroom (somehow), and when Barrett texted me asking for my ETA, I was sitting on the living room floor organizing my bookshelf. To be fair, I firmly believed that the house had to be clean and organized before I could leave and go write; it was procrastination at its finest.

BARRETT: Get your ass over here. Let's write.

Thirty minutes later . . .

ME: I'm on my way. Still have our booth?

BARRETT: Yes, but the barista is eyeing me like I'm an asshole for taking up a whole booth when there's obviously groups waiting to take it from me. Hurry! ☺

ME: Be there in a sec, see you soon. xo

I bustled into the café and saw Barrett right away talking to an aggravated group of four. From what I could hear, he was trying to explain that he wasn't alone. As soon as he noticed me, relief visibly washed over him like a waterfall.

"See, there she is!" His voice rose an octave, and he pointed in my direction.

I waved with an apologetic grin. "I'm here, I'm here. Sorry about that, guys. I was delayed." I smiled politely and took my seat next to Barrett, who gave a triumphant glare to the group leader, an old man with long gray hair pulled into a low ponytail. His curly mustache was truly impressive. At my official arrival, the man rolled his eyes in annoyance and stormed off with the rest following suit.

"Thank you for holding down the fort," I said sheepishly. "I'm sorry it took me so long to get here." I pulled my laptop out of my tote.

"My pleasure." He took a quick drink of his coffee and placed it next to his laptop.

"What are you working on this fine Monday morning?" I asked, curious. He had nothing but spreadsheets and figures pulled up on his screen.

"My dad and I have a big real estate investment opportunity coming up, and I'm going through the financials and such of the deal. Boring shit, really." He waved it off, clearly not interested in discussing it further. "You ready to write your bestseller?" he asked, looking over at my notebook I'd placed on the table with scribbles all over the page.

"Yep, right after I get my usual." I took a big breath and shot him a quick smile as I stood up.

"Honey lavender latte, hot, with almond milk," he repeated as if he were reciting a poem.

"Don't forget my dash of vanilla if I'm feeling fancy. Wait, I never told you my usual." I tilted my head and narrowed my eyes, along with a subtle pout.

"I have my ways." He gave me a devilish smile. "I just told the barista, who happens to know exactly who you are, that I was waiting on Elle Watson and that I would like to order your usual order. He said he knew what that was and that he was going to have it ready as soon as he saw you walk in. So I think that's it up there now?" He pointed to the pickup counter, and John, my usual barista, winked mischievously my way.

"You're good, B, you're really good," I commended him.

Barrett chuckled, then his phone vibrated on the table. He looked down and I saw his face fall.

"Sorry, Elle. One sec." He started typing furiously with his lips pressed thin.

I took that moment to turn and head toward John and my honey lavender latte. "Thanks, John." I grabbed my latte from the bar.

"Welcome, Elle. I like the new guy." John wiggled his brows while his lips curved into a playful smile.

"Me too." I gave him a sly pucker and shimmied my shoulders.

I sat back down next to Barrett, who was no longer texting but using his phone as a calculator. Without a word, I leaned over and kissed him on the cheek. He was warm and smelled of fresh linen and pine. His lips curved upward at the touch of my lips.

I opened my laptop, then held my latte to my nose before taking a quick taste. The lavender sent waves of calm throughout my body. I could do this. I hovered my fingers above the keyboard and started typing.

A little while later, Barrett stood up and reached toward the ceiling to stretch, exposing his lower abdomen for my eyes to devour. My brain malfunctioned as I caught a glimpse of his natural smooth contour and dark masculine happy trail. Change of plans—I did not want to write right now.

He noticed my hungry eyes, and a wicked grin spread across his face. "Hey, babe, I have to get back to the office. My dad is blowing me up this morning." He sighed and started to pack up his work. "I swear, it's not a true Monday morning until my dad reminds me I'm not him and that I have a duty to the family, so don't fuck it up." He rolled his eyes and shoved the last folder into his bag.

"I'm sorry, B. Is there anything I can do to help?" I felt helpless and wanted to make him feel better.

"Oh, I have some ideas. But later, okay?" He winked, hiding the frustration I knew was underneath. "I'm living vicariously through you, okay, Elle." He leaned in and I met him halfway. His lips against mine felt soft and teasing. "Fuck, I don't want to leave you right now," he growled.

"Don't worry, Mr. Henry." I kissed him again. "I think I can pencil you in between writing, writing, and, oh, writing."

"I'll see you tonight, Ms. Watson," he whispered.

And then he was gone.

27

Our love was an easy love. Not always perfect but easy. It was our first Mardi Gras together and we were meeting Jude's mother in Uptown to watch the parades. If there was ever a mama's boy in this world, it was Jude Ashford. He talked to his mother every day, and every Wednesday they went to lunch together. On Mondays, the three of us gathered at her Uptown home and enjoyed a New Orleans staple—red beans and rice.

"You let the beans sit overnight, Elle. That's the trick. And a generous amount of Tony's once you're ready to set the slow cooker. Don't forget the Tony's, all right?" she'd tell me as if passing down a family recipe.

Mrs. Ava Ashford lived on Prytania Street in an enormous plantation home that had been divided into condos. Jude had purchased the condo for her shortly after he won his first big case.

Even though it was a regular Tuesday everywhere else, Jude and I both had the day off for Mardi Gras. Mardi Gras was much more than throwing beads to women who took their shirts off; it was a way of life. It included weeks of parades and balls, along with wild costumes and wild enthusiasm. In NOLA, they took the phrase "laissez les bons temps rouler" very seriously.

Jude's mother was animated and warm. I loved visiting her and sharing a cup of espresso on her porch. She must have been watching out the window as we parked, because before I could gather the king cake in my arms and shut my door, she was rushing through the iron gate to squeeze me into a hug.

"Hey, Mama Ava." My voice was muffled by the closeness of her hug. She pulled away and gave me a kiss on each cheek. Her own cheeks were rosy, and her mouth spread into the biggest joyous smile.

"Elle! My darling, Elle. I'm so glad you are with us today. It's a good day. A beautiful day." She grabbed my hands and gave a gentle squeeze. "It's Mardi Gras." Her excitement was contagious.

I felt my own smile spreading across my face.

She was beaming as Jude walked around the front of his Range Rover and pulled her into him. "Oh! My boy, my boy." She hugged him tighter.

"I'm glad you're excited to see me too and not just our girl here." He winked over at me above his mother's head.

"Let's go inside, come, let's go." She shuffled us into the quaint, decorated condo. I stole a glance at Jude. His smile made my body tingle, and his wink—now that was just plain deadly.

"I love your decorations. It's so festive in here!" I exclaimed as we stepped across the threshold. She still had her Christmas tree up, but instead of Christmas decorations, there was purple-green-and-gold garland, oversized beads, and—were those . . . ? Yes—even king cake ornaments spread throughout the branches.

"Oh, my girl. Thank you." She beamed and looked to Jude. "Isn't the tree pretty? The sweet girl upstairs helped me decorate it."

"Yes, it's very beautiful, Mom," he said with a heartfelt sparkle in his eye. There was never any question about how much this man loved his mother.

"Oh, my boy." With a warm smile, his mother reached up and patted his cheek. She loved to call him "her boy."

The sun dipped below the horizon, and the parade was only beginning. We watched flambeaux, marching bands, and so many extravagant floats. It was overwhelming and thrilling to see all of the beads flying through the air and wrapping around oak trees and power lines. Children sat on their ladders, seats included, and parents stood with them to help them catch all of the parade's goodies. A marching band was approaching, and I felt someone's arms wrap around my stomach.

Jude smelled of whiskey and sweat. Even though it was getting dark, it was still over eighty degrees outside. I smiled to myself and leaned back into his broad chest. His heart thumped steadily into my back. He leaned his mouth to my ear, and his breath sent goose bumps down my arms.

"My beautiful girl," he whispered. The world didn't exist; it was just me and him, our little bubble. I couldn't hear the band playing or the crowd yelling. All I heard was his voice swimming through my head. "My Elle Belle, I love you."

"I love you too," I whispered back.

My Jude. All mine.

And I was his.

28

Now

'd been writing all morning, but I'd reached a stalemate. Nothing creative was coming out of my brain. I knew my grandparents' story, I knew I could make it into a fantastic romance novel, but when I got to the part where Grandma Di abandoned her writing dreams, I became stuck. And I hadn't figured out how to get rid of the writer's block, so I leaned back into my couch and typed out a message to Sarah.

ME: Hey, girl, you busy?

SARAH: Elle! Just got done with car line. What's up?

ME: I'm stuck with the book. I thought I had it all together and planned out, but it's not flowing. Something isn't working.

SARAH: What feels wrong about it?

ME: I'm not sure. I can't put my finger on it, but it doesn't feel interesting to write, so I can't imagine it's interesting to read. Every time I check my word count, it's hardly moving. I know I have more to write, it's just not showing up on the pages.

SARAH: Still writing the romance book? The one about your grandparents' love story?

ME: Yeah, I thought I had enough inspiration from it, but I got to the point where Grandma Di walks away from her dreams to become a wife and mother, and yeah, I'm stuck.

SARAH: Gotcha, well, I would keep trying. It's going to be hard. But if you don't feel the flow and the inspiration by the end of the month, let's figure something else out. It won't be too late.

ME: Seriously? That's insane. That's way late.

SARAH: No, it's not. I think if you have the right idea to run with, then you'll surprise yourself with what you can accomplish.

ME: All right, well, I'll keep you posted. I'm gonna try a little more, but if I can't make progress within a week, I'm gonna scratch this idea. I think waiting till the end of the month would send my panic into overload.

Sarah: That's fair. Good luck, Elle. You've got this, just keep writing. Writing SOMETHING is better than having nothing at all. It's just a first draft, perfection isn't the goal, completion is!

Me: True. OK, I'm going back in . . .

♥

Later in my therapy session, my Wi-Fi cut out as if it had a personal vendetta against me. Tina's screen was buffering, but her voice was clear despite the connectivity issues. "So, Elle, tell me, how have you been since our last session? Twice a month seems to be working, yeah?"

After texting with Sarah earlier, I'd felt my anxiety flutter intermittently at the thought of starting over. It was meant to be that I had a therapy session scheduled for that afternoon. I settled cross-legged onto my oversized white sofa and held on to an oversized pillow for support. My chest rose as I inhaled deeply and then fell with a slow release.

"Oh, I think so. Twice a month is great. Thanks so much for getting me in with you virtually." Truly, Tina was the reason my transition was working so well. She helped my mindset stay positive, even when overwhelming and passive thoughts crept in. I pulled my mouth in, trying to contain my smile, but the dimples in my cheeks gave me away. "I've met someone." My heart fluttered at the thought of Barrett. I closed my eyes and saw his face, clear and smiling. "I've met someone, and I can't believe I feel like this."

"Elle, that's amazing! Where is your mind going right now? What are you feeling? I can sense your brightness all the way through the screen."

I took another deep breath and said the first word that came to my mind: "Safe." I wrapped my arms around the pillow and squeezed. "I feel safe and giddy and I can't stop smiling." Admitting Barrett felt safe meant that now I could get hurt, that this was real.

"It's been hard for you to feel safe with people, hasn't it?" Tina's voice was warm and encouraging.

My mind lingered on the word *safe* as I answered slowly, "Yesss, but I'm trying to think why." I furrowed my brow and scratched my head slowly. "My grandparents were safe for me, and I never felt unsafe with them. My childhood wasn't terrible." I paused. My childhood was something I never really thought about. "I'm not the only child who's ever been left by their parents. I had my grandparents, so it worked out." I felt my cheeks start to burn, and anger flushed momentarily through my chest, catching me by surprise. Why were my eyes stinging?

"It's all right, Elle. I can see we are digging up powerful emotions, and that's okay."

"What's wrong with me?" I groaned with frustration. "This hasn't bothered me in years. I never think about my parents and that whole situation. Why does this feel like so much all at once?" I looked at Tina, pleading for an answer. This was unacceptable. Why was I getting angry over something that happened years ago, that I'd put behind me and forgotten about?

She replied calmly, "Sometimes we put things away but never really work through the pain they caused us as children. Events in our childhood shape our values, our thoughts, our ideas as we grow up, even if it's subconscious."

I stared at her, my cheeks getting hotter and my hands feeling clammy.

"Elle, let's take a deep breath and then try to exhale slowly as if we are blowing out a candle." I furrowed my brow and looked at her curiously. "This will help to calm the anxiety you might be feeling. You are not doing anything wrong; you haven't done anything wrong. Your childhood does not define you, and you have so much to be proud of, especially the woman you've become."

That was it. I was crying and I couldn't stop. With a shaky voice, I spoke to my screen, to Tina. "Why am I crying? I don't understand, Tina! I don't understand." My body shuddered with every sob.

She pulled her screen closer so that she appeared bigger on my laptop. "Elle, listen, we will work through this together. I think you're crying not only because of these suppressed feelings but because you are being validated today."

I stared at her while tears continued to stream down my face. "What?" I asked, disbelieving what she'd said.

"Yes, you are hearing validation. You have done nothing wrong. You have become an amazing woman. You have made it through very dark times. You are not behind the curve, Elle. If anything, you are extremely resilient, and whether you realize it or not, you inspire others."

I was back to ugly-crying. The screen resolution was finally crystal clear, but Tina was distorted and blurry as I tried to keep my eyes open and look at her.

She continued. "We will overcome this. But first, let's focus on our breath and understand this reaction your body is having. You have to inhale." She watched as I took in a deep breath. "Now hold, Elle. Hold for a few seconds."

I held my breath.

"Good, good." Her voice was reassuring, solid. "Now," she said, "I want you to let it all go."

So I did.

29

Eight years ago

"Babe, want to go see a play this weekend at the Saenger?" Jude scrolled through the Saenger's Instagram feed while he enjoyed his morning cup of coffee.

I sat down next to him at the table and lifted mine to my lips. I set my mug down and gave him a dismayed smile. "I can't, I'm so sorry." I hung my head and sighed.

When I looked back up, he was staring at me with a blank expression. He'd expected this answer.

"I'm really behind and the emails never stop. I can't seem to get ahead, even a little bit."

Disappointment flickered in his eyes. While he was also a busy person and sometimes slept in his office, I was much worse with coordinating my work-life balance. I never slept in my office, but that wasn't for a lack of trying. Mr. Landry caught me sleeping one morning after I'd fallen asleep at my desk the night before, and he immediately sent me home to change my clothes and freshen up. Come to think of it, he was kind of rude. This was no longer a nine-to-five job. It was constant.

"I really am sorry." My pleading gaze softened his features.

"I mean, that's a good thing though, right?" he asked calmly, patiently. "When you're busy, you get more accounts, and you make more money."

I nodded.

"I just wish it wasn't so crazy." He reached for my hand and lifted it to his lips. "I miss you, Elle Belle."

I turned his hand over and pressed it to my cheek. "I miss you too, my love." Resting my cheek in his hand felt warm and secure. Safe. "I just want to prove myself, you know?" I placed his hand back on the table and intertwined our fingers. "This guy Chris in the office is such a dick." I groaned and rolled my eyes.

"Why's that?" Jude looked at me with a quirked eyebrow.

"Well, he's always coming over my shoulder and telling me how to do things with my work. His mansplaining makes me want to bang my head against the wall." I put my coffee down and rested my chin on my other fist. "Believe it or not, I actually know how to do my job."

"Never doubted you." He lifted his mug in acknowledgment.

"I know, I know. It's just . . . I don't know." I groaned and tried to find my words. "It's just that he makes me feel small. I don't like him, and I definitely don't trust him. His words aren't authentic, if that makes sense?"

"No, I get it. There's one of those in every company." His smile was apologetic and understanding.

"Yeah, I guess." I sighed. "Corporate culture and all that, right?"

"Oh absolutely. And it's just as bad for lawyers, trust me." He stood up and walked to my chair. He motioned for me to stand, and I reluctantly agreed. He pulled me close and held me in his arms. His chest was warm, and his heart a steady *thud, thud, thud.*

When he spoke again, I felt his voice vibrate through his body. "You're strong though, Elle. And I know you take zero shit from people. You wouldn't be your grandmother's granddaughter if you weren't spicy." He kissed the top of my head and released me. "Now, how do you want your eggs?" He smirked as he walked into the kitchen.

"Sunny-side up, please," I said over my shoulder.

"Anything for you, Elle Belle."

For a moment, I forgot about work. I forgot about my emails and my coworker Chris. I loved when Jude called me Elle Belle. I loved him. His words were still whispering through my body when a phone call scared the shit out of me. I noticed Jude glance over at me from the stove, and I looked at the phone.

Work was calling.

30

Now

couldn't get enough of Barrett Henry. Every kiss, every hug, every text was a Cupid's arrow to my heart. I fell harder for him every day, and when Emma casually mentioned his ex was Margaret from the office, I finally understood why he would avoid coming into the Boston Social office with me. He didn't want to run into her. I thought I might be jealous of her, especially since they were an item for a few years, but she wasn't the one going to the Henry family Thanksgiving dinner. I was.

Barrett wasn't off work yet, and I was sitting on my balcony with my legs propped up on the railing and my computer on my lap. He was staying over more often, and then occasionally I'd stay with him at his fancy Seaport condo. Barrett wasn't oblivious, he knew how much I loved my condo, so he stayed with me more often than not and never asked for us to go to Seaport. I had a feeling Seaport didn't feel like home to him. He hadn't been there long before I moved to Boston, so when he was with me, he was home. I was his home.

First his toothbrush stayed behind, then a pair of shoes, then suddenly I was dog-sitting Louie and sharing my couch with him permanently. Barrett told me he felt bad leaving Louie at home all the time, and since I was home regularly, we decided that Louie would stay with me and live at my house. And not that I thought of this right away, but it also meant Barrett wouldn't have to go home to let him out or feed him. He'd just come right to my condo, and the three of us would be together.

I gave a frustrated sigh and shut my computer. This wasn't working. I grabbed for my phone and opened my text messages.

ME: Sarah, it's time.

SARAH: OK, make your list of ideas and send them over. You've got this, Ellz. How many words do you have right now?

ME: Forty-five thousand.

SARAH: Shit, OK, that's going to hurt, but we can manage. Don't delete anything! You might use it one day for something else. Send me over your ideas, OK?

ME: OK, OK. Actually, I have an idea. It's crazy as hell. What if I wrote a rom-com loosely based on mine and Jude's story?

SARAH: Um, what?

ME: Not like "us" exactly, but girl meets boy one summer while interning, and then their paths cross again later on in life. I can get an outline together super fast; I mean, our story is straight out of a Christina Lauren book and could be really cute.

SARAH: Oooh, I love it. It's something you know, and you can play with plot and character development so easily since you are already familiar with your main characters and their story.

ME: Exactly.

SARAH: I'm not gonna say don't stress, because that'd be stupid, but I think your forty-five thousand words will come back way easier this time around.

ME: Me too. I know how it ended in real life, but per the rules of romance, I'm going to give my characters a happily ever after. It's something I can work with. I think I've got this. Check your email tonight.

SARAH: Ellz, wait. What about Barrett? How is he going to feel about you writing a story based on your relationship with Jude?

ME: I'm just going to say it's a rom-com idea based on my life before I met him. I'm not sure why my grandparents' story hung me up so badly. I really wanted to finish it, but I think I have some mental blocks to work through with how Grandma Di left it all for a life that I don't really understand. I wish I did, but I just can't wrap my brain around such a talented woman leaving it all behind. It felt like it was missing something, and I couldn't figure it out.

SARAH: Honestly, she sounds like you but reversed. You see it right?

ME: Eh.

SARAH: Oh, it's totally there in plain sight. She left something she loved and was talented at to become a housewife and caregiver for her husband. You, on the other hand, left a work situation for something that you love and are talented at. (Don't @ me, you're a talented writer!)

ME: I don't think what she did was wrong, it's just what she wanted (I think). I know she loved being a mother. It's hard for me to picture that for myself though, so it was tough to, I don't know, articulate in writing without sounding like a bitch. If anything, you're like Grandma Di. ☺

SARAH: Such an honor! Love you, Ellz. To the moon and back. ♥

I closed my first project for the last time. Ideas and words for my new manuscript were fighting to get onto the screen. When I finally looked up from typing three hours later, my outline was done. This worked. Everything worked. I shot off an email to Sarah and got a quick reply:

Oh my God. Keep writing.

So I did.

Barrett walked through my door that evening with Chinese takeout in one hand and flowers in the other. He walked right over to me, placed everything on the coffee table, and took my face in his hands and kissed me, desperate, hard. The subtle hint of crisp pine needles and cotton lingered in the air.

"Hello, beautiful," he murmured.

I could still taste him on my lips. A delicate smile spread across my face. Our relationship was growing quickly and so was my word count.

♥

"Elle, I have this idea, but I want to run it by you." Barrett turned onto his side and faced me. His hair was tousled, and his head was resting on his arm. The bed dipped slightly, and my body fell closer to his. I would never get over the warmth that emanated from him.

I was about to reply when a little cardinal landed on my windowsill and let out a chirp.

"Ellz, are you listening?"

I readjusted my eyes and turned my gaze back to him. "Yes, of course. What's your fabulous idea?" I said with my morning lisp. My mouthguard was still in, and Barrett's mouth pulled into a cheeky grin. He wrapped his other arm around my body and pulled me into his bare chest.

"What if"—he kissed the tip of my nose—"we went away to Nantucket for a weekend?" Another kiss on my cheek. "After Thanksgiving?" He placed another kiss on my forehead.

Surprised, I arched my eyebrow and gave him a playful glare. "Nantucket? Wait, are you serious, or are you messing with me?"

"I'm totally serious." He let go of me and rolled onto his back and stretched his arms toward the headboard. "We have a townhouse there, and I think it'd be nice to get away for a weekend, just the two of us. What do you think?" He paused for my reply, but I was too stunned to form words, so he continued. "The island is incredible the whole month of December. We'll get to see the Festival of Trees and do the Christmas Stroll since they start right after Thanksgiving."

I snuggled my head into his shoulder and emitted a low anticipatory groan. I'd always wanted to go to Nantucket, especially after the *Gilmore Girls* revival showed Emily Gilmore living her best life there. It had always seemed like a magical place to visit.

"I can't believe you want to take me to Nantucket!" I rolled my body on top of his and thoroughly enjoyed watching his wide smile appear, reaching both eyes. I leaned forward and held the tip of my nose just above his. My hair fell over our faces and hid us from the rest of the world. I could smell the mixture of his warm skin and my fresh lavender laundry detergent. Anticipation glistened in his eyes, and he groaned in excited frustration. A wry grin spread across my face. "I say yes."

His arms wrapped around my body and held me bent over, straddling his waist. Then he rolled over and flipped me onto the bed, the white duvet swallowing me in warm goose down. He gently pinned my arms above my head and used his knees to hold my thighs apart. His breath was shallow and fast. He leaned in as I lifted my head to meet him, my body vibrating with raw energy. Our lips met, and my mind blurred with lust. He left my lips tingling, then began kissing and nipping at my neck. Barrett kept going down, down—*oh my God.*

Barrett and I danced and floated as one. Every thrust, every moan, every touch was ecstasy. I was an addict for Barrett Henry, and there was never going to be enough of him.

He moaned my name with raw need, then collapsed on top of me.

With my knees still pulled into my chest, he rested his head on my shoulder, his nose nuzzled into the crook of my neck.

"I love you." The vibration of his voice tickled my ear, and his breath softly brushed my neck.

I love you. My mind spiraled as I tried to justify what he'd just said. My adrenaline rose again, and every movement, every touch shocked my sensitive body. *I love you.* Oh my God, he loves me. Barrett Henry loves me! It was terrifying, but I had yearned for this comfort, this safety, and this connection for a long time.

I lifted my head and nibbled his earlobe. I rested my head back down and gazed at him from under my eyelashes. "I love you too, Barrett Henry."

We lay there for a few moments more, and then we heard the bedroom door open. Louie had a nasty habit of forgetting to knock. He sauntered up his doggy stairs and squirmed between us. Moment ruined.

Barrett rolled off the bed and walked into the bathroom to dispose of the condom and take a shower. I let Louie jump over me and find his favorite spot in the center of the covers. I sat up and petted Louie, who quickly started snoring. His white fur was soft, and his little pink nose wrinkled with every inhale and snort.

"What do you have planned for the rest of the day?" I asked casually as I got out of bed and walked into the bathroom to pee.

"I'm headed to the office today. Dad and I have a conference call with a high-net-worth client in Miami. He's been giving me more responsibility and the lead on accounts since he allegedly wants to retire next year," Barrett said while the hot water steamed up the bathroom.

Despite his confidence, I thought I could hear hesitation in his voice.

"Barrett, are you okay?" I was standing naked by the glass shower door trying to hear him. He'd gone completely quiet.

He opened the door and walked out to grab his towel hanging on a hook. I stepped back as he wrapped it around his waist, then leaned against the wall. He had one hand on his chest and the other on the wall. He was heaving and struggling to breathe. He removed his hand and leaned forward, hands on his knees with his head down, taking quick, heavy breaths with his eyes closed.

"Barrett!" My high-pitched voice echoed throughout the bathroom. I grabbed his upper arm and bent over with him. "What's wrong?" I rubbed his lower back in large circular motions. "Sit down, Barrett, sit down. Breathe. Take big, deep breaths."

I guided him over to the toilet and had him sit down with his head between his knees. I kept rubbing his back and guided him through the breathing that Tina taught me.

"Elle, I can't do this."

My heart plummeted. What did he mean, he "can't do this"? Us? After he just said *I love you for the first time?* "Do what?" I asked. "Breathe, babe. C'mon, big inhale, now slow exhale. I'm here. I've got you."

"I can't keep pretending. I can't keep doing this with my dad." He sat up and reached his hand over his heart. "Elle, my chest, it hurts. I can't breathe. Right now. I can't breathe." His eyes were wide and his pupils dilated. He was scared.

"Barrett, I'm here. I love you. I'm here."

Louie woke up because of the commotion and waddled over to his daddy. He whined and licked Barrett's shins.

"Barrett, do you think you're having a heart attack? This might be a panic attack. Have you ever had one before?" I held his hand and intertwined my fingers in his, firm and supportive. "Inhale, two, three, four—exhale, two, three, four," I repeated.

"No, no, this happens sometimes. It goes away, the chest pain goes away, but—" He was hyperventilating again. "It's not working, the breathing!" He was gasping for breath. "Elle, Elle, I'm . . ."

I grabbed both of his hands, moved to the floor in front of him, and looked him straight in the eyes. "Barrett, focus on me."

He held my gaze. I didn't blink. His eyes were wild and his body was trembling, but I held his face between my hands and never broke my stare.

"Okay, inhale deep. You *can* breathe, you *are* breathing. Barrett, you are not dying. I won't let you. Now, inhale deep. Do it."

He fixed his eyes on me. His bright blue eyes were red-rimmed and watery, but he took a large inhale. I saw his bare chest rise.

"Now exhale, slowly, as if you are blowing on a flame but trying to make it flicker, not extinguish. Do it, I'm here." I let go of his face and grabbed both of his hands in mine. They were clammy and shaky.

He blew out slowly through his pursed lips. The lightest breath brushed my face. "Exhale as long as it takes, then inhale again. Remember, you can breathe." I watched him take each inhale and release each exhale.

After a little while, his panic started to abate. His chest stopped heaving, and he stopped sweating. He closed his eyes in obvious relief and his heart slowly returned to a normal rate.

"A little better?" I asked, still holding on tightly to his hands and kneeling on the bathroom tile between his knees.

He nodded, appearing exhausted, and leaned forward to rest his forehead against mine.

"Elle," he whispered.

"Barrett, I'm here," I whispered back.

Louie was still whining and gently nuzzled my naked thigh.

"Elle, that wasn't the first one," he admitted.

"Barrett." I reached back up and cupped his cheeks in my hands. He sighed and tilted his head into my open palm.

"When that happens, I always think I'm going to die. Sometimes I wonder if that would be better." His voice was soft and raspy.

"No, Barrett. No. Never. Promise me." I pressed up on my knees and kissed his forehead. "I know what that feels like. That darkness and anticipation of no more pain, no more anything. I know how awful panic attacks can be. But dying isn't the answer. Living is."

He opened his eyes and met mine.

I wrapped my arms around his wet body and held him. Nuzzling my face into his neck, I whispered softly into his ear, "Please, Barrett, continue to live."

31

Now

"Barrett, you said your dad is going to be there tonight but has to leave early, right?" I was reaching for my purse as Barrett stood up from his couch. I'd arrived at his condo earlier to write while he got some work done before dinner. "Wait, where did you say they live again?" I knew it wasn't technically in the city but was still pretty close.

"Correct. Dad has to catch a flight out to Miami for a large real estate deal and won't be joining us for dessert." Barrett rolled his eyes and scoffed. "And they live in Weston. It's about fifteen minutes or so away, so not too far." He reached into his hall closet for a blazer. "Are you sure you don't want to borrow a winter jacket? I'm sure Emma left one here, and it's frigid outside. As much as I love looking at you in your black dress and pearls"—he walked over to me and kissed my cheek—"you're not wearing anything very warm." The concern in his tone made my heart ache in the best possible way.

"I'm good, I promise. We're just going to be in the car and then their house. How bad can it be?" I said with a nonchalant shrug.

"Oh, Elle Watson. Those will be your famous last words." He pulled me into a firm hug, and the vibration of his deep chuckle spread throughout my body as I held him tighter.

I knew Barrett and his dad weren't close, especially since the conversation of retirement was thick in the air, and after his panic episode yesterday I knew it was getting to him. He was being pressured—no, forced—into a career he didn't want to pursue. He told me he asked his dad after their conference call yesterday to leave the business to his uncle—his dad's brother—to let him run the company. His father vehemently refused and told Barrett it was his responsibility to the family to be the next Henry in charge. Barrett came back to my condo that night a shell of himself and lay on the couch with his head on my lap for hours while I ran my fingers through his hair and kept *The Office* playing.

I believed the only reason his parents were having this show of a dinner tonight was so that they could finally meet me, the new girlfriend. Barrett had confessed that Thanksgiving was never a huge deal for his family, and usually his parents would travel out of the country, leaving him and Emma to celebrate by themselves.

We were moving toward the door when I added, "Well, even if your dad is there and it's a little tense, I'm sure we will have a great time with your mother." I smiled at him reassuringly.

Barrett stepped in front of me and shook his head in disbelief. "Elle, I don't know where you get your positivity from, but I love it. My mom will be thrilled I'm visiting for dinner, that's for sure. The faster we get this dinner over with, the better. I'd rather be on the couch watching the Red Sox as usual, but with you of course."

He winked, then opened the door, holding it open for me to walk through. "We should hurry. My mother has a strong aversion to tardiness." He checked his phone one last time and then slipped it into his coat pocket. His slim navy blazer accentuated his broad shoulders.

Winter was in full force, and a fresh blanket of soft snow dusted the ground. The sun was beginning to set over the horizon, and the ice crystals on the bare trees sparkled. The cold caught me by surprise, and my gasp left a cloud of breath that lingered while we walked to his Lexus SUV.

"I told you you'd want a jacket." He smirked as I pulled my arms in for warmth.

"Oh, shove it," I teased back. "I'm . . ."

He opened the door and in his other hand was a heavy winter jacket.

"Just in case, I thought I'd grab it," he said confidently.

I rolled my eyes and smiled as he helped me put the jacket on over my outfit and get in the passenger seat.

"I didn't know you had another vehicle?" I said as I turned the seat warmer on high.

"Well, my Porsche prefers less ice on the roads." He laughed, then pressed the ignition button.

About twenty minutes later, we pulled up to a large iron gate. Barrett put in a code, and the gate rolled back. The driveway turned over on itself for at least a mile before the house finally came into view, a mansion and sprawling estate with heavy original stone and meticulous vintage details. There was a fountain in front of the home, and the driveway looped around it, placing us right at the enormous wooden front door.

"Oh my God." My mouth was ajar as I stared at the mansion before my eyes.

"Yeah, it's nice on the outside," Barrett remarked, "but it's probably colder in that house than it is out here." He gave me a quick eyebrow raise and put the car in park.

An older man with short white hair and a uniform walked from the door to greet us. Barrett made his way around the Lexus and opened my door as the man stopped in front of us. "Welcome home, Mr. Barrett." He bowed his head.

I watched, transfixed.

"Good evening, Harold, how are you?" He gave the man a crooked grin and embraced him. Barrett looked genuinely pleased to see him. His smile spread naturally, and his energy relaxed as the old man, Harold, hugged him back with a tight squeeze.

"Very well, sir. Thank you." Harold smiled and stepped back. His eyes went from Barrett, back to me, then back to Barrett. He beamed and then bowed to me. "It's a pleasure to host you, miss."

"Elle. Um, my name is Elle," I replied shyly.

Harold chuckled and straightened. "Welcome, Miss Elle. We are delighted to have you with us tonight." He pointed to the house and looked to Barrett. "Your mother is waiting just inside, sir." He bowed his head again and then walked around the SUV to go park it in the garage.

The front door was larger in person, and as we walked up, Mrs. Henry swung it open to greet us. "Darling, so good to see you!" She wrapped Barrett in a tight hug. "Oh, my boy, I've missed you. It's been too long." She backed up slightly and her eyes captured mine. I knew exactly where Emma and Barrett inherited their crystal-blue eyes from. She extended her arms toward me in excitement. "And this must be your Elle!" She grasped my forearms with cold, firm hands and proceeded to give me an air kiss on each cheek. I was in way over my head.

"Yes, ma'am, nice to meet you." I smiled, shy and slightly intimidated.

She stood up straight and stared at Barrett. "Ma'am?" She raised her eyebrow in disapproval.

"Mother, she's from New Orleans. It's nothing offensive." Barrett smiled warmly at his mother, but when she looked back at me, I caught his gaze from behind her and saw him mouth, *Sorry!*

"Oh, right, right. They do say that there, don't they?" Mrs. Henry smiled coolly at me and motioned for us to follow her into the house.

Great, this was going to be a fantastic evening. I rolled my eyes to myself and felt Barrett's hand grasp mine firmly. I looked up and he smiled down. A quick squeeze let me know that he was still with me and wasn't going anywhere.

We were led to a large den, where his father was waiting with scotch and cigars. "Barrett, my boy." His voice boomed in the antique room.

Floral wallpaper and the smell of aged wood surrounded us as we walked in to greet Mr. Henry.

"Hello, Father." Barrett's voice was short and crisp.

The tension in the room was thicker than the cigar smoke. My heart ached for Barrett and the person he had to become around his parents, mainly his father. His mother was quiet, seen but not heard. I had a feeling, though, for no particular reason, that Barrett was her baby and she loved him dearly. A few times I saw her look from Barrett to her husband, and her eyes were heavy, her forehead creased with concern.

The Henrys, they had all of this money and all of this financial success, yet I knew all Barrett wanted to do was run home with me and watch baseball. I guess you can be financially successful but still lack in other areas of your life. Barrett had told me that his big dream was to own a sailboat and have a tour company off of Nantucket. He just wanted to sail. He was excited to bring me there, because for him, that was his happy place.

"Good evening, Mr. Henry. Nice to meet you, I'm Elle Watson." I extended my hand, hoping it was the right thing to do.

"The pleasure is all mine." His smile was forced, his face tense with a lack of genuine joy.

After a few cocktails, everyone seemed to relax a little more. Mrs. Henry talked more to me instead of through Barrett, and she even gave me a few somewhat genuine smiles throughout the evening's conversations. To be honest, it was hard to tell, but I'd accept any smile that woman gave me.

Dinner was delicious—a baked ham with all the usual Thanksgiving sides—but also, smoked salmon?

Barrett leaned over and whispered in my ear, "Dad has a poultry allergy. I saw you staring at the salmon." He chuckled lightly and his breath sent a tingle through my spine.

While I was still a little insecure, I felt so incredibly special that Barrett had brought me to meet his family. Emma was supposed to be at dinner, but Olivia had her on assignment in New York and she hadn't made it back yet. Mr. Henry's voice was soft and proud when he spoke about Emma. I wasn't sure, but the way his eyes lit up at the mention of her name, I had a feeling she was his favorite.

"So, Elle, I hear you work with Emma. Is that right?" Mrs. Henry asked casually before looking over at her husband.

"Yes, that's correct." I smiled. "I'm a freelancer for the magazine she works for and see her in the office pretty often. We also do yoga together." *We also do yoga together? C'mon, Elle,* I told myself.

"A freelancer?" Mr. Henry interjected. "So you aren't actually employed with them?"

Well, that wasn't where I thought this was going. I hesitated for only a moment, trying to gather my thoughts. "I'm employed, but more so on my terms, I guess you could say. I work as an independent contractor while Emma is actually a full-time employee."

He didn't skip a beat. "So you don't work full time?" He looked to Barrett. "Margaret is *employed* at that magazine your aunt runs. Isn't she the art director or something high up like that?"

Barrett's face blanched at the mention of his ex-girlfriend. I could feel the frustration and anger rising in my chest. His dad was twisting my words. And also, *aunt?* Olivia was Barrett and Emma's aunt. *Holy shit!* Before Barrett could reply, I chimed in again.

"Yes, Margaret is there still. She does a wonderful job for the magazine with layout and design." I was going to kill with kindness. *I repeat, kill with kindness.*

Sitting next to Barrett, I could feel him getting uneasy and noticed his shoulders draw up toward his ears. Tension was gathering in his shoulder blades, so I placed my hand on his upper back and made soft, circular motions to help him relax.

"I see. So as an independent contractor, you're not entitled to benefits or retirement then, correct?" Mr. Henry continued arrogantly with his twenty questions.

I was beginning to feel defensive, like he was attacking me for something I did wrong.

"Dad, I really don't think this is appropriate," Barrett said, his voice tense and low.

"Barrett, I can ask Elle about her work. It's fair game, right, Elle?" Mr. Henry asked with an overly sweet voice.

What is wrong with this man? I thought to myself.

While holding her wineglass with glazed eyes and a content smile, Mrs. Henry chimed in to the conversation. "I'm so glad you've met Margaret. We love her. You know, she and Barrett were a hot item? We thought for sure they'd be announcing an engagement, but—"

"Mother!" Barrett's voice was hot and firm.

Mrs. Henry closed her mouth abruptly and looked at Barrett with a confused and slightly annoyed expression on her face. "What, Barrett? It's true. We all thought—"

He cut her off again. "Mother, that's enough. We aren't here to talk about Margaret. That relationship is over." I could feel the heat radiating off his back, so I moved my hand to hold his underneath the table. His palms were sweaty, and I squeezed gently as our fingers interlaced on top of his thigh. I had to keep him calm. If he lost control of his emotions, they'd eat him alive. We were definitely going to need a stiff drink after this dinner.

I couldn't look away from Mrs. Henry. I didn't think she hated me, but she was a little cold earlier. Now she was acting aloof. After Barrett reprimanded her outburst, she began to pout and kept looking over to Mr. Henry, then to her glass. Sip, pout, sip. In that glimpse of a moment, I couldn't be angry with her; I felt bad for her. She was coping with this very uncomfortable situation, and she was coping with her wine. I wondered how often that was the case for her.

I turned a challenging gaze back to Mr. Henry. He didn't scare me; he annoyed the fuck out of me, and I wasn't intimidated by this small-minded, narcissistic man.

"Mr. Henry."

He looked over at me, surprised.

"You are correct in your assumption."

His eyes widened and his brows rose in question.

"I do not have retirement benefits or any other benefits with this current position. However, I had a very successful, very financially rewarding career for many years prior to moving to Boston. I do, in fact, have a 401(k) and an investment portfolio, but forgive me, I don't typically brag about it at the dinner table."

Barrett whispered in my ear, "Elle . . ."

But I kept my fierce stare on Mr. Henry. Fire was burning in my eyes, and Mr. Henry wasn't going to treat me like Chris or Mr. Landry had. I wouldn't allow it. I deserved better as a woman trying to be enough in a society that was rooting against me.

"Elle, please, you don't have to justify yourself here. Please. It's not worth it." Barrett squeezed my hand and tried to assuage my anger.

I ignored him.

"You are very interesting, Elle Watson." Mr. Henry held my gaze; he was a powerful man, after all. "You chose to work for less. Or did you think you'd meet someone? Someone like my son?"

Okay. This made sense now.

"Dear, stop. Who wouldn't want to meet someone like Barrett? He's simply the light of my life—and such a good boy." Mrs. Henry waved her hand whimsically in the air.

"Motherrr," Barrett groaned. Though, it was pretty cute the way she doted on him.

"I'm not questioning that, my dear." His voice was sarcastic and crass. "But someone like our son, who is very wealthy and from a *good* Boston family, is quite the catch. Wouldn't you agree, Barrett?" He turned to his son and gave him a cold grin with thin pressed lips and a maniacal head tilt.

"She's happy, Father. Sometimes all the money in the world can't buy happiness," Barrett said tightly.

"Happy?" Mr. Henry sneered with laughter. "This must be a new generational thing. Right? Happy? I've never heard of such a thing." Then Mr. Henry lifted a finger and smirked at Barrett. "Well, almost never, right, Barrett, my boy? Didn't you once say you weren't happy?" He looked right at me as he spoke. "I set him straight. Right, Barrett?"

Barrett was trembling, his eyes were narrowed, and his nostrils flared. I squeezed his hand tighter and pulled slightly to keep him seated.

Mr. Henry continued with his harassment. "Something about sailboats and Nantucket—what an idea." Mr. Henry waved his hands dismissively. "You were born to lead this company, and it took a while, but we've come to an understanding. Right, Barrett? Happiness? What do they teach you at college these days?" he said with disdain.

At the other side of the table, Mrs. Henry was staring at her glass, nodding silently, barely listening.

"One day, you kids will figure it out. You need to be successful and have money like we do. You don't want to end up on the streets or, worse, be forced to fly commercial. These hobbies and such, they won't do for long. They don't pay the bills. You can't be a successful writer." He glared at me, then back to Barrett. "And I refuse to allow you to do anything that will jeopardize our family legacy or our company. Do you hear me, boy?"

Barrett was stone-still. He didn't give his father the satisfaction of a reply. I didn't expect Mr. Henry to be so savage. He had thrown back quite a bit of scotch, but still, this man was awful.

We continued to sit in silence for what felt like an eternity but was only a long, agonizing minute. Mr. Henry kept checking his watch, and Barrett was inhaling and exhaling deeply and controlled. I could feel the rage emitting from his body.

I shouldn't have said anything, we were almost done with this fiasco, but I became brave for a few seconds and ran with the opening. "I'm also writing a book," I declared with a lift of my chin.

Barrett's neck whipped around and he stared at me, his eyes pleading with me to stop. But I couldn't. I was pissed, and no one was going to make us feel like we were less than.

"A book?" Mrs. Henry finally spoke.

"Yes, a book," I replied, noticing her interested stare. "With all due respect, Mr. Henry, I don't believe a corporate career is for everyone."

He rolled his eyes as if my voice inconvenienced him further. "And yes, I did leave security and money and comfort. I did it because it was right for me, and not everyone needs to lead the life others dictate for them." At that, I looked over at Barrett and felt his grip tighten. "I'm experiencing unfiltered joy with your son." I didn't break eye contact with Mr. Henry. "I love your son."

Mrs. Henry sat silently with a curious look on her face. Her eyes darted between me and Barrett, and I noticed the tiniest smile appear on her lips. She reached for her wine again. The room was heavy, and the tension could be cut with a butter knife.

"Oh, look at the time. I must be going." Mr. Henry tossed his dinner napkin on his plate and rose to his feet. "My driver is outside. See, Barrett, you won't get a driver until you start making those big deals." And with that, he nodded to me and Mrs. Henry, turned around, and never looked back.

Harold came in through the doorway moments after Mr. Henry rushed out. I had a feeling he'd been waiting for the atmosphere to cool down. He walked up next to Mrs. Henry and made his announcement. "I'm sorry, madam. Miss Emma called to say she is staying home for the evening. She just got in from the city and won't make it in time." He bowed his head in regret, but Mrs. Henry just waved her hand in indifference.

That was our cue. Barrett squeezed my hand, and we exchanged a glance that said we were on the same page.

"Mother, I'm sorry, I don't think we can stay for dessert." Barrett looked across the table at his mother. "Elle and I need to get home to Louie."

Mrs. Henry didn't argue. "I think that's best, dear. Maybe next time." She gave us a defeated, pitiful look. "I'm sorry, Barrett. I thought he would behave." Tears glistened in her eyes.

Barrett walked over to his mother and gave her a kiss on the top of her head. I couldn't hear what he said, but he muttered something to her, and a tiny smile appeared for just a second. She reached for his arm and gave a quick squeeze. I saw her mouth, *I love you.*

Harold walked us out of the dining room and toward the heavy front door.

"Harold, I'm sorry." Barrett turned and hugged the old butler.

I noticed Harold had a tear in his eye and hugged Barrett back, a firm and loving embrace—a father's embrace.

"It was a pleasure to meet you, Harold," I offered before he opened the door for us.

He looked to me with warm eyes and a soft smile. "No, Miss Elle, the pleasure is sincerely all mine. Take care of my boy."

Barrett and I walked out into the frigid night air. It felt like escaping an enemy's castle. We walked across the stone path and fled back to the safety of our own kingdom.

Once in the car and on our way, I turned to Barrett, who was staring blankly at the road in front of us.

"Harold?" I asked.

He immediately picked up on my question. "Yeah, he was always around for Em and me. He's more of a father than the other man you had the *pleasure* of meeting tonight." Anger laced his words, and as we passed under a light, I noticed his cheeks were wet.

"Hey, B?"

"Mm?" he hummed back.

"I love you, like a lot." I smiled in the dark and placed my hand on the back of his neck, twirling his thick hair between my fingers. He released a deep sigh and let his body relax under my touch.

"I love when you touch me," he moaned as my fingers massaged his neck.

"I love to touch you," I replied low and sweet. "You know you always have a choice, right?" I asked seriously.

His sigh was long, and the tension returned to his neck and shoulders. "You do, Elle. I'll make sure you always have a choice." He grabbed my hand and placed his cheek in my open palm. "But I don't. My choices were made a long time ago. The best choice I ever made, though, was sitting next to you at that Pats game and pretending I'd never seen you before." I felt his cheek lift with a smile.

"I mean, I will say this. Leaving Marrrrgaret wasn't a bad choice either," I teased.

He let out a soft chuckle. "Yeah, well, actually, she left me. But you're right, not going back when she asked was another good choice." He took my hand and held it on the center console.

"She wanted you back?" I asked, curious. "You've never really mentioned your relationship with her."

"There's not much to tell. We dated for a couple years, but I never truly loved her. My parents did, though. They really loved Margaret, especially because her father is a senator and her family was here during the Revolutionary War as well."

"A real OG Boston family," I whispered.

"Yeah, my parents enjoy comparing social status, in case you missed that part at dinner." He turned his head and smirked.

"So, okay, she wanted you back. When was that?" I wasn't mad, just curious.

"Right when you and I started dating, actually."

My eyes went wide, but he couldn't see them in the dark.

"Emma told me that Margaret had asked about me in the office. Emma really loves you and said that you and I were 'talking'—whatever that means." He laughed softly. "In my mind, all I could think about was you."

"Oh, B." I laughed. "You're such a noble man."

"Right, well, Margaret texted me later that day. I'd had a heads-up, though, because Em called me right after Margaret left her office."

"Dear God. You know, I don't talk to Margaret that often in the office when I'm in there. She does her thing and I do mine." I shook my head. "I didn't think she was so, so . . ."

"Manipulative? Passive-aggressive? Entitled? Pick one," he said. "Anyway, she called me and, after bitching me out for God knows what, begged me to get back together. It was the same emotional roller coaster we'd experienced in our relationship."

I rubbed my thumb on his palm, encouraging him to continue.

"I told her no. I wouldn't do it anymore. We were over and I was finally happy . . . with you."

"I'm happy with me too," I joked and let a smile show. "No, seriously, I'm so happy with you."

"Good—otherwise, sitting on the couch and watching a replay of the game with Louie in our laps would be very, very awkward."

I laughed along with him, then fell quiet. We had to talk about the dinner. "Hey, B?"

"Yeah, babe?"

"That dinner was rough." My voice was cautious; I didn't want to overstep any more than I might have already.

"That's the understatement of the century." He laughed. "But you know what?"

"What?"

"Watching you put my dad in his place made me harder than you can even imagine."

I rolled my eyes. *Hard?* "Oh my God, Barrett!"

"Elle Watson, you are one sexy firecracker when someone upsets you. If you ever need to pretend you're mad at me in bed, I won't hate it." His deep chuckle made a warm sensation spread through my core.

I leaned over the center console and whispered into his right ear, "Not a problem, Mr. Henry."

32

Now

After a tough Pilates class with Finn, I recounted the Thanksgiving dinner to him, and his big gay heart was fuming. "Okay, other than the fact I rarely see you these days and you're a writing queen, what the actual fuck, Elle? People can't treat you like that." Finn was wiping down his reformer as I took a small drink of water.

"I know, I was more shocked than anything at first. Like, I've never had anyone completely ambush me like that." I moved my machine bar back to the front. "I mean, Mrs. Henry was a tipsy mess and then Mr. Henry was a demon from hell—a very rich demon from hell, I guess."

"Well, there are people like that here, everywhere really. And that opinion isn't uncommon. Ya know, go to college, get your degree, and get the nine-to-five." Finn walked away to throw his towel in the bin. "It's the perpetual cog in the wheel, rat race, all that jazz." He shrugged and rolled his eyes.

"I know, and for the longest time, I thought that was my story, Finn. I really did. And it's some people's story for sure, like my friend Rachel. She's a corporate queen. I just can't do it, though. And his dad couldn't wrap his mind around it at all."

Finn and I walked into the lobby of the studio and took a seat by the smoothie bar he'd just opened. "You know, I really like this smoothie bar idea," I said while I looked at the menu.

"It was Jackson's idea." Finn shrugged. "But yeah, I like it too." He ran his hand over his sweaty hair and turned back to me. "So, dinner was a shit show. The important thing is this: What does Barrett think of it all?"

"He supports me and says he understands. He knows I'm not dating him for the money. God, that's so tacky to even say out loud."

Finn laughed and his dimples made me smile.

"He likes to say he's living vicariously through me and that he wishes he could have a choice. He feels trapped. I don't know." I sighed. "He supports me one thousand percent, that I know for sure. He's told me that."

We grabbed our bags and made our way out of the studio.

"Ellz, just remember, Jackson and I love you, and you'll always be enough for us, even if the Henrys think you're a moochy millennial freeloader. 'K?" Finn leaned over with a big smile and gave me a quick peck on the cheek. "Oh, by the way, put this on your calendar: Marley and Laura, our good friends from Pennsylvania, are coming over the weekend before Christmas. It's an early mini Christmas party, if you will. Bring Barrett. It's going to be so much fun! Please say you'll be there?" He squeezed my arm.

I rested my head on his shoulder and sighed. "Finn, I wouldn't miss it for the world."

"You guys leave for Nantucket soon, right?"

"Yep, we leave Friday. Funny enough, I wanted to live there when I first moved up north."

"No shit, that's hilarious. You know it's fucking crazy expensive, right?"

"Literally the exact reason we are here together right now." I bumped into him teasingly. "But we are just going for the weekend to relax and see the huge Christmas tree and all that fun stuff. He says it's really magical." I beamed, thinking about how it would be my first white Christmas in more than a decade.

"You're going to have a blast," Finn said. "When we go in summer, we love the sailboat tours—they're the best and so fun."

"Wait, no way! That's so funny you say that!" I let go of his arms and squeezed his hands.

"Huh, why?" he asked, confused.

"Barrett tells me all the time that he'd rather own his own business, a sailboat business, in Nantucket and do tours. I've just never heard anyone else ever say anything about it. I didn't know that it was a thing." I was excited by the revelation.

"Oh, God. Elle, it's a huge fucking thing. You have to reserve it days in advance. Too bad he doesn't do that. I bet it's way more fun than what he's doing now." Finn shrugged and continued walking.

"Finn, why did you open up the yoga studio?" I asked as we turned onto the next street to go to our coffee shop. I was going to write, and he was going to do a little administrative work for the studio.

"To be honest, I never had the intention of being a fitness studio owner."

I kept staring at him, waiting for him to go on as we walked.

"I had a degree in education and was a physical education coach for a high school here. It was all right, but super political. Later, I became the cheerleading coach and fell in love with it. I loved my girls and training them for competitions and all that stuff."

We arrived at the café, went inside, and got in line for our usual orders.

"Anyways, after a few years, I realized that even though I loved cheer and my girls, I hated dealing with the school board and all the bullshit that went with working in the school system. At that time, I was taking yoga classes here and became good friends with the owners."

Finn gave our orders to John, and we walked to the end of the counter.

"Thanks for the latte," I said with a soft elbow bump.

"No problem. So anyways, I was talking to the previous owners one day after class, and they mentioned they were going to sell the studio because they wanted to retire and travel, but they also wanted the new owner to keep the name and continue the legacy they'd built. Jackson and I had been dating for about a year, so I went home and told him I wanted to buy the studio. It just felt right."

"Holy shit! Were you scared?" I asked with eyes wide.

"Fucking terrified. But Jackson believed in me and really made the dream possible. He had a little money from his parents and some more saved up. We added it to whatever I had, and it was enough to make an offer."

"Wow." I was in awe of Finn and Jackson. "I actually didn't know Jackson was part owner."

"Oh yes, absolutely. He has more money in this than I do. He's the brains behind it, really. I'm the instructor, social media guru, and face of Align. But Jackson, he makes sure we're good financially."

"You guys make a perfect team. I literally had no idea he's so involved."

"Oh, one hundred percent. The LLC paperwork has his name on it too, ha ha. Anyway, we went with our money to the owners, and they accepted our offer. Jackson got all the legal shit taken care of, thank God, and I started getting my fitness certifications. Also, since I was a student and the instructors knew me, most of them stayed on the schedule, so that was nice."

"Yeah, for sure," I said.

"I quit my job right after the contracts were signed," said Finn.

"Do you miss your girls and cheer?"

"All the time," he admitted. "But my hands were tied. I couldn't be their coach anymore with the way the school system was handling internal affairs. Over the years, some of the ones who stayed in town have come to the studio and said hi, and it makes me happy. But I had to make a trade-off—stay miserable but keep my girls, or do something that scared the shit out of me but felt right. I know I made the right choice, though."

"Definitely."

"Elle! Finn!" John called our names from the bar.

"You took one hell of a risk, Finn," I said as we grabbed our drinks from the pickup counter.

He turned, gently grabbed my elbow, and held me in place. "Elle, you're not risking peanuts either." Then he let me go.

33

Now

couldn't stop crying. My tissue was crumpled in my hand, and my laptop screen was blurred from my tears. Tina and I started my session five minutes ago, and I started crying less than sixty seconds into the video chat. I continued telling her about the tense Thanksgiving dinner with Barrett's parents and how they'd attacked my and Barrett's life choices and desires—well, Mr. Henry was the real aggressor.

"It wasn't even the fact that his dad seems to think so little of me—it's the fact he thinks I'm after their precious family money!" My voice was shaking with fury through my tears. "I don't want their fucking money. I can make my own. And the way Mr. Henry talked down to Barrett—oh my God, I thought Barrett was going to explode." The tears were streaming down my face, hot and constant. My head throbbed, and the pain radiated around my eyes and temples.

"We both know you are more than capable of taking care of yourself and making your own money. You've proven that to yourself before *and* now." Tina was calm and firm with her words. I knew it deep down, but hearing this validation from her, this reminder that I could provide for myself, felt reassuring.

I know I'm an independent and strong woman, I thought to myself.

"You're right, and I know that too. I forget more often than not, but I know I'm capable. It's just—they made me feel so small. So wrong. And Barrett feels the same way. It's why he and his dad don't really get along. His dad just belittles his dreams and calls him foolish." I took a deep breath; I could feel my mind being torn in so many tangents and directions. Me, Barrett, success, his family, my book, my grandparents. It was as if my brain was scanning through traumas, decisions, and relationships and hadn't chosen a station yet. I continued, staring at Tina on my laptop. "Mainly, his dad made me question my worth, and I've never felt so inadequate."

"What do you think your worth is?" Tina asked thoughtfully.

I considered her and my thoughts. At first, my negative thoughts broke through. *You're nothing. You know you're faking this. You don't really belong here. You're not a real writer. You don't have nearly as much money as Barrett does. You can't support yourself like him.*

But then I flipped it around. I shifted my mindset and let my real voice speak the truth. "I have worth. I'm not a gold-digger faking achievement or success. I belong here. I am a real writer with worth because I create. I'm vulnerable yet brave. I had financial success, and I will have it again. I am worthy. I know I am enough. I am simply enough." It felt like a chant, affirmations repeating in my mind as my words echoed in my living room.

"You are certainly enough. And you are more than worthy of the life you are living. I'm so proud of you, Elle." Tina was beaming on the screen. "I know the situation you came from in NOLA, but now, in Boston, do you feel happier? Have you thought about what your success might be?"

I let my heart answer her questions again. "Yes." Nights with Barrett came to the forefront of my memories. Yoga with Emma and Pilates with Finn. Running on Comm Ave and writing in coffee shops and the library. "Yes, I'm happier, and I know that this was the right decision."

Tina nodded as I continued to stare dreamily over my laptop, thinking.

"I was almost to that dark place again." My voice hitched. "When that email came, when I quit, when everything felt ungrounded. I didn't want to be there; I didn't want to be here."

"Here?" she prodded.

"Alive." I turned my gaze to hers on the screen. "The little scandal with Chris and Mr. Landry was the straw that broke the camel's back, but the camel was already broken."

Tina nodded in understanding.

"If I hadn't left when I did, even though it felt like it was out of nowhere and I was devastated, I don't know how much longer I could have stayed strong. I was exhausted. Even now, I'm tired of being resilient. But there in NOLA, I was alone." I hugged my decorative pillow close to my chest and rested my chin on top. The pressure of the pillow against my body was calming and grounding.

Tina opened her mouth to speak, but I continued my train of thought, cutting her off. "I know I have Rach and Sarah. Again, my brain knows that, but I felt so isolated. The grief of Grandma never really went away, and Jude—I needed to leave. I'm happy here. I'm free. I think for the first time in a long time, I'm alive and living instead of simply existing."

"I tend to agree with you. You seem better mentally since you left New Orleans. Of course, we are human. We are never going to be perfect or feel one hundred percent.

We have anxiety, we have doubts, and we have hard times. The ebbs and flows of life will always exist." She paused and drank a small gulp of water. "This life, while better, isn't going to be easy. And I know you are aware, but I also want to remind you that you are a resilient woman who will handle any obstacle head-on with fortitude and perseverance. You don't quit. You don't give up. Your worth is not dictated by your productivity or what someone's father thinks of you." She raised an eyebrow to make her point.

I stared at her with a shy grin and more tears gliding down my cheeks. My mind was trying to comprehend all of Tina's validation and truths.

"And you know what?" I added. "It's been a while, but in addition to you, of course, I have so much support. Sarah, Rach, Finn and Jackson, Barrett, and Emma—I have real friends. Real support. I don't need his parents to understand. Barrett already does." I smiled to myself as I talked my thoughts into existence.

"We all have different callings in life, Elle." Tina smiled, her eyes empathetic and understanding. "And you're lucky enough to know what yours isn't. You never belonged behind a corporate desk; you belong behind a writing one."

♥

Later that night, I was typing away on my couch and listening to a rom-com podcast when I got a text message from Rach asking if I was free to FaceTime. Since it was after eight p.m. her time, I knew something was up and immediately called. She answered on the first ring.

"Elle!"

"Rach, is everything okay? It's late, and we don't talk this late unless one of us is having a midlife crisis and quitting their job, so I hope that's not the case and obviously that no one is dead. Actually, I'm sure you would have led with that, right? Because that's kind of morbid and—"

She cut me off before I kept going down the rabbit hole of possibilities for what prompted this video chat. "No, no, nobody is dead." She let a small grin peek through her lips, and then she pressed them back together in a serious way. "I'm up for a promotion at work," she said quickly.

"Oh my God, Rach! Congrats! That's awesome, isn't it?"

She wasn't smiling. Why wasn't she smiling? "And Josh just found out that his job is transferring him to New York."

"Oh fuck." It slipped out before I could censor myself. I noticed her cheeks glistening on my phone screen. "Rach, you're crying!"

"No shit, Sherlock," she said with a tearful grin. "But, um, yeah, and if he doesn't take the transfer, then there is no job here in Saint Louis for him." Her voice quavered.

"What about your job? Is the promotion available in New York? Your company has an office there, right?" My heart was breaking for her. I knew the pain and anxiety this decision brought with it. Last time, I chose my career and so did Jude. But Rach and Josh, God they'd been together for years. Would this be it?

"That's the thing, the promotion isn't guaranteed and it's only for the Saint Louis office. New York doesn't have the position open."

"Rach?" My voice was full of contemplation and reflection.

She replied with a throaty "Yeah?"

"So what exactly are you leaning toward? What about if you kept your current position in New York and skipped the promotion? Is that option available?"

"That's the thing—I don't know, Elle. I'm so fucking torn, and I asked already. My position is full there. I don't know what I would do." Her frustration was beginning to peek through the grief of the decision. "I want to move up. I want to break glass ceilings in my career. But Josh and I are serious. I mean, shit, we're talking about marriage! You don't throw that away. We have to think of each other, right?" Her eyes were pleading, and I felt like I was suddenly in a very small room. Jude and I had been lightly discussing marriage as well, but we did throw it away.

"I mean, that's what they say," I replied lightheartedly. "We both know I'm not the pro of this kinda thing." I felt shame heat my cheeks as I remembered my conversation with Jude. Remembered choosing to end things . . . again.

"Right." She looked at me with a quizzical lift of her brow. "So I have to think of his career now too, but what do you do when they're at odds? I really don't know, Elle. I want him to take the job, but at the same time, I want my promotion. I've worked so damn hard, I deserve it." She sighed as she lifted her arms up and rested her clasped hands on her head. "Jesus, how do things get so complicated?"

"Josh is going to support you, and you know I will too," I said after a few quiet moments. "When do you officially talk to your boss about the promotion?"

"We have a meeting set for this Thursday, the first," she replied with a hopeful tone.

"Oh, okay, that's the day before I leave for Nantucket. I'll have my phone on me, waiting. You'll have to keep me posted and let me know what happens!"

"Again, no shit, Sherlock." Her wry grin was sassy, and her brown eyes were bright and almost caramel against her jet-black hair.

"You'll make the right decision . . . for both of you. You're too good for anyone to lose. Josh included."

34

Now

Bundled up in thick jackets, Barrett and I held hands on the bow of the ferry. I stepped a little closer so that I could rest my head on his shoulder and felt a tiny kiss on top of my beanie.

"See that over there, Elle?" He pointed to a long blur in the horizon.

"Yeah, I see it," I whispered dreamily as the wind rushed against my face and the smell of sea salt made my body relax.

"That's where we're going." He wrapped his arms around me and held them across my chest. His hands held mine, stabilizing me on the ship. "You're going to love it. I can't wait to show you the townhouse we have off Main Street." He squeezed my hands a little tighter and tilted his head on mine. The scent of sandalwood and spice made me close my eyes and sigh.

The ferry sailed up and down, following each wave as it broke against the boat. My wavy brown curls whipped across my face, so Barrett turned our bodies to block the wind. I turned around and wrapped my arms around his middle. He took one hand, brushed my hair from my face, and kissed my nose with the tiniest little peck. I rested my head on his chest and felt his heartbeat against my ear. His body was warm, safe.

He moved unexpectedly, making my eyes burst open. He shifted his arm and pulled a coin out of his jacket pocket.

"Elle, here's a penny." He offered it to me with a huge smile, and I stared at him with my mouth open and my brows pinched together. "Seriously, take it. We're passing Brant Point Lighthouse."

"Ah, I love lighthouses! What's the penny for?" I asked, turning the penny in my fingers and looking to where Barrett was pointing. "Is that it?"

"Yep, you're looking at one of the oldest lighthouses in the US. And if you throw a penny into the water as we pass it, you'll ensure your return trip back to Nantucket, or so the locals say." He took another penny out of his pocket and held it. "On the count of three?" He looked at me with an eyebrow raised.

"Okaaay," I said.

Together we counted, "One, two . . . three!" I held his gaze, smiled, and threw my penny into the ocean with his, hoping for a return trip to Nantucket—together.

♥

It was just as I had imagined, if not better. The cobblestone streets, lines of Christmas trees, and the feeling of cheer filled my soul.

We both had mulled wine in our hands to keep warm and walked the streets of downtown for hours. The shops were quaint and bustling, and I imagined that Nantucket was a modern-day fairy tale. I could feel the magic Barrett had told me about.

It was in the crisp air brushing our faces, the taste of pastries along Main Street, and the smell of pine and mistletoe from candles burning in all of the little shops.

"The summer months are packed with tourists, but my favorite time was always coming for Christmas with my mom and sister." Barrett put an arm around my shoulders and held me close.

"What about your dad? Didn't he come spend the holidays with you guys here?" I took a sip of my mulled wine and felt the warmth spread through my chest.

"Once or twice he did, but he was always working. He's not much of a Christmas guy anyways. But my mother—oh man—it's her favorite holiday." He laughed and then stopped walking. "Hey, wait just a minute. I want to run into this store really quick."

Confused for a moment, I glanced at the quaint little gift shop and shrugged.

"Go ahead. Do you want me to come? Or I can wait here." I pointed to a wooden bench situated next to a coffee cart that was currently serving hot cocoa to a little girl and her grandma. I forgot I asked Barrett a question and stared at them, the little girl so happy and the grandmother smiling joyously. The little girl noticed me staring and gave me a shy smile. I instantly smiled back.

"No, I want to see something, and I don't want you to see it just yet." He winked and walked off toward the shop.

No cars were allowed, and the Christmas spirit was making me eager, and I regretted telling Barrett I'd stay on the bench. I pressed my lips together, then decided I'd just walk to a few local booths while he was in the store. I wouldn't wander far, and I'd keep an eye out for him. I've always been confident and fine being alone, but after a terrible news story broke out in 2018 where a girl was found dead in New Orleans in her apartment, I started to make sure that all my friends could have access to my location. Within a few weeks of dating Barrett, I made sure he had access on his phone too.

About ten minutes later, while I was looking at some dainty rings at a booth across the street from the gift shop, Barrett walked out of the store holding a gift bag. I watched him hustle across the street to me.

"Elle, here!" His smile reached both eyes, and his cheeks were rosy red. "In honor of your first Nantucket Christmas, will you please do me the honor of opening this small brown recycled gift bag?"

We both laughed. The cute little paper bag had a glittery green bow on it and, sure enough, was made from one-hundred-percent recycled materials. My cheeks hurt from smiling so much. As soon as he was close enough, I threw my arms open and lunged into a hug. I pulled back and reached for the bag he was handing me.

"Yes! Of course." We sat down together on the bench I was supposed to be sitting at, and I untied the vibrant bow and carefully pulled out the gold-foiled tissue paper. Inside was a small navy-blue box.

"Open it." He nudged me with a contagious smile. I grinned back up at him and crinkled my nose with excitement.

I carefully opened the small box, and inside, delicately wrapped, was a glass Christmas ornament. My breath caught. It was stunning—and all too familiar. The glass was a soft gradient blue with hand-painted reindeer, a sailboat, and a minimalistic outline of Nantucket. My eyes narrowed in on the very bottom of the ornament. There in elegant gold cursive read *Barrett and Elle, Christmas 2022.*

My throat started to close; I couldn't catch my breath. "Barrett, it's . . ."

A memory of a boy giving me an ornament came back to me: Jude. New Orleans. The Christmas before he left. I shook my head free of the memory and came back to the present.

I reached for Barrett's cold face with my mittened hands and held his crystal-blue gaze. "It's absolutely perfect! I love it." I closed my eyes and leaned in for another delicate yet passionate kiss.

"I knew you'd like it," he said with a smile as he fluttered his eyes back open. "I listen to the way you talk about Christmas, and I knew this would be a great way for us to celebrate our first one together." Beaming, he reached for my hand. "I know it's only a few days after Thanksgiving, but we can decorate our own tree when we get home, yeah?" he said with hopeful eyes.

"Absolutely." I beamed back. "Also, if you're free, Finn invited us over to have an early Christmas with him and Jackson and their friends. I'd love for you to come with me." I squeezed his hand and kissed the tip of his nose.

"I think I can make that work." He scooted closer to me on the bench and pulled me into his warm, safe embrace. "Dad's working on a lot of accounts right now, but he can handle it. I think he hardly needs me. He says he's training me to take it all over, but it's a bunch of bullshit. He does all the work anyways. Plus, I'd rather be with you guys." He gave a small squeeze and then his eyebrows lifted. "Oh, I have another surprise!"

"Oh? What do you have up your very sexy sleeve, B? Now, I asked for a pony once, but I really don't need one now. Louie is just fine. And by the way, I'm so glad he's spending the weekend with Emma. That was so nice of her to watch him for us."

"Ha, right. No. Definitely not a pony. And yes, she claims she's not a dog person, but she must have forgotten that Louie is a dog." He shrugged with a soft grin. "But this surprise, this one is for me, but kind of for *us*. I took something you told me to heart. Follow me." He took my hand, and we went down toward Nantucket Harbor.

"The pier?" I asked.

"Not quite," he said, looking at me mischievously.

"B, what did you do?" Now I was concerned. "You're not the mayor or something and I don't know about it?"

"You really do have an imagination. I can't wait to read your book."

I crinkled my nose and narrowed my eyes in a playful pout. We walked for a few more yards and then came to a dock at the end of the pier.

"Here she is." I followed his gaze and saw a breathtaking sailboat floating in the water. It looked like a scene straight from a Nantucket postcard. With intricate craftsmanship and a polished shine, she was timeless, moving with the waves and the tide of the harbor.

"Look at this." Barrett pointed toward the back of the vessel. My gaze followed his finger: *Elizabeth*.

"Oh my God!" I yelled. "Barrett, you did it!" I was ecstatic. I grabbed his arm. "You're going to start your business?" I wanted, no, needed all the details.

He shook his head with a sheepish grin. "Not quite. But I did buy myself a sailboat so that I'm one step closer. I also named her after the person who inspired me to start following my dreams, even if I have to modify them for a bit." His eyes sparkled as he smiled down at me.

I started crying. I couldn't help it. This whole evening was incredible.

"Barrett, I'm so honored. I'm so happy for you, that you did this for yourself!"

"I may have to run Dad's company, and I may be stuck in the family business for now, but at least I can get away on the weekends and be on the water." He laughed.

"I've always been able to buy my own sailboat, but I never thought to actually do it. I never thought I could dream and make any of it a reality. Thank you, Elle. You've brought so much light to my life, and I seriously don't know—just, God, I'm so glad I found you."

I jumped up and hugged him. My heart was so incredibly happy that he was trying to be happy.

"Wanna see her up close?" he asked while holding me snug in his arms, my body pressed up against his chest.

"Is that even a question?" I pulled away to grab his hand. "Take me to your ship, Captain." I winked and he chuckled.

From our point of view on the harbor, we looked out over the side of *Elizabeth*'s hull at Main Street, where the king of Christmas trees was glistening. Snow fell gently as Barrett stood behind me and rested his chin on the top of my head. I leaned back into him and continued to stare at the Christmas tree and the beautiful sight of Nantucket.

♥

The next morning, light trickled through the curtains, and snow was falling as we opened our eyes. Barrett's arm was lying heavily across my body, possessive and strong. I was holding his hand by my side and turned my face toward his. His espresso-brown hair was tousled, and his cheeky grin was half hidden by the oversized duvet.

"I'm so comfortable, I don't want to get up, ever," I mumbled, curling closer to his body.

He pulled me into him and rolled onto his side, our bodies flush against each other. "Me either, but you've got writing to do today, and I'm going to drink coffee and watch Netflix while you slave over your bestseller." His husky whisper made goose bumps erupt down my neck.

"I mean, I might reward myself with a little Netflix and chill with you too." I pursed my lips together and flirtatiously pouted.

He rolled onto his back but kept his arm around me. With my head nestled on his shoulder, he negotiated with me. "Every thousand words, you get a kiss. Every two thousand, a kiss and an episode of any show you'd like."

"Fifteen hundred and you have a deal, sir."

He bent his head and kissed my forehead. "Deal."

When we got out of bed, I started toward the kitchen out of habit. I needed coffee, and I planned to make Barrett a cup as well. I was surprised when he interrupted me as I went to grab the coffeepot.

"I've got it, Elle. Here, go ahead and sit down so you can write. I'll be the barista today," he insisted with a cheesy smile and a proud puff of his chest.

"You're sure?" I asked, skeptical. "You know I'm very particular."

"Yep, I've got almond milk for you and everything." His eyes caught the sunlight and glistened in the morning glow.

"Perfect, you know just how I like it, then."

"Oh, do I?" His voice became deep and mischievous.

I groaned and rolled my eyes. "Oh, shut up. I totally set myself up for that." I smirked and sat down on the couch. "Hurry over here. This couch is too big without you."

While writing, I kept gazing up at Barrett, at this charming home. It was open and bright, with large windows and weathered wooden floors. A massive stone fireplace anchored the living room, creating a cozy, intimate atmosphere, while pops of navy and sandy beige echoed the nautical essence of Nantucket. I thought about what his childhood must have been like. Lonely, I assumed. With my legs crisscrossed on the couch and my laptop in my lap, I sat up straight and figured I'd find out.

"What was it like coming here as a child? Did Harold come with you guys?" I asked as I made sure my manuscript autosaved.

Barrett grabbed his coffee from the side table and then slightly pursed his lips in thought. "Yeah, he was always with Em and me." He readjusted his seat and turned toward me; I motioned for him to put his legs across my lap. He smiled as I closed my laptop and put it on the coffee table, then I helped place his long muscular legs over my thighs. Without thinking, I began to massage his calves while he continued talking.

"My mom asked him to watch us a lot, and she would go off and do social events with the ladies on the island. She was actually really involved with the museum. Harold would take us to go see the tree every year, and we'd get hot chocolate from the local booths, because of course we were just kids." He chortled to himself, then continued with a wistful smile. "He really treated us like his own."

"Did he ever have any children?"

"No. His wife died before he worked for us, and he didn't have any family close by, so he always stayed at our house. He has his own room and lives there. I'm not sure if that's common or not, but for us, it was nice because he was always there when our parents weren't. He's the reason Emma and I aren't monsters."

I considered Barrett for a minute. "Hmm, that's interesting." My hands stopped massaging his legs while his words lingered in the air, pulling my focus away.

"What is?" Barrett was looking back at the TV. *The Office* was playing because he knew that I could still write even with it on the television. He laughed at something Michael Scott did and then turned his gaze back to mine.

"Well, I guess the fact that here I was, thinking you had a perfect family, ya know? Mom and dad and all that. And I was the one who wasn't 'normal.' My grandparents adopted me and raised me—not normal. But your butler raised you and your sister. It just goes to show, things aren't always what they appear."

His lips pulled to one side, and he crossed his arms over his chest and appraised me with his quirky grin. "Elle, you're something else. Jealous of *my* family dynamic? Oh my God. Normal?" He snorted and shook his head.

I was confused.

"Yeah," he said with a soft chuckle, "our butler raised us, but things are certainly never as they appear. And just so you know"—his face became serious and firm—"you are most certainly normal. Just because your grandparents raised you doesn't mean you didn't have a real family."

I looked away, shy about the conversation. It wasn't easy taking compliments or validation. That's probably why Tina tried to do it as much as possible in our sessions. Even if I knew I wasn't abnormal, sometimes it still felt that way. Not to have the perfect family, the mom and dad who were always there, it made holidays like Mother's Day and Father's Day a real bitch.

"Very true," I replied slowly. "But I still feel differently about it. There was no mom and no dad." Then I whispered, "Barrett, they didn't want me. They left me." My shoulders sagged and I hung my head as the words floated into existence.

His face changed instantly and became protective and angry. He took his legs off my lap and sat on one as he scooted closer to me on the couch. Then he gently placed his arm around my shoulders and hugged me toward him. "Elle, fuck your mom and dad." His voice was firm and strong. "Your grandparents loved you, and that's all that matters. They wanted you, they loved you, and as far as I'm concerned, they were your parents. If anyone else says otherwise, then fuck them too."

I looked up, tears glistening on my cheeks.

"I'm serious. They loved you, Elle. And I love you. And I'm not going anywhere." His grip tightened and I relaxed into his embrace.

"I love you," I whispered with my eyes closed. I wanted to drown in his masculine scent and strong arms. So safe. I felt him kiss the top of my head.

"Did I tell you I have a surprise for us tomorrow? Assuming you want to take the day off writing, I think you'll like what I have planned." He rested his head on mine and took a deep inhale. "Also, did I ever tell you that I love the way you smell? Weird, right? But you smell so good, like coconut and something, I don't know, but it's just so good." He chuckled, and his chest expanded under my head. I sat up with narrowed playful eyes.

"What? Another surprise? What are you up to, Barrett Henry?" My voice was incredulous and sensual.

"You'll have to wait and see," he whispered into my ear.

Then he kissed me.

35

Seven years ago

Jude was heavily involved in the BP litigation from the Deepwater Horizon spill. I rarely saw him and woke up alone in our bed most days. I was to blame too. Work was my priority. Always.

My morning chats with Grandma Di were shorter, and lately I'd been antsy to hang up so I could get to my desk. Whenever I talked to her, she asked if I was writing. I wasn't. For her to ask if I was writing, it made my stomach hollow out. I *wanted* to write, but I wanted to make her proud and to be financially secure. I wasn't brave enough to be a writer, and every time she asked, I'd gently change the subject and ask how she was feeling instead. She never remembered telling me at the beginning of the conversation anyway.

Tonight, I was alone at the dinner table while *Friends* played in the background. Around 12:30 a.m. I turned the TV off and went into our bedroom. I lay in bed under a soft goose-down comforter and tried to turn my brain off; I couldn't stop thinking. No matter how hard I meditated or literally tried to count sheep, I couldn't doze off. I was staring at the ceiling and watching the fan rotate when I finally heard the key in our front door. I turned my head to look at my phone—two a.m. His footsteps echoed across the hardwood floors as he went into the kitchen. Then he came toward me.

"Are you awake?" he whispered, tiptoeing to my side of the bed.

"Mm," I murmured, staring at the ceiling again. He perched on the edge of the bed next to my right arm.

"Hello, beautiful," he whispered and kissed my forehead. I closed my eyes and allowed a soft smile to ghost over my lips. He stood back up and walked slowly to his side of the bed. I watched him take off his shirt, then strip down to his boxers. With a loud groan, he lifted the covers and crawled into bed.

I turned on my side to face him in the middle of the bed. He extended his arm, signaling for me to nestle into his embrace. I couldn't resist.

"I miss you," I whispered with my head on his solid chest. "We keep missing each other." I kissed the inside of his shoulder and snuggled closer, craving his warmth and affection.

He sighed deeply and traced small circles on my exposed arm. "I know. I miss you too. This case is draining me, but I'm hoping it won't be like this much longer." He focused on the ceiling and avoided my gaze.

"Fingers crossed," I murmured.

He tilted his head to the side and kissed the top of my head again.

"I'm sorry." His voice was barely audible, but it was amplified with my head on his chest.

I should have acknowledged it, but instead, I stayed silent and let his inhales and exhales gently lull me to sleep.

36

Now

The next day in Nantucket felt like déjà vu.

"I could get used to this. God, that coffee smells good," I said as I walked up behind Barrett in the kitchen and wrapped my hands around his waist. I kissed him right between his shoulder blades and watched as goose bumps appeared on his warm, soft skin.

"We have a busy day, so drink up. We leave in an hour." He grabbed my hands, lifted them to his mouth, and kissed my fingers. Then he picked up his coffee and went to the bedroom. I heard him opening and closing drawers and a few "ahas" sprinkled in with groans.

"What are you looking for?" I shouted across the house.

"Just some things, and I know Emma left snow boots here. I wanted you to have them to wear." Another drawer closed.

An hour later we were hand in hand, enjoying the Christmas Stroll through Main Street. My rosy cheeks and chapped lips were entirely worth it, as the Christmas trees brought joy to my heart. I couldn't think of anything better right now than holding Barrett's hand and walking through a Christmas wonderland. We made our way into a local bakery and sat down by the window.

"Wait here. This isn't the surprise, though," he said as he got out of the booth.

The Nantucket Christmas Stroll was surprise enough for me. It's an event that happens the first weekend every December, and it's a big deal, like huge. There are even horse-drawn carriages, though I'd had my fair share of those in New Orleans.

Barrett came back holding a picnic basket.

"Barrett?" I asked, my voice tinged with curiosity.

With a huge smile, he extended his hand. "Let's go, we have to walk a little bit."

Excited, I stood up and took his hand in mine. I could smell fresh bread through the basket, and my mouth started to water.

"What's in there?" I asked as we walked through the fresh powdery snow on Main Street.

"You'll have to wait and see," he said with a smirk.

The suspense was killing me. Eventually, Brant Point Lighthouse came into view. It wasn't that far from the town, and I squeezed Barrett's hand as soon as I realized we were walking toward it.

"Ahh, Barrett!" I yelled, excitement thrumming through my body.

He laughed and readjusted his grip on the basket. "We actually get to go inside," he said, his voice layered with excitement.

My eyes widened and my mouth dropped. "No way! Oh my God!" I covered my mouth with my free hand, and my eyes stayed wide in pure shock.

"The mayor's a family friend. What can I say?" He shrugged as if it was no big deal.

"Of course he is." I rolled my eyes and giggled. I squeezed his hand tighter and skipped with delight.

Once we got to the historic lighthouse, Barrett opened the door and motioned for me to walk up the stairs. "Let's go to the top."

I followed him to the very top of the lighthouse, the whole time wondering why he was still holding the basket. When we arrived at the top, I looked out over Nantucket Harbor. The ocean extended for miles into a gray snow-filled horizon.

"Okay." Barrett was behind me, fumbling with the basket. "I actually asked Mrs. Moffat, who owns the bakery, to put together a nice lunch with some mulled wine for us so we could have a picnic. So without further ado, let's dig in, shall we?" He started to pull items out of the basket and put them onto a blanket he'd placed on the floor of the lighthouse.

I couldn't stop smiling. Barrett had gone to so much trouble to make this a beautiful, memorable day. I couldn't remember the last time I'd felt this special. It had been way too long. We sat next to each other eating paninis filled with stuffing, turkey, cranberries, and gravy. My tastebuds were assaulted with flavor.

"God, this is delicious! How did you get this idea?" I asked around a mouthful of panini.

"Emma and I have done this a few times over the years. Harold would arrange the picnic basket, and the two of us would come up here." He shrugged. "Like I said, the mayor is a family friend, so we spent a lot of time here. I just love being on the water I guess, and I only have happy memories in this spot."

I'm not going to cry. I'm not going to cry. The combination of warmth and spices from the wine had me relaxed and comfortable.

"What are you thinking about?" he said.

"I'm not sure." I shrugged with a sideways grin. "I guess I'm thinking about how truly happy I am right now." I shook my head and lifted my hands, looking around. "Like, is this even real life?"

"Oh, it's definitely real." He laughed and lifted his cup to mine, then took a sip.

"Oh, look, there's one more thing in here," he said excitedly.

"Did she pack dessert?" I asked, hoping for one of the brownies I'd seen in the bakery window. But it wasn't dessert.

"Elle . . ." His voice trailed off.

"Oh my God. Is that . . . ?"

He reached into the basket and pulled out an old green book, like ancient. "I know how much you love to read, and I asked Finn if you had a favorite fairy tale. I didn't want to ask you and spoil the surprise."

He extended the vintage green book toward me, and I could barely speak. My eyes were wide, and my heart was pounding.

"It's a first edition *Beauty and the Beast* from the 1700s. I pulled a few strings and got it out of good old boy George Vanderbilt's collection." He released the book into my careful grip.

"This is the most thoughtful—oh my God, I don't even know what to say. Barrett! Oh my God!" Holding on to the book, I flung my arms around him and hugged him tight. "Thank you," I murmured into his neck. I sat back up and gave him a playful smirk. "You know, I totally thought you were going to pull something else out of your magical basket of treats."

"That was the point, my dear." His playful eyes turned my stomach into knots.

"Oh my God." A lighthearted headshake and I held the book to my heart. "Thank you." I gazed into his crystal-blue eyes and beamed.

After an unusually long pause, Barrett asked with a soft, slightly nervous voice, "What if it was the other thing?"

I went still, the book clutched to my chest. I was fine teasing him about marriage, but wait . . . Was he seriously considering it—and after only a few months? Did I want to marry Barrett Henry?

In that moment, a picture of Jude smiling and holding me came to the forefront of my mind. Jude and I had talked about marriage, and we had picked out a ring. I almost said yes once before to a boy I loved. Was I ready to say yes this time? And with someone else?

I gave Barrett a coquettish smile and leaned across the few inches between us to put my face in front of his, our noses barely touching. "Well, I guess you'll have to ask to find out." Then I kissed him.

37

Now

Nantucket was a dream I never wanted to wake up from, but once I was back home in Boston, reality was like a splash of cold water to my face. A week had passed since our trip to Nantucket, and time was running out for my writing competition. Fifty-five thousand words in, I was about twenty-five thousand words short of my goal for my first draft. I'd read that eighty thousand words was acceptable for a contemporary romance, and so my goal was born. How had Grandma Di done this? What was her story about? She'd never mentioned it, and I'd never found anything when I cleaned out their New York home. Actually, that wasn't true. I'd found her old working typewriter. I had it on the desk in my bedroom, but I never touched it.

When I glanced at it, I thought about how she'd been alive, real, and her fingers had touched those keys. If I didn't touch it, part of her was still in the world. Those hidden fingerprints had created a story on that typewriter that had won this competition. Sometimes—and I wasn't sure if it was grief or if something was wrong with me—I thought of my grandmother and questioned whether she'd been real. Had she really existed? Now, of course I knew she'd existed. But she'd been gone for more than five years, and without her in my life, all I had were pictures that didn't feel real. They felt like history and longing. It didn't make sense. I wasn't sure how to articulate how it felt to lose someone who was such an important part of your life and then try to keep living without them.

My mind would still play games with me; it made me question which of my memories were real. Did Grandma Di really buy me all of the Nancy Drew books and fuel my love for reading? Yes, I still had them on my bookshelf. Real, tangible books with her love notes and handwriting on the inside covers. How could all of that exist without her here anymore? My memories of her and my grandfather and my childhood felt like a life that happened hundreds of years ago. Maybe even another life completely. My grandmother's typewriter was a tangible reminder of the woman I loved most and lost. One of the last reminders I had.

As I typed in my favorite booth at the coffee shop with a honey lavender latte by my screen, I thought about my grandmother. I kept wondering, had she kept a copy of her manuscript? I wished she had so I could read it and feel her presence, hear her voice, be a part of the world she'd created.

Lost in thought, I almost missed my phone vibrating with notifications on the table.

BARRETT: Are we still putting up the tree tonight?

ME: Yep, that's the plan! I even got Louie a Santa hat so he can join the festivities.

Barrett: Okay, don't be mad. I'm still coming over, but it's going to be a little later than I thought.

Me: B, it's a Saturday. Your dad still has you at the office?

Barrett: I know, Ellz. I know. I promise, I won't miss this.

He kept his word. He walked through the door at ten p.m. and saw all of my Christmas decorations and boxes spread out in the living room. I'd purchased a beautiful eight-foot flocked tree online and had it set up as well. All we had to do was hang ornaments—and drink hot cocoa, of course.

"Where did you get all of these ornaments?" he asked as we decorated.

I could tell he was tired, but he was still decorating with me because he'd promised earlier. His eyes were tired, and noticeable dark circles had appeared. He yawned and hung another ornament.

"Oh, I don't know. Just over the years. Some were my grandmother's and some courtesy of Hobby Lobby." I laughed as I continued to string oversized ribbon and get the tree somewhat closer to my vision of a Pottery Barn tree.

"Damn, Elle. You're pretty good at this." He sat on the couch and watched as I went to work fluffing and putting ornaments in the precise spots I had imagined for them.

"It takes years of practice, and not to mention, I've watched many tutorials on how to make your tree look like it was professionally decorated." I winked at him and then got back to work. I grabbed our bag from Nantucket and pulled out our ornament.

"Barrett and Elle," I said with giddy delight. "You ready to put this gem on the tree?"

I looked back, and he was taking a deep breath with his eyes closed. A temporary look of relief graced his features.

"Hey, Barrett?" I whispered and walked over to him.

"Hmm?" he hummed with his eyes still closed.

"We can go to bed, babe. I know you've had a hard day."

He opened his eyes slowly and kept his mesmerizing gaze on mine. "Let's hang our ornament first. Deal?" He leaned forward and kissed me softly.

We walked to the tree together, traditional Christmas music playing low, and picked a spot on the tree for our Nantucket souvenir. *Barrett and Elle.*

About an hour later, we were lying in bed, my arm across his chest and his arms wrapped around me. My eyes were closed, and I let my head move with the rise and fall of his chest. Then the peaceful quiet disappeared and his phone was blaring.

He startled awake and reached for his phone but knocked it to the floor. He rolled out of bed and got on the floor to find it. It had stopped ringing by the time he had it in his hand. He sat on the edge of the bed and went still.

I was still trying to get my bearings, and when my eyes focused, I saw Barrett staring hard at his phone, frozen. "Barrett, what's wrong?" I sobered up from my sleepiness and put my hand on his shoulder as I leaned over to get a look.

"Elle?" He looked up and I could see the fear in his wide eyes.

"What? What, Barrett?" I pleaded. "What's wrong?"

"Elle, I have a voicemail from my mom. I read the transcript. My dad had a heart attack. He's in the hospital." Barrett stood up and stumbled while looking for his pants on the floor. "I need to go." He looked lost, confused. Fight-or-flight was taking over his body.

"Oh my God." I couldn't comprehend the news fast enough. "Go, go! Do you want me to come with you? Drive you?"

What else could I do?

He nodded absentmindedly. I don't think he really heard what I said, because within minutes and without a word, he threw on shoes by the door, grabbed his jacket and keys, and ran out. Louie stopped snoring and stood up on the couch to see where his daddy had gone. I stood in the living room in only his boxers, my chest hurting and my mind reeling.

"What now?" I looked at Louie, who stared back at me with big brown eyes. I texted Emma, but she didn't answer. I texted Barrett—nothing. Finally, I called Finn and he answered after the second ring.

"Elle? Elle what's wrong?" he asked in a sleepy voice. I heard shuffling and Jackson in the background.

"I'm sorry, Finn, I know it's late, you know I never call, but—"

"Elle, what happened?" This time his voice was firm and awake.

"Finn . . ." I was trying not to cry. My body wasn't listening to me; I was officially freaking out, and my chest was getting tight. *Fuck*. My head was pounding, and my throat felt like it was closing. "Barrett's . . . dad . . . he had a heart attack!" I said between sobs and choked breaths. My chest hurt and I was hungry for air. "Barrett left, he had to go. He's at the hospital. I didn't go. I didn't know, he didn't ask. I—"

"Elle, we're coming. We'll be right there." Finn hung up without another word.

Breathe, damn it. Breathe! Slow it down, Elle. Slow it down. I tried to coach myself through the anxiety. I had to; it was just me at the house. *Inhale, two, three, four, exhale two, three, four.*

♥

About twenty minutes later, Louie started yapping. *That was fast*, I thought as I ran over to the door to open it.

"Stop, Louie, stop. It's just Uncle Finn," I pleaded with the Frenchie, who kept barking.

The knocking didn't stop. It was panicked and fast.

"I'm coming, Finn, I'm coming!" I yelled out. Overwhelmed by all the noise, I grabbed Louie and unlocked the door.

Barrett was standing there. He was leaning against the doorframe, eyes sunken and skin pale. His jacket was covered in fresh snow, and small flakes sprinkled his hair.

"Oh my God, Barrett, you're back?" He looked up sheepishly. "Why didn't you text me you were on your way? I was so worried!" My heart was racing, and I embraced his cold body.

I steered him into the condo and helped him to the bedroom. His eyes were vacant and lifeless. He was present but somewhere else at the same time.

"B, B, how's your dad, your mom?" I asked eagerly as he sat on the edge of the bed and shed his coat.

"I forgot my key. Sorry I knocked like an idiot." He didn't answer my question. "I wanted to get back as fast as possible. It was a shit show back there, and I wasn't needed." He took a deep breath and lay back on his side of the bed. His hands spread over his face and he let out a vicious groan. Then he kept taking deep breaths. "So Finn is coming over?" he asked after a few moments.

"Yeah, I think Jackson too." I moved to lie beside him. I reached my top hand over to grasp his. His fingers welcomed mine and held on like I was the only thing keeping him here.

"They got worried when I called crying, and you and Emma weren't answering. I felt helpless. Actually, I felt scared . . . for you." I lifted his hand to my lips and kissed the back of it gently.

"I get it," he said, staring up at the ceiling. "I'm scared too."

"Yeah?" I said. "Is he okay, Barrett?" I didn't like his dad at all, but I certainly didn't wish him dead.

Louie, who'd jumped on the bed as soon as his mom and dad were in it, cuddled between us and began to lick Barrett's face.

"Yeah, he's okay. It was a heart attack, but they saved the bastard with an emergency procedure. Angioplasty, I think they called it? They put in a stent too."

"Oh my God, that's crazy." I squeezed Barrett's hand again and whispered, "Is he going to recover?" I stared at him while he continued to take deep breaths and stare at the ceiling.

"He will," Barrett said in a short, brisk tone. I knew their relationship was strained, but he was acting distant, hot and cold. I didn't have to wait long for an answer. "Elle, if he died, I'd be in charge. That's the last thing I want in this fucking world."

His voice changed so quickly, dark and fierce, that I flinched.

"But he's still alive, and of course I don't want him dead, but God, I don't know how to explain it." He sounded frustrated and brought his hands to his face again.

"Try," I coaxed in a soft, hushed voice.

"Elle, I'm not close to my dad, and I would say I love him in a very loose way. Like the fact that he's my father, and that's all. But then knowing he could have died tonight scares the shit out of me. To be in charge of the company terrifies me. It's inevitable, but it feels like this faraway thing, like my dad is immortal. Does that make sense? I don't expect him to retire—I think he's full of shit. I don't want to be in charge, Ellz. I don't want to become my father." With his hands still over his face, his body shuddered with sobs and frustration.

"Barrett, this means you're human. Of course you can care, but you don't have to. The fact that you do means you're an incredible person." I slid closer and put my arm around his tense body. "I love you, Barrett. I know you don't want to take over the company, and you're right, it's terrifying. But I'm here, okay? We can make it through the tough days together." I kissed his cheek and nuzzled my head back into his shoulder.

"Barrett, he's okay," I said after a few minutes.

"Yeah, he is," he said in a choked tone.

We lay there a little longer with Louie snoring soundly between us. I grabbed my phone and texted Finn.

ME: He's home. His dad is okay-ish.

FINN: Thank God. We are almost there. Do you still want/need us?

ME: No, it's okay. Thank you for coming. Thank you for answering. Thank you for being you (+ Jackson). I love you both, but I'm lying here with Barrett right now, and I don't think he's getting out of bed after the night he had.

Finn: Understood. Text me tomorrow, K Ellz? We love you.

I put my phone down on the bed and turned it on Do Not Disturb. I don't know how much time went by, but I fell asleep holding Barrett close in my arms.

38

A few days later, I woke up at eight a.m. and discovered a text from Rachel on our group chat. She'd quit her job, "pulled an Elle," and they were packing their bags to move to New York. Barrett was snoring—or maybe it was Louie or both? I sent a heart to the chat and cuddled up with my boys under our fluffy duvet.

Louie licked my face as Barrett's alarm went off again. I thought I'd heard something ringing, but I also thought I was still dreaming. Barrett stretched and gave me a quick kiss before going straight to the shower. He had to be at the office for a ten a.m. meeting with his dad and the owner of the Miami property. Once he got dressed, he met me in the kitchen, where I was pouring coffee.

"How much writing do you plan on doing today?" Barrett asked as he rushed to get his briefcase ready for the day.

"At least three thousand words." I sipped my coffee. "I can't believe your dad is back at the office today." I trod lightly on the topic. "It was less than a week ago."

I glanced over the rim of my coffee cup to see Barrett shaking his head. "From your mouth to God's ears."

"Mm," I mumbled.

"He won't stop. I talked to Mom—believe it or not, she called me—and he's acting like nothing happened." Barrett shrugged as he put more papers into his briefcase.

"Wow, seriously?" My forehead crinkled as my eyebrows lifted. "How is Em doing since the scare?"

"Emma was always dad's favorite. She's taking it hard and is at the house with him more now." His tone became clipped.

"Oh," I said and then brought my coffee back to my lips.

"Yeah, don't worry. I've had plenty of years to get over it. Em and I are close, but she's Dad's shining star, you know? The baby girl of the family."

"I can see that," I said.

Frustrated his briefcase wouldn't zip up, he tossed it onto the coffee table and sat on the couch next to me to breathe. "Fuck, today feels crazy. When we were growing up, Harold took care of Em and me."

"Right, right, I remember you mentioned that in Nantucket."

"Yeah, so Dad always made time for Emma's things. If Emma had a dance recital, he was there. When Emma graduated Yale, he was there." Barrett stretched his arms overhead and put his hands behind his head, elbows wide.

"You graduated Yale too." I smiled at him.

He gave me a bittersweet grin. "Dad was in London."

"Wow," was all I managed to mutter.

"Don't worry about it, babe." He stood up from the couch, walked closer to me, and leaned over. His arms boxed me in, and his fresh scent made my heart constrict.

"Oh, don't forget, we have our early Christmas with the boys later."

"No problem, I'll be home in time. Good luck on your book today—I can't wait to read it." His lips drew closer to mine. One soft kiss and he was gone.

♥

We parked in front of Finn and Jackson's apartment about thirty minutes late. First I couldn't find my phone, then Barrett forgot to feed Louie, then I forgot my white elephant gift. Needless to say, we finally made it.

"You know Louie loves me more, right?" I teased as we started to walk to the boys' front door.

"It's not a proven fact, Ellz. I refuse to believe it," Barrett said. Out of the corner of my eye, I noticed his pocket flashing.

"Barrett, is that your phone?" I pointed and his eyes followed my finger.

"Shit, you're right. Hang on a sec." He stopped and pulled his phone out.

At that moment, Finn opened his front door.

"Ellie, Elle, Elle! Barrett! You're here!" His voice carried through the dark snowy evening.

Barrett's face was blank, his lips were pressed together, and I could feel the tension rolling off of him.

"Babe? Babe, what is it?" I turned my body completely to his, trying to get him to look at me.

"Elle, Barrett, is everything okay?" Finn called out. I saw him shut the door and start to head toward us.

Barrett turned his phone for me to see. The texts were in all caps.

"It's from Emma," I choked out.

Barrett was staring at me with a fierce expression.

"Oh my God, Barrett, it's your dad," I whispered in shock.

Barrett pulled his phone back and looked over my shoulder as Finn ran up behind me.

"I have to go." Barrett turned back to the car. "I need to meet Emma at the hospital—she can't be alone. Not with my mother. Not with my father . . . in that condition."

"Barrett, I don't think . . ." Idiotically, I wanted to say that I didn't think his father was going to make it. It was a coronary artery blockage—one of the nurses called it a widow-maker—and it was serious. But he seemed to read my mind and whirled around, his face flushed with anger.

"He's still alive. I need to be there. I don't care if his chances are slim. I have to be there for my family." His lips pressed together, and I saw rage building in his beautiful eyes. He was shaking, burning. I noticed vapor rising from his body in the cold Boston night.

I wanted to reach out and touch him, comfort him. "Barrett, I want to come. Let me go with you, please."

He scoffed. "Elle, you don't get it. You can't understand this thing with me and my dad." He looked back to his car and ran his hands through his hair. He always did that when he was flustered.

Finn was standing next to me now, his hand on my lower back, letting me know he was there.

"You never knew your father. You didn't have this fucked-up relationship because he disappeared. You're lucky, you know that?" His voice was shaking, spite lacing his every word.

"Then tell me. Tell me what I don't understand!" I pleaded, heart sinking with every outburst from his lips.

Finn moved his hand and pulled me into him, holding me tight.

"You don't have a father leaving you a huge fucking company to run with real goddamn responsibility." Barrett's tone seethed with . . . something. I couldn't put my finger on it. Was that jealousy?

Speechless, I put my hand over my mouth and felt his verbal knife pierce my heart and twist. Who was this person spewing out venomous rage? He'd never spoken to me this way before. He would never say these things.

He continued with the final blow. "This is serious, and I'm serious. I have to go. I'm sorry, I have to go." He hurried to the driver's side of the car, jumped in, and sped away.

Finn's face was dark, lips tight and eyes narrowed. "Elle, I'm right here." He gave my shoulders a squeeze and didn't let go.

I hadn't realized tears were rolling down my cheeks until I turned into Finn's shoulder and began to sob uncontrollably. I thought I heard Finn saying my name or talking to me, but everything was an echo. I felt myself falling, maybe floating? All I knew was that my world went completely dark.

"Elle? Elle? Can you hear me?" Finn was shouting.

Where was I? I blinked a few times and then stared into my best friend's face. I was inside his house lying on the couch. Fear spread through my veins. What happened? I was standing outside . . . and now what?

"I don't know what just happened." I sat up and lifted my hands to my head.

"You just kind of went limp in my arms, so I hurried you inside to get warm." Finn's tone was soft and comforting.

"I'm sorry. That's so embarrassing," I groaned. "I think I just became overwhelmed, and then, well, then . . ." I rolled my eyes.

"I know." His firm voice made my eyes lift to his.

"He's never done that before. He's never spoken to me like that. I thought he believed in me. Do you think that's what he really thinks?" My voice cracked as I remembered Barrett's horrible words.

"I can't answer that because I don't know. But I will say . . . I was two seconds away from punching him in the face for the way he was talking to you. That was unacceptable." Finn brushed a piece of hair out of my face and gave me a soft smile.

Jackson was standing behind me, behind the couch. "We're here, Ellz. Just tell us, what do you need from us?"

I sat up all the way and crisscrossed my legs. Leaning forward, my head resting on my hands, I looked at Finn, then Jackson.

"I need to get to the hospital." Even though I was devastated, I knew I had to be there for Barrett. I wouldn't bolt on him.

♥

Within the hour, Finn drove me to the hospital. Barrett didn't answer his phone, and when I texted Emma, she told us which entrance she'd be waiting at for me. I called her as soon as we arrived.

She answered after only one ring. "You're here?" There was an urgency in her voice.

"Yeah, what floor, what room?" My mind was racing with the various situations I could be walking into. I looked over to Finn as I got out of his car and mouthed, *Thank you, I love you*, and made a phone signal to let him know I'd call him later.

"We're in 314. Hurry, it's not good," she said and then hung up. Before the call was disconnected, I heard Barrett's voice. He was in the room.

I found my way there with a nurse's help. Mr. Henry was unconscious. Mrs. Henry was frozen in the corner, sitting in a chair. Barrett stood like a statue, staring at his dad, and Emma was fidgeting with her nails, pacing from one side of the room to the other.

I entered the room cautiously.

"Elle!" Emma ran to me with her arms outstretched.

I instinctively opened mine and embraced her. She started crying, and I looked over her shoulder at Barrett. He'd glanced at me coming in but was staring at his father again. Barrett was talented at compartmentalizing his life, but we all have our breaking point.

"I thought you were coming with Barrett, but he said you weren't," Emma said in a small, delicate voice.

Before I could reply, Barrett's voice carried across the room. "Can I talk to you outside for a moment?" he said in a clipped tone.

I nodded, and Emma let go of me and sat down in a chair by her dad's side. I saw her reach for his hand and begin to sob as Barrett and I walked out of the room.

Once in the hallway and a few doors down from Mr. Henry's room, Barrett released a deep sigh and looked at me with tired eyes. "What are you doing here, Elle?"

"What am I doing here?" I put my hands on my hips and hissed, "I'm here to be supportive. I'm here to be with you."

"Elle, I wanted you to stay with Finn. I don't want you to be here if this goes bad." He leaned against the wall and brushed his hand down his face. The dark circles under his eyes were prominent in the fluorescent lighting. "He might die." His choked tone had my body reacting before I could think.

I dropped my hands from my hips, stepped closer, and wrapped my arms around his tense, shaking body. "Barrett, I know. Do you think I don't know that? Do you think I don't know what death is? Let me remind you, I'm very familiar with it." I stepped back and took both of his hands in mine. "I'm not leaving, I'll be here. Whether it's in that room or the waiting area, I'm here." I brought his hands to my lips and gently kissed his knuckles. "I won't let you do this alone."

Tears were streaming silently down his face. I could tell he was breaking. "He doesn't have much of a chance. I don't want Mom and Emma to hear, but I talked to the doctors. They can't do a bypass; he's too high risk. I think the stress, the work, the never stopping, it got him."

I leaned in again and held him firmly against my body.

"I'm scared," he murmured into my hair. "I'm so fucking scared."

♥

I fell asleep in the waiting room. Around three a.m. I felt a gentle shake. It was Emma.

"Hey, Elle. Wake up." Her eyes were puffy, and her mascara was running down her cheeks. A sense of dread crept through my body. I knew before she even told me.

"Barrett's in there talking to the doctors and Mom, but Dad didn't . . . he . . ." She kept choking on her words.

I wrapped my arms around her and let her cry into my shoulder. Her whole body convulsed with each new wave of tears.

"He's gone, Elle, he's gone." I could hardly make out the muffled words, but they were there.

I mindlessly rubbed her back while she held me tight. I caught Barrett's eye as he walked toward his sister and me.

"He's dead." I felt Emma flinch in my arms as Barrett echoed the words the doctors had confirmed only moments before. The Barrett I loved wasn't standing in front of me. Instead, I was looking at a vacant, lost human who'd just inherited the weight of a Fortune 500 company and the role of "man of the family."

Emma peeled herself away from me and turned to Barrett. She clung to him, and in that moment, he came back to us. He squeezed his sister and held her tight to his chest. She fell apart again, and he let her.

I couldn't ask if he was okay; I knew he wasn't. "How's your mom?" I asked cautiously.

He looked at me and with a bittersweet pull of his lips murmured, "She's making arrangements."

♥

A few hours later, I was in bed with Louie. Emma and I had been texting ever since I left the hospital.

EMMA: Mom was hammering him about the company. She and Dad were apparently arguing about it before he collapsed. She knows Barrett doesn't want to run it, but now he must. There's no other plan.

ME: Jesus, does Barrett know?

EMMA: That they were arguing? Yes. About him? No. But I couldn't believe what I was hearing. Mom was trying to get Barrett out of this. She never interfered with Dad and this whole Henry legacy bullshit. I don't know what changed her mind, but she was adamant that Barrett be allowed to do what he wanted to do.

ME: Fuck.

EMMA: Yeah, I was in the kitchen trying to ignore it. Harold and I could hear them arguing in the dining room.

ME: Omg! P.S. How is Harold taking this?

EMMA: He's with Mom right now. He's holding it together. Remember, he wasn't the biggest fan of Dad. But poor Harold, he's the one who called 911 because I was with Mom and really just in shock.

ME: You didn't want this for your brother either?

Emma: No, none of us did. Dad was the only one oblivious. I tried to tell him. I was the only one he'd kind of listen to about it. But he said it was Barrett's duty and his place to take over the company. I can't imagine that pressure.

Me: But aren't you taking over the magazine?

Emma: It's not the same. I love the magazine, I love writing. I've been working in that building ever since I can remember. Well, not really working. Aunt Olivia would bring me to work with her a lot, and I basically grew up with that magazine. I WANT to take it over and be involved.

Me: Fair point. Definitely a difference.

Emma: I don't know how Barrett deals with it. To be honest, before he met you, he was miserable. He and Margaret were the most toxic couple I've ever seen. If the job didn't kill him, she would.

Me: How do you think your mom is going to handle all of this?

Emma: Honestly, I think she'll go home and drink a vodka tonic, wake up tomorrow, put on makeup, and go about her day. She'd die herself before she let any of us see her get emotional.

Me: Seriously? Just like that?

Emma: Seriously. Just like that. She's already made the arrangements. It's what the Henrys do.

39

Now

Instead of Christmas dinner, we were at a funeral. I arrived early with Barrett so he could pay his respects without the eyes of strangers bearing down on him. We walked into the historic church and slowly made our way to the open coffin, where Emma stood looking over her father. The room exuded grandeur and spaciousness with its high ceilings and circling balconies. An oversized chandelier sparkled over the aisle, and Mrs. Henry sat still as a statue, alone in the front pew. Even though her black veil hid her narrow face, I noticed her shoulders shudder with every sniffle.

Barrett looked handsome yet solemn in his black suit. I'd donned a new black dress with an elaborate fascinator. My red lips gave my face contrast in a room full of pale grief.

This was the last place either of us wanted to be. I'd never been to an open-casket viewing before, so I was already very uncomfortable. Both my grandparents wished to have a closed casket. My heart rate rose the closer we got to Mr. Henry and Emma. Barrett squeezed my hand tighter. I wasn't sure how many funerals he'd been to. I didn't ask. But I saw the tension in his shoulders and his jaw set with concentration. How did someone say goodbye to a parent with whom they'd shared a complicated and often tumultuous relationship?

Emma turned around as we stepped close to the coffin. My throat immediately tightened. I didn't like this. I couldn't stand here. I had to get away.

Mr. Henry's eyes were closed, his lips pressed into a firm line. I'd done my research. I knew why his mouth stayed closed. My stomach squeezed and began to cramp. *Oh no.* I was going to be sick. *Oh my God, I can't do this.*

I squeezed Barrett's hand and gave him a quick, panicked glance. He furrowed his brow and whispered in my ear, "It's okay, go have a seat. I'll be right there."

I felt my throat release a little when I dropped his hand and turned away from the dead body.

Within the hour, hundreds of people showed up to pay their respects. The Henrys stood at the front and received the blessings of strangers, friends, and employees. Emma kept her head down, and the few times she lifted her eyes, I saw her splotchy red cheeks. Barrett's face was unreadable. Serious and professional, he shook hands with the assembly line of people and kept glancing at his mother to check on her.

He'd mentioned earlier that morning that he was worried if this funeral would be too much for her to handle. She'd been aloof and in a frail state ever since the hospital. All the arrangements had been made, sure, but personally, I thought that Mrs. Henry was a shell of a woman trying to put on a smile for the masses. I pitied her.

When the service began, I was seated in the front row with the family. I looked behind me to take in the audience. Every pew was packed, and it was standing room only in the back.

"I never imagined so many people would come on Christmas Eve," I whispered to Emma, who was seated on my left. Barrett was on my right with his hand on my thigh, mindlessly drawing circles with his forefinger. Mrs. Henry was flanked by Barrett and Olivia.

"It's a Henry funeral," Emma whispered back and gave a slight shrug.

"Hey, did you notice Margaret is here?" I murmured as the flowers were laid across the top of the coffin.

Emma looked back at her, pretended to search for someone else, and then turned back around.

"Way to not make it obvious," I said with a small grin.

"Oh shit," she muttered.

"Shit?" I asked.

"Yeah, I mean, of course she's here, but since she and my brother split up, they haven't been in the same room together," she whispered behind her program.

My face blanched. I didn't realize they hadn't seen each other since the breakup, and now she was here when he was feeling vulnerable and upset.

"No, don't worry. They were awful together. She was manipulative, and in case you haven't noticed, Barrett's a people pleaser. She owned him." Emma rolled her eyes and cleared her throat quietly.

"Oh no, it's not that. I'm just worried how Barrett will react when he sees her," I admitted.

"I can't imagine she'd start anything at the funeral. She knows better." Emma glanced back again, this time looking right at Margaret, who met her stare with a blank expression.

I never went out of my way to talk with Margaret at the office, especially after the dinner from hell with Barrett's parents, when they couldn't stop singing her praises. However, I felt slightly uncomfortable knowing she was seated a few rows behind me and could possibly cause Barrett more distress.

After the funeral service concluded, I stayed seated while Barrett circulated, shaking hands and accepting condolences on behalf of the family. Mr. Henry wished to be cremated and his ashes spread in Boston Harbor, so there wasn't going to be a funeral procession.

Out of the corner of my eye, I noticed a flash of red hair pass through the aisle. I looked up and saw Margaret heading straight to Barrett. I watched as he became aware of her stalking toward him. Someone was talking to him, but he ignored the conversation and had his narrowed eyes set on Margaret's prowl. I was stuck in the pew; my body wouldn't move. What was she going to do? I watched the inevitable scene unfold, a spectator just like everyone else.

Barrett excused himself from the conversation, never taking his eyes from Margaret. She stood close to him, too close, and sneered at him with her arms folded across her chest. I felt like I was watching a bomb tick down to zero as the tension rolled off their bodies.

They weren't arguing, but then I noticed she said something that caused Barrett to jerk backward. His eyes went wide, and his handsome face drained of all remaining color. I noticed him look down, and Margaret handed him a ripped piece of paper.

Then she whipped around, gave a quick smile and nod to Olivia and Mrs. Henry, and left Barrett standing ashen and motionless except for shallow breaths.

As she walked by me, her eyes met mine, but they weren't angry. They weren't malevolent. They were full of pity, and I didn't understand why.

I made my way to Barrett, zigzagging through fellow mourners. He was reading the note in his hand and didn't look up as I approached.

"Elle. Hey," he said, voice distant.

"Barrett, are you okay?" I reached up and stroked his forearm. "I saw Margaret talking to you and I wanted to get over here, but—"

He cut me off before I could finish explaining why he'd had to take her on alone. "Yeah, I, um"—he brushed his hand through his styled espresso-brown hair—"it's just a lot to figure out, that's all." He offered me a feeble smile and slipped the note into his coat pocket. He lifted my hand to his lips and kissed it gently. "Let's go home—oh, wait. Really quick, I promise, I need to go see my mom."

I nodded and let his hand drop again so he could find Mrs. Henry.

I'd had enough of dead bodies, overcrowded rooms, and ex-girlfriends. My anxiety was in rare form, I was overstimulated, and I needed to get a breath of fresh air. I reached for my purse and made my way to the exit.

I walked to the right of the building. Snow was still shimmering on the ground, and I followed a brick path toward some iron benches. I stopped short when I noticed Margaret's red hair. She was sitting on one of the benches, her back turned. I heard her speaking but didn't see anyone nearby. I assumed she was on the phone. I didn't move. I didn't want to bring her attention to my presence.

"No, Mom, I'm okay. Yes, I told him. No, he didn't say anything. I gave him the paper." Her voice was clear and crisp. I couldn't ignore it if I wanted to.

Told him what?

"He knows. Yes. He knows. I don't know. Okay, love you too. Okay, bye." She sighed, and a cloud of warmth clashed with the frosty temperature outside. She slipped her phone into her purse, and before I could make my legs move, she stood up and turned in my direction. She saw me right away. Surprise rushed across her face, her lifted eyebrows and open mouth confirming that she'd had no idea I was steps away while she talked to her mother. The shock on her face matched the horror on mine.

"What did you hear?" she demanded, her lips lifted into a fierce snarl.

Dumbfounded, I didn't say anything. I stared at her with my mouth moving and no words coming out.

"It's his, you know," she seethed. "He'll take me back. I know it. He won't leave me alone knowing it's his."

My brain was malfunctioning. I couldn't find the words. I couldn't even think straight. She wasn't saying what I think she was saying. Right? "What?"

"You heard me. You heard the whole conversation, didn't you? It's his baby, and he won't have a choice after his mother and Olivia get ahold of him." Her voice was shaking. Was she really angry? She seemed . . . scared.

I felt the warm tears roll down my cheeks and turn to stiff ice. I felt every crack of my heart as it broke with every word Margaret uttered. "No," I whispered, my eyes pleading. "No, no."

"Yes," she said and put her hand on her now visible rounded stomach, protective and proud. "Just because you say no doesn't make it go away." She grabbed her purse, held her stomach, and stared at me. "I never hated you, Elle."

I was trapped in her stare.

"But he was never yours."

Then she walked away.

I felt my stomach turn upside down once she was out of sight. I rushed to the closest bush away from the crowds beginning to file outside and heaved. I have no idea how long I threw up. I don't know how long I was outside. Mid-heave, I felt Barrett's hand on my shoulder and then looked up into his beautiful eyes.

"Elle?" Barrett pulled me into him, warm and secure. "Are you okay? What happened? C'mon, babe. Let's get you home."

"Barrett," I sputtered. "Barrett, I know," I choked out through my tears. I wiped my face and mouth on my jacket and sniffled back more tears.

Barrett's face dropped, and before he could say anything to me, his mother walked up from behind him with Olivia and Emma.

"What is it you know, dear?" Mrs. Henry remarked with cautious concern.

I didn't want to do this—not here, not now. Instead, I heaved one more time and let Barrett pick me up and carry me to the car. His strong arms cradled me, and his woodsy scent soothed my overactive mind. He gently lowered me into the passenger seat and snuck a soft kiss on my forehead before closing the door. I watched him walk over to his family, and all of them argued with animated gestures and loud voices. I couldn't hear them clearly, but a few times, Emma looked over at me with big blue eyes full of pity.

Barrett's jacket was on the seat next to me, and since he was a few feet away with the others, I slipped my hand into his coat pocket and grabbed the note.

10 a.m. Jan. 7

Dr. Sillos

Be there.

♥

The majority of the drive home was uncomfortably silent. Not only was my love life an episode of *Real Housewives*, but my manuscript was due in seven days and I still had to write the third-act breakup and happily ever after.

"Elle, how did you know?" Barrett finally asked as he turned onto my street.

Eyes puffy and head pounding, I looked over at him with exhaustion consuming my entire body. I didn't want to talk about it. I mean, what the fuck? We were happy and everything was going so well. The only fight we'd had was about custody of Louie should anything happen. Now it felt like we'd foreshadowed our own fate.

"I walked outside to get some fresh air, to wait for you." I exhaled a weighty sigh. "And I ran into Margaret. She told me . . . accidentally." I kept my eyes forward, watching the bare trees pass us by.

"Accidentally?" He quirked an eyebrow and glanced my way.

"Yeah, I was walking to the benches and noticed she was on the phone, so I stayed hidden, hoping to avoid her. Well, she saw me and thought I heard everything and knew about the baby." I leaned forward and massaged my temples. I sat back up and continued, my right hand lightly massaging my forehead. "Spoiler, I didn't know until she raged at me." The frustration was winning over my exhaustion, and my voice felt hotter, like a momentary burst of adrenaline rushed through my body.

He released a heavy sigh, then trailed his hand from his weary face down to his neck, where he rubbed his tense muscles.

"Look, I'm really sorry. It was before I met you. I swear. You know I'd never cheat on you." He looked over again, this time his eyes pleading.

"I know it wasn't while we were together. I gathered as much," I said wearily. The adrenaline was waning again.

"I had no idea until she approached me at the funeral. I'm still—my mind is reeling." He groaned and hit the steering wheel. "Fuck!"

His voice vibrated through my chest, and I kept my eyes on him.

"But, Elle, I . . . I'm sure we can make arrangements. I . . ." Slow tears trickled down his face.

"I know," I said again, my voice feeling heavier as my headache intensified.

He parked in front of my building and shut the car off. "Are we okay?" His voice cracked at the same time as my heart. I reached for one of his hands and gently squeezed.

"Barrett, I have to write." I gave him a tender grimace and kissed him on the cheek. "I also have a headache from hell, so this all feels so bleh."

I turned to open the door, but he continued in a whimsical manner. "It could be cool, I guess." He kept his eyes unfocused and straight ahead. "Maybe Margaret and I can split custody or something. There has to be a way this will work for everyone."

Irritable and ready to go inside, I spoke before I thought about what I was saying out loud.

"I don't want to be a mom. I didn't ask for this. I don't want to raise a child. I don't like Margaret, and I don't want her to be a part of our lives." Fire was burning in my chest, and my head felt like someone had a dagger in my temple. Oh my God, I was going to be sick.

"You don't want to be a mom?" he asked quietly.

"Seriously, that's the only thing you got from that rant?" I snapped. I sighed and squeezed my eyes shut. It was fine, I was going to be fine. "No. I've never wanted to have children. I don't dislike them; I just don't want to take care of one or to be responsible for them. I want to have my own life."

His expression fell, and he lowered his head to the steering wheel and groaned. He sat back up and looked at me with heavy eyes. "Just because your parents left you doesn't mean you wouldn't be a good mom."

"Excuse me?" My voice rose an octave with his assumption.

"It's a parent thing, right? You don't want to be like them or something?" he said, trying to explain himself.

"No, it's a me thing. I choose my life over having kids. I don't want them, and it's my choice, and now with Margaret, I feel like the choice has been made for me in our relationship."

Something in Barrett snapped. "Sometimes we don't have a choice, Elle. Sometimes life deals us a shitty hand and we have to take it. I don't want to be a dad right now."

"I refuse to accept that. I refuse to believe that we have to accept what life gives us," I replied irritably.

"Stop living in your dream world—or whatever you're writing about—and come back to reality for a minute. Shit happens you can't control, bad shit. You have to deal with it and do your duty. I don't want to run this company, but I have to now.

I don't want a child with Margaret, but I have one coming." His jaw was tight and his knuckles were turning white on the steering wheel.

I felt the angry tears streaming down my cheeks. "How dare you! I know the real world. I choose to acknowledge that everything is a choice, because otherwise, what the fuck are we doing here? You had a choice to sleep with her. Now you have the choice to raise your child. I also have the choice not to."

"What does that mean?"

I was fuming. I couldn't think straight, and I couldn't see straight. "Barrett, I think you should go home tonight." My chest constricted as I felt a surge of anxiety. I winced as my head viciously throbbed.

"What? You aren't serious?" he stammered.

"I can't be with you right now. I can't think. I don't want to argue anymore. I don't want to talk about the baby or Margaret. Please just leave." I opened my door and got out of the car.

Before I shut the door, he shouted, "Elle, tomorrow is Christmas!"

I started running and didn't look back.

Once inside, I collapsed on the floor and heaved. I couldn't breathe. I couldn't stop crying. Louie came to me, licking my tears and nudging my head up. I was finally strong enough to crawl to the bathroom and lie on the floor.

I was in between sleep and awareness, still on the bathroom floor. I thought I heard the front door open but was too tired and sick to care. I felt a warm hand touch my forehead and then lift me gently into strong arms.

"I'm sorry, Elle. I couldn't stay away." Barrett's voice was the last thing I heard before sleep overcame me.

40

Six years ago

Jude walked into the kitchen wearing nothing but boxers and a soft smile. He fell onto the white oversized couch that took up most of our living room and groaned with his hands over his face.

"You okay?" I looked over the couch at his long, lean body. "Don't forget, we have dinner plans at Galatoire's tonight, yeah?"

He met my eyes and raised his eyebrows. My Jude, my everything, had a look in his eyes I'd only seen once before. It was the summer of my senior year. Red flags materialized in my head.

"Oh my God, Jude, what's going on? Tell me." I fumbled around the couch and took a seat beside him. Even while only wearing a pair of blue-striped boxers, heat radiated from his bare body. He took a deep breath, then sent a caring look my direction.

"Elle, I . . ."

"Yes?" I prodded. The emotions of that summer resurfaced, and I felt jittery and uneasy. He sighed and shrugged.

"I got an amazing job offer," he said, "and before you ask, no, I wasn't looking."

"Oh." I relaxed a little. This wasn't terrible news. "Well, that's awesome. Congrats, babe. Why are you so upset?"

"You know I wanted to make partner here, but over the past year—maybe longer if I'm being honest with myself—I realized I'm miserable." He glanced at me with wide teary eyes. "I've been so miserable fighting about Chinese drywall and going up against oil companies. It's not rewarding to me, and I went into law to make a difference." A gentle grin graced his lips, then he continued. "One of my law school buddies in New York reached out, and his firm is looking for someone to work in contract law, specifically creative contracts and negotiations."

My eyes went wide. *No.*

"Elle"—he sighed again—"the offer is in New York City." He held my stare, waiting for my response. Did he expect me to be angry? Sad? Joyful? Even my brain couldn't figure out what it wanted to be in the moment.

I jumped off the couch, panicking and irrational. I don't remember what I said. I felt ice consume my body, fear flood my veins. He couldn't leave. My Jude, my love, the one I thought I'd marry. *No, this can't be happening.*

He stayed on the couch and listened; he didn't yell back. He didn't move. He kept his eyes fixed on me and watched as I fell apart. He never told me if he'd accepted the job or if he was moving. I'll admit, I jumped to the conclusion right away. I felt the pain in his eyes when I finally sat down and held his hands in a tight grip.

"You can't go, you can't. We're here. I'm here." My voice was beginning to crack, and he gave me a look of understanding. "I can't leave my job," I finally whispered.

"That's why I wanted to talk to you about it. I don't want to leave you. I don't want to be without you. I want you to come to New York with me."

"Come with you?" I replied. "To New York City?" I had to be sure that's what I'd heard him say.

"Yes, come with me to New York. I don't want to do this without you. I don't want to let you go."

I should have felt calm, but the decision to leave felt heavy and thick in my stomach. Either I would lose Jude, again, or lose my career I'd worked so tirelessly to build. If I went to New York City, I'd have to completely start over. I'd be dependent on Jude until I found someone else to hire me. I didn't know if I could handle that loss of independence, of money, of my success. But then, could I handle the loss of my life?

Sensing I couldn't answer him immediately, he sat up and kissed me on the forehead. Then he reached for my cold hands and held them tightly against his chest.

"Think about it, Elle. Please? But just know that I want to take this job. I want to leave and take you with me."

My stomach dropped. He was seriously considering—no, accepting this job.

"Jude . . ." I paused; the words didn't want to come out of my mouth. "You know I can't." My chest tightened and my throat felt thick as I tried to keep my emotions bottled up for a little longer. "I'm making lots of money now, and I've worked so hard to have this life. I can't take it with me. I can't lose my independence. You know that about me. I can't mooch off you in one of the most expensive cities." My heart was racing, and every thud felt like a punch to my chest.

"Is it success if you take a Xanax every day and hardly see the people you love?" he whispered, looking down at our hands in his.

"I think so," I replied with delicacy. "I mean, obviously I wish we saw each other more, I miss us. But the Xanax is fine; it calms me down. This is what work is. It's not easy and success isn't easy."

He let out a small sigh. "I'll agree to disagree with you, my love."

I didn't know what to say. I didn't want to fight with him, and he wasn't forcing me to go. He was asking.

"What is it for you?" I asked curiously. "Success?"

He looked up for a second, thinking, then his warm amber eyes held me breathless. "I'm not entirely sure, but I think helping others and having more free time and less stress will be part of mine. Taking you to Europe, waking up next to you every morning, and having our coffee on a balcony. You are part of my success."

My mind was short-circuiting. "What about Ava?" I knew his mother would probably have the final say on this. She couldn't possibly be okay with this idea of moving to New York.

"I talked to her when I got the offer yesterday afternoon." He sounded so casual.

"Oh?" My eyebrows rose and I was at a loss for words.

"She supports me and thinks I should do what makes me happy." I noticed by the way he was speaking that he wanted me to support him too.

"I support you, babe. I really do." I released my hands from his and placed them on his thigh closest to me. "But how do we do this? We aren't college kids anymore. This isn't summer break."

"Elle, I love you. Think on it, okay?" His eyes, his golden-brown eyes pierced through my heart. "They won't need me in New York until I finish my current case. I can't leave it undone. It's not fair to my client when they went out of their way to hire me as their counsel. It's looking like it will be around June."

"So you're definitely accepting? No matter what I decide?"

"Yes." He didn't hesitate. "I'm happy with you, I'm in love with you, but my job is killing me. I don't want to stay there till June, but like I said, I feel obligated to my client." I nodded in agreement, and he put his hand over mine, rubbing gently with his thumb. "After I was approached, I looked to see if they had a division here, and they don't. Then I looked for other companies who may need someone for media law." His empathetic eyes told me what I needed to know. He shrugged and continued. "The place for me to be is in New York City. New Orleans doesn't have anything for me anymore, except you." He leaned forward and kissed the tip of my nose.

"What are we going to do?" My voice was barely above a whisper. The tears were threatening to break through, and then I'd be lost.

"Come with me. Let's start over together," he whispered.

I couldn't speak. He was serious. Everything was about to change.

"But you've got plenty of time to think about it. It won't be until June, after all, and before any of that . . ." He stood up from the couch and walked over to our hall closet, where he pulled out a small felt box.

"Oh my God!" The words fell out of my mouth.

He looked at me, then down at the box, confused. "Ohhh." He shook his head from side to side in understanding. "Well, glad to know *yes* would have been the first word out of your mouth." He chuckled playfully. "This is a bit different than a ring box, okay?"

I nodded in relief. I mean, yeah, I would marry him in a heartbeat. But this job thing had me tied in knots.

"I love you, Elle. Merry Christmas." He handed me the box, and I realized it was a bit bigger than a ring box.

"My mistake." I gave him a bashful grin and opened my mystery present. "Oh my God." I held up a hand-painted ornament and admired the delicate design of a New Orleans streetcar on St. Charles Avenue.

At the very bottom written in silver lettering, it read, *Jude and Elle, Christmas 2016*.

41

Now

told Tina everything that had happened since our last visit. I recounted every detail and feeling. There was Mr. Henry's death, the funeral, the baby news, even throwing up behind a bush.

"I have no idea what's going to happen." I squeezed a white linen pillow to my chest and looked at Tina on my screen. I wanted her to fix what was happening, but how? How could she make everything go back to the way it was before his father's funeral?

"So Margaret is definitely having his child?" she asked.

"Yes, or so she says. See, I'm not so sure. I was going to tell Barrett to get a paternity test, but I couldn't get it out of my mouth. I'm hoping he's smart enough to do it. At the end of the day, it's not my choice." I groaned into my pillow.

"That's true, but it does affect you, Elle. You are his girlfriend, maybe even wife one day, right? You are part of his life and he's part of yours, so both of your decisions will affect the other. True, you can do things independently, but now big decisions are ahead." She wrote something in her notebook and then sat back up, readjusting herself and grabbing for her cup of coffee.

"What did Barrett say to you about all of this? I'm curious to know if Margaret proves the baby is his child. Is that what you want, Elle? Have you both spoken about this further since that night?"

My chest squeezed a little tighter. I didn't want to admit to myself or out loud that our future came down to my desire of being a mother or not, specifically regarding a child that wasn't mine. And truly, I did not want to be a mother. But I didn't want to lose Barrett. I squeezed the pillow tighter, and my upper back spasmed with new tension. Saying words out loud made them real, and I was terrified.

"He hasn't been home much over the past few days. It's just been Louie and me at my condo because he's working so late at the office. So, no, we haven't talked about it in depth since the funeral. I'm scared, Tina." A tear trickled down my cheek as I stared at her on my screen. "I'm scared that if we talk about it, when we talk about it, things aren't going to work out."

"Elle, I know this is a very hard decision to process, but it is something that deserves your attention and thought. Your feelings surrounding parenthood are important, as are his. Both of you honestly sharing your feelings surrounding this change, and the future, is an important part of the process in making the decision that is best for both of you."

"You know, people always told me I'd change my mind. But this feels forced upon us. Upon him. I love him so much that every time I think about what our future will be like if he decides to be a part of that baby's life, my heart cracks and my stomach drops. I never wanted to be a mother because I wanted to live my life in whichever way my future partner and I decided. Travel whenever we wanted.

Be financially secure. There's so much responsibility with little humans that I don't desire. Being a mother, it never appealed to me. The day I decided I didn't have to do what was expected of me as a woman, I felt this huge burden lift from my shoulders. It's simply not my cup of tea." I chuckled to myself before continuing. "But being the cool aunt at a T-ball game? Yeah, that I would like to do someday."

"You have a few choices here, but ultimately, if you don't want to be a parent, you need to talk with Barrett sooner rather than later. If that baby is going to be a part of his life, then it's going to be a part of yours. If that's not something you want for yourself, then you need to ask yourself if this relationship is what you want. Are you settling? Are you giving up your ability to choose? What do you want and what is okay for you? You aren't stuck, you aren't married, and you have some say in this matter. It's your life too."

♥

I woke up earlier than usual and watched the sunrise from my balcony. The streets were quiet, the city was still sleeping, but today was my big day. It was New Year's Eve and my manuscript was due.

I'd finished my first draft around eleven p.m. the night before. Barrett had been sleeping. Most nights lately, he didn't make it home before midnight, and he was exhausted as soon as he walked through the door. Barrett Henry, CEO. It had a ring to it, but damn did it have contingencies too. Late nights, high stress, limited time for himself. The list went on.

I knew he needed the sleep. He left for Miami just a few hours later—four a.m. I think? But I'd had to tell someone that I finished my first draft! I had texted the girls and Finn last night. I knew Sarah and Rach would be sleeping, but Finn was a fifty-fifty shot.

He'd texted me right back.

AHHHHHH! You did it, Ellz!! I'm so proud, so fucking proud! We need to celebrate! xo

I told myself that today would be a spell-check-and-send-it kind of day. After weeks of writing, I felt confident that even this amateur first draft could catch an acquiring editor's or agent's attention. Yet, even with my confidence, I felt the weight of imposter syndrome. As the sun rose higher, light came through my French doors and into my living room, gently reaching onto my couch and kissing my knees.

I'd written the book, but how could I share it? I'd never done something so incredibly vulnerable. I felt exposed and I hadn't even submitted it yet. I wasn't even sure I'd finish the novel in time—that was my biggest fear until today. Now, what if no one liked it?

The validation of this competition was turning me inside out. But so was the fact that my grandmother had won it years before me. I wanted to make her proud, make myself proud. Finish her story and live the life of a writer, like she had dreamed.

Once I submitted my manuscript, then it would be up to the judges—a Harvard literary professor, an acquiring editor or two, and a few agents. They didn't release names, which makes sense, or the exact number of judges. *At least Margaret isn't on the panel,* I thought to myself and laughed as I lifted my morning coffee to my lips and Louie jumped onto the couch beside me.

I'd vaguely heard Barrett leave this morning, and I already missed him. We still hadn't discussed the baby. It was almost as if avoiding the discussion kept us in our safe little bubble. It was going to pop, I knew it. But until then, I was going to cherish every ounce of our relationship as it was now.

I pulled out my phone and looked at my recent texts: Finn, Sarah, Rach, Em, Barrett . . . and Jude was at the very bottom. I hadn't talked to him in ages, and for some reason, I wanted to tell him so badly that today I was submitting my book. My finger hovered over his name, but I decided better of it. I scrolled back up and went to Instagram instead.

I looked through my feed and noticed that my Instagram had become a place for baby announcements and Christmas decor sales. I rolled my eyes and shut the app.

After changing clothes and gathering my computer and notes, I grabbed Louie and left for the coffee shop. I felt bad leaving him while I wrote and Barrett was away. I told myself he was used to being home alone, but it hurt my heart too much to leave him. After a few visits to the café and management's approval, Louie was officially their unofficial mascot. The little guy had been extra clingy and needy lately, so I made sure to give him lots of kisses and keep him in my lap while I wrote.

"Heya, Elle, same as usual?" John, my barista, asked as I walked up to the counter. "Oh! Little guy is with us today? Does he want his usual too?"

Louie's usual was an espresso cup of whipped cream, and he borderline expected it every time he came to the café with me. I adjusted my backpack on my shoulders and nodded, giving John a thankful smile. My table was open, so I set my things down, placed Louie to my side, and started to get my laptop out of my bag. While my head was down, I noticed two feet standing next to me. I looked up, and it was John smiling with my latte and Louie's puppacino.

"Oh, you deliver now?"

He laughed and set my latte on the table, carefully away from my laptop.

"Only for you, Elle. How's the book coming? Still working on it?"

I let out a large sigh and slumped into the booth.

"Yessss. I'm done with the overall draft. But oh my gosh, this was so much harder than I anticipated. Today is editing and submission day!"

His eyebrows lifted in amazement. "Wow. Way to go!"

"Yeah, but it's not quite ready to be submitted. I need to make sure it's formatted correctly and that spell-check doesn't catch anything too obnoxious, ya know?" I brought my latte to my lips and melted into the first taste of honey and lavender.

"Gotcha. Well, let me know if you need any more fuel along the way. We're rooting for you." He winked, and the girls behind the counter waved and gave a thumbs-up.

"They all know?" I asked, surprised.

"Oh yeah. Finn's been in here bragging on you, saying you're writing a bestseller. We can't wait to read it. Though, I knew you were already writing it, of course." A gentle chuckle escaped his lips.

"Well, I can't wait to get you all copies, then. Thank you again for bringing me the latte. I so appreciate all of you." I gave him the biggest smile I could muster and then slipped my headphones in my ears so I could start looking over my draft one last time.

I had to hurry, and I felt all the pressure start to come down on me the second I tried to open the file from Dropbox. But as I scrolled through my manuscript, something felt wrong. I skipped to the last chapter, and that's when I saw it. This wasn't my most recent version! Where was my happily ever after? Where was my last chapter?

Panic pulsed throughout my body. I had no idea what to do. I restarted my computer. I tried to find any possible way to open a different version. They were all the same or older. *Oh my God. Oh my fucking God!* I started sweating and getting hot flashes. I was going to be sick.

Hysterical, I called Finn. "Oh my God, oh my God! It's not here! My finished version, everything I did last night, it's gone!"

John was staring at me, concerned, and I waved him off, even though my face must have told a different story. I was known for my face giving away anything I was thinking, so when John kept glancing over to check on me, it was certainly warranted.

"I'm not sure I can help, but I'll be right over. I'll bring Jackson. He knows Dropbox better than me." Then I heard the call end.

I texted Emma. I called Barrett. Nothing. John walked over and sat down next to me.

"Elle, you're worrying me. What's wrong?" he asked quietly.

"Do you know anything about computers? I tried to open my most recent version in Dropbox, and it's gone. My last chapter is nowhere to be found, and I don't know what to do! It's due today. Oh my God!" I threw my hand over my mouth and hunched over, squeezing my stomach. My latte was not sitting well with this influx of anxiety.

He grabbed my arm and patted my back forcefully, murmuring that it would be all right.

"Let me see it." He took my computer and messed with it for what felt like an hour.

"Is this it?" he asked, pulling up a Word document from Recent Projects.

I scrolled all the way to the last page. "The End."

"Yes. Oh my God, John, you did it!" I screeched. "Oh, thank you. Thank you!" I leaned over and gave him a huge kiss on the cheek. His face went bright red, and his hand went right to where my lips had touched his face.

He couldn't speak. He just nodded with an impish grin and got up to go back to the coffee bar. I scrolled through to make sure everything was all right. Finn and Jackson walked in and rushed over to my booth to sit by me.

"Did you get it back?" Finn asked, looking at me and then my screen.

"I think so. Look, John did it." I squealed and pointed at the ending on my screen.

"Oh, thank God! Well, that will make tonight even more fun."

Confused, I looked up from my spell-check and raised an eyebrow. "What's going on tonight?" Finn's lips pressed together in a smile, and his nose crinkled as if he was trying to hold in a secret. I couldn't handle the anticipation. "What is it, Finn?"

"Okay, so before our minor heart attack this morning with your missing words, Jackson and I made spontaneous plans to go into New York tonight for New Year's! It's ridiculous, I know, so many people, but I don't know, we were feeling it. Aaaand, we want you to come!" He had the biggest smile on his face, and Jackson was cheesing right next to him. I was too stunned to respond. First, I'd forgotten it was technically New Year's Eve, and second, what about Barrett and Louie?

Finn continued with excitement radiating from him. "The train leaves around five. And remember, we still need to celebrate the fact that you finished your first draft of your first ever book! Submitting it is the cherry on top. We're so proud of you, Elle." Jackson nodded along as Finn pulled me into a hug.

"Okay, okay. I'm in. I think after I hit submit, I'll need a stiff drink anyway, right?" I smirked at the two boys, who were overjoyed with my acceptance. "But I still need to ask Emma if she'll watch Louie for me. Barrett is in Miami."

I noticed Finn's sideways glance to Jackson. "Wait, Barrett left for Miami?"

I tried to act as if it was okay. I mean, it was. He had to get this deal done. I was a little bummed we wouldn't have our first New Year's together, but there would be plenty more.

"Who's going to kiss you at midnight, girlfriend?" Jackson probed.

I shrugged. "Well, I was thinking Louie, but now that I'll be out, I'll have to get my puppy kiss when I get home."

"You didn't answer me, Ellz," Finn replied.

"Oh, right. He left this morning, like around four a.m. It was a brutal wake-up call. Actually, I'm pretty sure he was sleepwalking out the door."

"Elle, that's bullshit. It's your first New Year's together. Couldn't he leave a day later?"

I felt heat flush my cheeks. Finn had a point, but also, he didn't see what Barrett was going through. The baby, the Miami deal, settling into his new role. I didn't want to make anything harder on him. We still hadn't truly discussed children and the baby because he'd had a string of panic attacks since the funeral, and I didn't want to cause another one.

"It's okay, Finn. Seriously. He's got a lot going on, and you know me, I'm a homebody. I was totally fine staying with my baby Louie tonight and watching the ball drop on TV. Honestly, we're kind of crazy going into the city tonight. Like, I refuse to wear a diaper. That's not happening. I won't be in Times Square."

Finn and Jackson both reeled back together. "Oh my God, eww, Elle. We would never take you to Times Square for their shenanigans." Jackson still had a look of disgust on his face as he nodded along with Finn's words. "We have a friend in the hospitality industry who got us on the list for a hot club tonight. We told him we'd have

a group, so I would have tried to convince you to come regardless of your response."
He laughed, proud of himself.

"Where are we staying?" I asked, realizing they'd never mentioned the full plan.

"Oh, duh, forgot to say." Finn waved his hand like it was a minor detail. "One of our friends lives in Dumbo, so he said we could crash there at the end of the night. He's in Paris with his boyfriend tonight, so the apartment is free."

"Paris? Damn, we should go there next, ha." I continued to click through changes on my spell-check tool.

"Seriously," Jackson said, and Finn nodded in agreement.

We sat together for another hour or two, ironing out details as I spell-checked and did a final once-over of my manuscript.

Emma agreed to watch Louie. She was going to come over to my condo and stay with him. She was still recovering from the funeral and the loss of her dad, which, honestly, I could relate. It took me forever to want to do anything again after my grandparents died.

After checking my document one last time, I went onto the competition website to submit. I felt my heart race as I clicked through the prompts to upload my manuscript.

As I was waiting for my book to export into a PDF, the boys went quiet and a stranger sat right next to me. I noticed her out of my peripheral vision, an oversized puffy blue jacket and short blond hair. As soon as I caught the scent of her perfume, I knew. Because after a decade of friendship, I'd know Vera Wang Princess absolutely anywhere.

In shocked disbelief, I turned my head toward my stranger. She was smiling from ear to ear and opened her arms wide to embrace me. I couldn't help it. I burst into tears and threw myself in her arms.

"Sarah!"

I couldn't believe my best friend was sitting next to me. A glance at my computer screen and I saw my manuscript was done exporting into a PDF. The file was ready.

"Oh my God! I can't believe you're here!" I was crying, laughing, and smiling all at the same time. "Is Rach coming?"

She hugged me again, tighter this time.

"I knew today was the day you submitted your manuscript. I wanted to be here. James is watching the kids for the weekend, and I got on the first flight out of Virginia so I could be with you when you hit submit. And no, Rach and Josh have plans in Saint Louis for New Year's and are flying in tomorrow to meet the movers at their new apartment."

I'm not sure words could describe the emotions fluttering through my body. My bubbly best friend was here. Finn and Jackson too. Oh, and heaven forbid I forget my pork chop, Louie. If only Rach and Barrett were here, but it was fine. It was okay. I'd see both soon enough, and I knew they were proud of me.

My exhaustion, fear, and joy poured out of me as tears streamed down my cheeks. It was okay, everything was going to be okay.

Sarah grabbed my hand and squeezed. "You haven't submitted yet, right?"

"No, actually, I was just about to do it. It's ready." I smiled as all three of my friends gathered into the booth with me, holding my arms, my shoulder, anywhere they could reach. Louie was now sitting in my lap.

"Let's submit this book and get ready for a brand-new year," Sarah declared as I lifted my finger to hit the button.

"Wait!" I shrieked.

John looked up from the espresso machine, eyebrows pinched in concern.

"I'm doing it, John!" I yelled across the café. "I'm submitting!"

"It's time?" He clapped his hands together and jumped. Turning to the others behind the bar, he yelled across the café, "Guys, it's time! She's submitting her manuscript!"

The café broke out in applause—baristas, strangers, everyone. They cheered me on as I lifted my finger to upload my manuscript.

"You got it, babe. Submit the damn thing," said Finn.

I met his gaze and gave him a curt nod. Then Sarah, Finn, and Jackson all placed their hands on mine. Together, we submitted my manuscript at 2:47 p.m. Perfectly imperfect and ready for the judges' eyes. The confirmation hit my email moments later, and I broke down into tears again.

"I did it," I cried into Sarah's shoulder.

Finn was rubbing my back and Jackson had his hand in mine.

"You did it," Sarah said, squeezing me tight to her chest. "And I'm so fucking proud of you."

"We all are," Finn whispered, and Jackson gave my hand a tight squeeze.

♥

I gave Louie an early New Year's kiss before leaving the condo and left him a treat on his dog bed. Emma would be by in a few hours, and he'd still have a New Year's kiss. Lucky dog.

As we got through the turnstiles and ran toward the train, Finn and Jackson waved me and Sarah on. We couldn't run as fast as them in heels.

"Let's goooo!" Jackson yelled. Finn was laughing by his side, watching us stumble and try to rush to catch the train.

"You two are a hot mess," Finn said as we caught up to board the train to New York's Penn Station.

We laughed with our hands on our sides, trying to catch our breath.

"And you two . . . are rude . . . as fuck," I joked.

Sarah sat down next to me on the train and took a deep breath.

"God, I don't even remember what it's like to celebrate New Year's without kids," she panted.

"Well, honey, there's no better time to remember than NYE in NYC," Finn said with a flirtatious smirk.

We all laughed as the train started moving. In three and a half hours, we'd be in New York, and I wouldn't be alone for New Year's Eve. I only wished that Barrett would be there with me.

42

Five years ago

Jude's flight was leaving at four p.m. We'd stayed up late the night before, and that last time in bed with Jude had felt like goodbye. We had to savor every kiss and every touch because this was the last time we'd be in our bed in our apartment in New Orleans.

When I kissed him goodbye this morning, he was expecting me to meet him at the airport after work. We talked about me going with him to see the city, to our new place, and to get acquainted with our new environment. He said he even had some finance contacts who could help me with interviews.

My mind wasn't made up, and he was treading lightly about my decision. He never tried to force me to give him a straight answer, but I could feel his anticipation. Fear was overwhelming me; I didn't want to start over. *What if I can't find a job that pays as well as the one I have now? What if it takes me months to find a job? What if we break up once I get there? What if . . . ?*

I loved Jude, but I couldn't stand the idea of having no purpose. What was my worth if I mooched off him because I didn't have a job or an established reputation? Leaving my job now would be career suicide.

It was two o' clock, and I was sitting in my office looking out at the Crescent City Connection bridge and the Mississippi River. I could still make it.

At the thought of getting on the plane, deep anxiety consumed me. I didn't want to leave. We'd have to figure this out. He'd understand; we just had to figure this out. I leaned sideways and turned on my shredder.

As I watched my plane ticket shred into hundreds of strips, my heart ripped apart along with it.

I texted him as he was supposed to be boarding.

ME: I love you, I just can't.

JUDE: I understand, I just wish you'd chosen us. I thought you were mine, but something else has stolen you away.

JUDE: I'll always love you. I just want you to be happy.

ME: I don't know how . . .

JUDE: You'll find your way, Elle. I love you.

I couldn't respond. He was gone.

He chose himself. I chose myself.

We both chose our careers.

43

Now

After dinner, the four of us went out on the city. Around 10:30 p.m. we made our way to Tightrope, an exclusive club that Finn's friend was able to get us into. It was the place to be if you weren't at a house party or the touristy Times Square.

I had on a Badgley Mischka two-tone metallic sequin dress with my brunette hair in a high curly ponytail. My silver stilettos sparkled against the club's vibrant atmosphere. Sarah was wearing a black sequin dress with black strappy stilettos. The boys were in black suits with a pop of flair. Finn had paired a glittering gold bowtie with his tailored black suit, and Jackson had opted for a sparkling silver one. When we entered the club, we were given 2023 headbands and accessories to celebrate the new year. I was overwhelmed with excitement.

My book was done. I wasn't thinking about winning or losing tonight, I wasn't thinking about my future as a mother or stepmother or wife or unpublished author. All I could think about was how lucky I was to have friends like these three and, of course, getting on the dance floor as quickly as possible.

Finn's friend went above and beyond in providing us with a luxurious experience. We had a reserved booth just for us and bottle service for the entire evening. It wasn't cheap sparkling wine either. We had Dom and Veuve spread out before us.

"What is this liiiiife?" I shouted across the table to Finn.

He grinned and raised his glass of Veuve Clicquot.

I placed my Dom Pérignon on the glass table and reached for Sarah's hand.

"Shots!" I shouted at her over the music and pointed toward the magnificent bar with shelves of gleaming bottles and fine liquor.

She nodded with excitement and stood up.

We shimmied our way through the crowd and found an open spot at the very end of the bar where the mixologist was creating one of their themed cocktails with gin, champagne, and elderflower.

"That looks amazing," I said as Sarah got the bartender's attention.

"Four tequila shots please, Don Julio," Sarah said.

The bartender nodded and hurried off to get the bottle and glasses.

I leaned in closer to Sarah's ear. "James would flip his shit. Don Julio? Who are you? I thought we'd do the good ole college Jose Cuervo?"

She turned her head and gave me an *Are you serious?* look. "This place would kick us out if we got Cuervo!" she shouted back. "And yeah, but he's fine. Though, I forgot to put beer in the fridge. Poor guy only has ginger ale tonight!"

We both let out contagious belly laughs.

"Oh my God, poor Jamesie," I cooed. "He's so lost without you, I bet. Tell me the truth, how many times has he called or texted you?"

"Honestly?" She giggled. "Called five and—wait, actually, he's still texting me." Her phone screen lit up, and I saw the bubbles from his texts on the screen.

The mischievous yet loving gleam in her eye had me throwing my head back again in laughter.

The love James and Sarah had for each other was pure, and I wanted that. I'd thought I had it. *Wait, no. I'm not going to let myself think about anything but the present. No relationship rabbit holes or babies or anything. It's just me and my friends bringing in 2023 like we are a couple of newfound celebrities.*

"Here you are, ladies." The bartender slid the shots toward us.

"To friendship and the nights we'll never remember." I lifted my shot glass to her.

"Cheers!" she yelled.

It was so crowded, the bartender forgot to give us any salt, so we only had the small lime wedges in the shot glass. The first shots went down fine. Sarah's eyes were glassy, and I was starting to feel the buzz of the alcohol. Now, the second shots were . . . something. I tossed mine back and grabbed my lime wedge and sucked hard on it to cut the taste of the tequila. Sarah threw hers back but forgot the wedge. I saw her eyes bulge and her body heave. I thought to myself, *Oh fuck!* Her hand flew over her mouth, and her wide eyes told me everything I needed to know. She ran through the crowd toward the women's restroom. On second thought, maybe the back-to-back shots of tequila were a little too much too fast.

I texted her to see if she needed me, and she responded right away.

> SARAH: No, no. I'm fine. I think my body was just shocked, but I'm good. I'm good, I swear.

> ME: I'll order you a water! I'll bring it to the table.

> SARAH: 👍🙂

I got the bartender's attention again and asked for a glass of water. While leaning on the bar, I checked my phone. Still nothing from Barrett. I guess I was expecting to hear something from him tonight, but I knew he was busy. Just wishful thinking on my part.

I grabbed the water, turned, and accidentally bumped into a man's chest who was standing right behind me. Embarrassed, I looked up and came face-to-face with eyes that I didn't realize still made me weak in the knees until that moment. His deep laugh was the same, and his voice made my heart race all over again when he asked, "Elle Belle? Is that really you?"

The plastic cup bounced on the floor and water splashed up my legs. The cold rush clashed with the heat that consumed my body just by the way he said my name.

I barely whispered his name, shock taking over my intoxicated body. "Jude."

"Elle." His lips pulled up and his golden eyes turned smoky. Seductive.

I couldn't speak. My tongue was literally paralyzed. We stared at each other for what seemed like an eternity but I'm sure was only a few moments. His gaze was magnetic, pulling me toward him.

He leaned down and tilted his head to the side so that his lips brushed my ear. An electric shock pulsed through my spine, and my body was alive. "Can I get you a drink?" His breath tickled my oversensitive neck.

"No, no that's okay. We have a table." *Way to go, Elle. Way to go. Say no, per usual, but tell him you have a table. Jesus, do better.*

He pulled back and looked down at me with narrowed playful eyes.

"A table?" His lopsided grin was about to murder me. I wasn't going to make it to 2023.

"Yeah, my friends, uh, well . . ." *Why can't I use my words?* "You should come over. Come sit with us!" I blurted out before my brain could say anything reasonable.

His lips pulled into a grin and his dimples made my body ache. Jude was an illicit affair in the making. *No, no. I'd never do that to Barrett*, I told myself. And, yeah, it was true, I'd never cheat, but my heart cheating was a totally different story.

Jude waved his arm in front of us. "Lead the way, Elle Belle."

44

Five years ago

One month. It had been one month since I last went to sleep in Jude's arms. The pain was devastating. When I thought my heart couldn't shatter any more, it would crack just a little deeper. To keep the grief from consuming me, I buried myself in my work and pushed the levels of exhaustion just so I wouldn't have to lie in bed at night and think about the loss of my life. It didn't always work. Sometimes, I'd lie in bed and scream until my throat was raw, my head congested, and my heart throbbing against my chest.

I couldn't stay in our apartment. Everything from the way the coffee machine sat on the counter to the way my clothes hung less cluttered in our closet was an agonizing reminder of Jude. So over the past month I'd searched for a new apartment near my office downtown. I only saw pictures before I put an application in on a luxury apartment on Conti in the French Quarter. It had a beautiful balcony with historic iron railings and floor-to-ceiling windows that connected the balcony to the open living room and kitchen. It was the perfect place to start over, or in all honesty, barely keep going.

I didn't reach out to him. I couldn't. And he only texted me to tell me he'd landed at JFK Airport. I replayed our entire relationship on a loop in my mind. I'd thought he was the endgame; he was supposed to be the endgame. Our alchemy was transformative and magical, and I was the villain who destroyed it all. I think that's why I was so fragile when Jude fluttered through my thoughts. I chose my career; I chose to let him go. I'd had the choice, and lately, I thought I'd made the wrong one.

I missed him. Desperately, deeply, and painfully.

Since he left, I'd been lost and ungrounded. Life felt so dark, and I felt so alone. I texted the girls and jokingly mentioned that I was so lonely. I couldn't tell them point-blank that I couldn't see the sunshine and felt like all the happiness in my life had disappeared. I would burden them, and I couldn't do that. I was the happy Elle. The one who had it together. The one who always made good decisions. Forever optimistic and glass half full. They'd never believe that there was a layer underneath the illusion. And it was darker than all the midnights I saw.

I began to resent New Orleans, I began to resent my situation, and I began to resent myself. Nothing was physically keeping me in New Orleans. Nothing was physically keeping me away from Jude. But he deserved better than me. What I did, was that even forgivable? I knew I broke his heart, but I refused to be the heartbreak princess. I wouldn't keep hurting him.

45

Now

Sarah was back at the table and drinking water when we walked up. I realized too late that I forgot to get her another water after I dropped the first one.

Sorry! I mouthed, but she wasn't looking at me. She was looking at the tall man next to me with wavy chestnut hair and his left hand on my lower back.

Sarah's eyes popped and her lips mouthed the words *Holy shit!* She knew exactly who was standing next to me, but the boys had no idea. "Jude!" She jumped out of her seat to give him a hug and then over his shoulder gave me a *What the actual fuck?* stare. *No*, she mouthed behind his back as she gave him one more squeeze.

I got her message loud and clear. *Stay away from him.* I was, in fact, still very much in a relationship with Barrett Henry. And last I knew, Jude had a someone. The memory of that late-night phone call and hearing a stranger's voice with him made my stomach drop all over again.

At the sound of Jude's name, Finn came to attention. He raised his eyebrows and made direct eye contact with me. I'd mentioned Jude here and there, and he knew that he was *the one* before Barrett. All Jackson could tell was that I knew this man and there was some juicy history in this entire situation.

"Sarah, hello, good to see you again." Jude's warm smile made Sarah look down. She was a sucker for good manners.

Finn stood up, eyes on me, then shifted his gaze to Jude. "Finn Bennett." He extended his hand to Jude, who took it in his free hand and gave it a firm shake. "And this is my boyfriend, Jackson." He released Jude's hand and pointed to Jackson, who waved with glee and continued to smile.

"Jude Ashford, nice to meet you all!" He motioned to the velvet booth and lightly pressed his fingertips into my lower back. "May I join you?"

"Of course you can!" Sarah was trying so hard to be nice. Truthfully, they got along, but I knew she was worried about me. Jude was the one who got away. The one I could never get over. Until I did. I thought.

"Jude, where's your plus one tonight?" Sarah asked nonchalantly. I gave her a side-eye that could kill, and Finn brought his drink to his lips. Jackson glanced over to Finn then back at Jude and me, eyes wide with curiosity.

I noticed Jude's shoulders tense for a moment, then relax again.

Our server returned with our orders and handed Jude his scotch.

After a slow sip, Jude looked at me while answering Sarah. "No plus one. Just me and some friends from work."

I didn't look away. I was studying him even though I knew every dimple, every mannerism. The unconscious lick of his lips and the slight pull of his smile. The way his sultry eyes stayed on mine made the room fall away. It was me and him. Always me and him. His energy was pulling me in—magnetic, addictive—and the group took notice.

Jude excused himself a few minutes later to find his friends, but he told us he'd be right back. The boys, more specifically Jackson, leaned in as soon as Jude walked away.

"Who the hell was that Casanova?" Jackson slurred with his Dom still twirling in his hand.

Sarah didn't skip a beat. "That's Jude! Oh my God, Elle!" Her wide-eyed incredulous stare made me feel guilty. "They have history, like major history."

Jackson rolled his eyes. "We've gathered that much, Sarah."

"No, you don't understand." She looked over at me before continuing. "He's like her Achilles' heel. She's never been able to resist him. He's her addiction, or at least he used to be."

Barrett, remember Barrett. I love Barrett, I told myself, reaching for my freshly poured champagne.

Jackson and Finn stared at me, waiting for an explanation.

I rolled my eyes dramatically and took a deep breath.

46

Five years ago

I was sitting on my couch listening to Spotify in my favorite pair of boxers that Jude had left behind and an old Nike sports bra. It was a tough day at the office dealing with my self-serving and oily coworker Chris Johnson. No matter the conversation, he always left me feeling manipulated and uneasy. As the song changed on my playlist, my phone started ringing. I looked at the caller ID and saw that it was my grandmother's neighbor, Suzanne.

This is weird, I thought as I answered the phone. "Hello, this is Elle."

All I heard were tears. She couldn't get anything but my choked name across her lips.

"Whoa, Suzanne, what's wrong? What happened?" I could feel it in my gut. This was going to be awful.

"Elle, Elle, we've lost her." Her voice was cracked and muffled.

"Wait, what?" I said. *Who was her?* "What the hell do you mean, 'We lost her'?" Adrenaline pulsed in my body and my head turned heavy. Dread was creeping through my thoughts.

"I went to check on her this morning—you know, the chemo was tough for her—and when I knocked, no one answered, and—"

I cut her off. "What chemo?" I shouted. "Who are you talking about, Suzanne!"

"You know, the chemo for her cancer." Her words were laced with confusion.

"Suzanne!" My head throbbed.

"Oh dear, you didn't know she was undergoing chemo?" Her shocked tone struck a chord.

"No," I growled.

"Oh, honey, Di had stage four breast cancer. She's been doing chemo for about three weeks. I'd take her to the infusions and assist at home since I was a nurse."

My ears rang. My heart passed the point of repair and crumbled in my chest.

"I can't believe she didn't tell you she was sick. She talked to you all the time." An awkward pause followed for only a few moments before she continued. "It was aggressive, dear. I'm so sorry you had to find out this way. She should have told you. I thought she told you. I'm so sorry, Elle. So, so sorry." Suzanne was sobbing on the other end of the line.

I couldn't yell. I couldn't fight.

"She's gone?" My voice wavered and my body went numb.

"Yes, dear." It was difficult to hear her through her sobs. I didn't cry. I wasn't allowed to cry yet. I felt my fight-or-flight kick in, and I knew I had to get to my grandmother. I had to take care of her arrangements. I had to start the process of getting her safely next to Grandpa. I couldn't really grieve yet. I had to take care of business.

"She went peacefully in her sleep, from what the paramedics said." Suzanne's delicate voice broke through my thoughts.

"I'll be there tonight," I replied with firm confidence.

After I hung up with Suzanne, I called the one person whose heart I'd shattered, seeking solace while selfishly hoping he'd help me put my broken heart back together.

"Elle? What a surprise," said Jude. I could feel the tension over the line. Yet the sound of his voice changed everything within me. Emotion overwhelmed me.

"She's gone." My sobs were raw and unfiltered. I could never hide from Jude.

"Wait, Elle, Elle. Who's gone? Please don't tell me it's Di." His strained voice made my throat tighten. He loved my grandmother too.

The guilt suffocated me. I didn't know she was sick. I didn't go home last month like I promised. I would have noticed if I'd gone. Maybe she would have told me? On our calls, she never mentioned being sick. Granted, those calls had been sporadic over the past few months, but she'd sounded fine—tired but fine.

Nothing changed the fact that she was gone, and during our last conversation, she'd randomly asked me if I was happy; I'd lied and told her yes.

47

Now

Everyone sat still, anticipating my story. All eyes were on me—lights, camera . . .

"All right, well, a few years back, I was severely depressed. Like, severely."
I stopped to clear my throat. I'd never told this story to anyone outside of Sarah and
Rachel. Even Barrett didn't know. "I'd just lost my grandmother unexpectedly, and
I didn't even know she was sick. I hated myself for not being there for her." I took
a sip of my champagne for courage.

"Right, you told me that before. You started therapy right after that," Finn added.

Jackson had tears slowly rolling down his cheeks.

"Well, that's not exactly why," I said. "See, I went dark. *Very* dark. I was
so obsessed with work, I blamed myself for my grandmother's death, and I hated
my life, my job, myself. Nothing was off the table. Anyways, I couldn't see a way out,
or a reason to live."

I caught Sarah's eye and her slight nod to continue.

"You know how they ask people who are suicidal to call a number or a friend or anyone? That, like, they aren't alone and they are loved and all that good stuff?"

Everyone nodded, waiting for me to continue.

"Right, well, I'm sure that works for some people, but me, I just wanted to be alone. I didn't want to talk to anyone, and the thought of talking to a stranger about my first-world problems made me cringe."

The alcohol was giving me the courage to say everything out loud. Finn and Jackson both reached for me. I took a deep breath and kept going. Each part felt painful but at the same time cathartic. It had been years, and I felt like in the smallest way I was regaining a little bit of myself by sharing one of my darkest moments with people who loved me. I wish Barrett were here so he could know too.

"You see, Jude and I dated for a long time. He was my boyfriend while I was in New Orleans, and one day, I was drinking rosé on my balcony in the French Quarter and decided that I didn't want to live anymore."

The boys gasped and Sarah held her gaze steady. She knew the story.

"Yeah, I just hit this dark wall, like it was the last straw for me. And really, it's so hard to explain the way the little voice in your head can truly convince you that you are alone and that you'd be better off gone. The little voice was wrong, of course. Depression wreaks havoc on your mind, and I wasn't immune to it."

"Wait, but what about Jude? Weren't you two together?" Jackson asked curiously.

I shook my head as the memory came back to me. I could feel the heartbreak as if it happened yesterday. "No." I looked up and gave a small, sad smile. "He'd left a few months before to take a job in New York. Anyway, in that moment, I remember I was negotiating with death. What if I did it, what if I jumped? I was pulling at straws to keep my feet on the balcony."

Everyone's eyes went wide, their attention on every word.

"I was standing on my balcony's edge and about to jump when a man's voice roared behind me."

I noticed Finn and Jackson glance behind me, a look of surprise washing over their faces. Sarah's mouth parted ever so slightly as she followed their gaze.

I could feel him before I saw him. I turned around slowly, and the ache in my chest returned. Jude was standing behind me with glassy, understanding eyes.

48

Five years ago

RACH: Elle, I'm worried about you.

SARAH: Yeah, Elle. We haven't heard from you in a few days.
Are you okay?

RACH: Ellz, c'mon, it's us.

ME: I'm not great, but I'm okay. It's fine, I'll be fine. Things always work out. Plus, it's the day before Halloween. How can I be sad when I have Hocus Pocus to watch? ☺

SARAH: Do you want us to come be with you? I know Jude leaving was hard and then Grandma Di. Elle, you aren't alone, we're here for you.

SARAH: P.S. Yes to Hocus Pocus!

Me: No

Rach: Are you sure?

Me: Don't come. I'm super busy. I wouldn't be able to entertain or take you two anywhere.

Sarah: Elle, you don't have to entertain us, you don't have to do this alone.

Rach: Right. You have us. You always have us.

Me: K

Rach: Elle, this isn't okay. I know you're not okay. Please talk to us.

Me: I have to get this email out. Love you both. Ttyl.

Sarah: Elle, please, tell me you're hanging in there . . .

Rach: Elle?

♥

They say acceptance is part of grief, right? This was my acceptance.

I didn't want to keep living life without my grandmother. Missing our last call continued to haunt me, and I was robbed of saying goodbye. I didn't want to keep living life without Jude; my bed was empty and cold without him. *Should I keep up the illusion? Should I tell the girls what's really happening?* My tortured heart, my tortured mind.

I hadn't talked to Jude since I told him about my grandmother. He'd stayed on the phone and listened to me cry for hours, but within a few days, I was ghosting him again. Hot and cold, I couldn't make up my mind. I was toxic, and so I texted him one last time before I assumed he went to work.

Me: I don't want to keep pretending. I don't want to live a lie anymore.

Jude: Elle, what are you talking about?

Me: I'm so tired, Jude. Exhausted. I love you, Jude, okay? You were the best part of me.

Jude: Elle, you're scaring me. Talk to me. What's happening with you? I'm still here for you, okay? I'm still here.

Me: Everything is dark. It's so hard. Breathing is hard. Jude, I'm tired. I love you, ok? I love you.

Jude: What's going on, Elle. You're not making sense.

Jude: Elle?

Jude: Elle, answer me!

Jude: Elle Belle, what the fuck? I just called you three times. Answer your fucking phone.

Jude: Elle!

I'd had a forced yet convincing smile on my face since June. Everyone saw it. They heard my hearty laughs. No one knew I was dying and fighting my demons on the inside. I felt alone with a shattered heart. I felt like the world would be better off without me. What did I matter in this world? I was merely a speck on our planet in a vast universe. What was our purpose, my purpose? What was the point?

For some reason, I waited. I convinced myself not to do anything stupid. Maybe I'd hang on, maybe I could do it.

I couldn't.

Seated on my French Quarter balcony, three stories high, I scanned Bourbon Street where crowds of tourists flowed in sync, and the smell of alcohol and cigars drifted through my fern-covered rails and around my heavy head. The music from a bar at the corner of Bourbon and Conti rumbled through the street and rattled the glass panes of my floor-to-ceiling windows. The humid October air was thick and uncomfortable; condensation slowly rolled down my chilled glass of rosé while I twirled it on the table.

What would happen if I did it? What would happen if I listened to this sweet song of surrender? I stopped twirling my glass, the stain of my bloodred lipstick still fresh on the side. Why did I feel so alone? My heart constantly ached, and all my emotions were void and empty. I was numb.

I slowly stood up and slipped my shoes off my swollen feet. I lined them up neatly next to my chair and lifted my chin as a slight breeze caressed my skin and brushed my hair away from my sweaty brow. I was aware of my body moving toward the edge of my balcony, and I felt my hips brush up against the iron railing. I leaned over, just to look, and my breath went shallow.

Memories rushed through my cloudy mind, glimpses of the life I'd thought was right. Now everything was wrong. Six years old and my grandparents officially adopting me. Fifteen years old and telling everyone I was going to be famous. Twenty years old and falling in love.

With blurry eyes, I pressed up on my tiptoes. My calves ached, my arches sore from my heels—stupid heels. Everyone was gone. I was alone.

My heart was beating through my lightweight linen dress. The orange one Grandma and I had picked together in Italy the last summer we had Grandpa.

My head spun and my vision tunneled as I gripped the cast-iron column with shaky, sweaty hands. My biceps began to quiver as I hoisted myself up, taller, higher.

I took a jagged breath and looked down one last time. A mother and her young daughter walked together hand in hand, the little girl taking two steps to her mother's one. The little girl looked up, and our eyes met. The mother stopped short and looked up to my balcony. Her face paled and her eyes went wide. I saw her pull out her phone, but I didn't care. My heart ached. I had to fix this feeling.

Would it hurt? How much longer could I keep pretending I was okay? No one would believe this. No one would think I was hurting. I never showed them.

A tear trickled down my cheek. No one would care. I closed my eyes and waited as a breeze, warm and muggy, tickled my face. I gave a small, delicate grin and leaned into the breeze. It would be okay. I leaned a little farther, and I heard a woman scream at the same time a man's voice boomed from behind me. Jude's.

"Elle, don't you fucking dare!" His voice vibrated through my body.

I held on.

"Elle! Elle!" His arms were open, fear etched on his face with wide eyes and sweat along his brows. "Elle, get down. Please. I'm here, please get down!" He stepped a little closer.

The woman on the street had her daughter's eyes covered and her phone up to her mouth.

"Please don't jump, Elle. Let me catch you. Please, I'll do anything, let me catch you!" Jude begged and stepped right next to me, inches away from my body.

Before my fingers lost their grip, before I let go, his strong hand clasped my sweaty forearm.

"I've got you." His voice was far but firm. "I've got you, Elle."

I didn't fight him. I was so tired. So fucking tired. I couldn't think anymore; the exhaustion and darkness were all-consuming.

So I let go. I let go of everything, everyone, and fell right into Jude's open arms. He squeezed me tight to his chest, my head cradled into his shoulder.

"I'll always catch you, Elle. Always." His voice cracked as he sobbed into my shoulder. His unwavering grip was a silent promise I knew he'd keep. "Thank God you still don't lock your doors. Thank God." He half chuckled, half cried into my ear. He gently stroked my head, and the strands of sweaty hair clung to his fingers.

I'm not sure when I completely disassociated and blacked out, but I do know that Jude was with me the entire time.

49

Now

In the roaring club, our table was silent. The tension was thick and heavy.

"Remember what I said to you, Elle Belle?" Jude was looking at me and only me.

I nodded slowly and said, "Let me catch you. Please, I'll do anything, let me catch you!"

"You saved her," Finn said, eyes wide with awe.

Jude didn't look away from me. It felt like if he did, I'd fall apart, and he knew it. He only nodded silently.

A tender smile spread across my lips. "He wasn't supposed to be there. He was supposed to be in New York."

"I was," Jude said, eyes on me.

"He caught me," I whispered as my heart throbbed with the memory of Jude's strong arms around my body as I collapsed, cold with shock and grief. I forced my gaze away from his and looked back to the rest of the party. "So, yeah, what was it you said, Sarah? We *definitely* have history." A shy smile crossed my lips as I glanced back at Jude.

Later, and after somehow avoiding all conversation of Barrett, Jude grabbed my hand and leaned over to my ear. "Dance with me?"

The boys were already on the dance floor, and Sarah was fielding texts from James and looking at pictures of her two girls in New Year's Eve glasses with their daddy. She really was the best mother.

I'd told myself earlier that I was sticking with champagne the rest of the night, but after sharing my almost-suicide story, I went back to tequila. I'd had one too many tequila shots and quite a lot of champagne over the course of the evening, so even though my head said, *No, no, no,* my heart said, *Get the fuck out on that dance floor.*

Jude led me into the crowd. It was 11:55 p.m. and everyone was getting ready to watch the ball drop. "Levitating" by Dua Lipa was blaring across the speakers, and my body instinctively swayed.

Jude yelled the lyrics to the song as our bodies moved together. His hands held my hips, and I leaned back, my arm up around his neck. It was sexy, it was steamy, it was intimate.

His body felt familiar, and his arms were still strong and safe as he ran his hands down my body. We fit perfectly together like we had all those years ago. His hips moved; my hips moved. It was hypnotic and sexual.

With less than a minute till the ball dropped, I turned to face him. "I Wish" by Joel Corry was playing. I pulled his head down, forehead to forehead, and sang to him while two tears crawled down my cheeks.

He held my face in his hands and sang back to me, the sweat on his forearms gleaming in the club lights.

Thirty seconds left before midnight, and someone tapped Jude's shoulder.

"Champagne?" It was Finn. He had champagne for us for the countdown, and Jackson was behind him, looking at me with narrowed curious eyes.

Realizing how close I was to Jude, I pulled away and took the champagne. The countdown began.

"Ten! Nine! Eight!" we all yelled together.

"Seven! Six!" Jude wrapped his arm around my waist and pulled me closer to him.

I couldn't resist. I was facing him again, my arms around his neck, one of his strong hands on my waist pulling me into him, the other cupping my face. It was just us.

He mouthed the remaining seconds: *Three. Two. One.*

"Happy New Year!" rang through the club. Confetti canons erupted and everyone was grabbing someone to kiss. To my left, Finn and Jackson were making out, and in front of me, Jude Ashford leaned down, our noses barely touching, his lips a whisper away from mine. I knew I shouldn't. I knew it was wrong. I had Barrett at home—well, technically in Miami—but hell, I had his dog at home.

I closed my eyes, anticipating Jude's soft lips on mine.

But nothing happened. He didn't kiss me. I opened my eyes and watched, confused, as Jude tilted his head away from my lips and gave me a gentle kiss on my cheek.

"Jackson said you're with someone," he murmured softly in my ear.

When did Jackson talk to him alone? I thought to myself.

"Guys talk in the bathroom too." His devilish smirk made heat pulse low in my belly.

My breath became jagged; I wanted him. My body ached for him. Jude, my Jude. *No! Barrett. Your Barrett. Get it together, Elle.* My mind was in anarchy, and my heart was in mutiny.

"Yes," I murmured, my voice barely more than a whisper.

His hand was still on my face, and I leaned into his warm palm. Then it was gone. "Then you're still not mine," he said, leaning back from me with a sad smile, eyes full of longing. "I'll have to catch you later, Elle Watson." He took his hands off me but reached for my hand and lifted it to his lips. He kept his golden-brown eyes on mine as he leaned down and lightly kissed the top of my hand.

He stood up and, with a sultry grin, lifted his champagne glass in a toast before turning away. Jude Ashford silently disappeared into the crowd of strangers from which he had emerged only hours before.

♥

Jude was back. Three days later, and he was still at the forefront of my mind.

Barrett had texted me on New Year's Day to let me know the Miami deal closed and he'd be home soon. When he got home last night, he gave me a kiss and walked straight to the bedroom. I followed him in and saw him stripping down to get into bed. He glanced over his shoulder, gave me an exhausted grin, and melted into our bed with Louie snoring beside him.

I grabbed my laptop and sat on the bed next to him so that I could work on some freelance work and be close to him. I'd missed him and hated his empty side of the bed. Louie was only snuggable until he started farting, then all bets were off for a good night's sleep.

This morning started off like any other day would for us. I made the coffee, Barrett drank it with me on the couch, and we put on *SportsCenter*. We still hadn't talked about the baby or Margaret, and unfortunately, reality couldn't be avoided. Her appointment was in three days.

"I know this is a bit of a touchy subject . . . ," he said after a deep sigh.

I was sitting sideways on the couch with my legs over his lap. Just by the tone of his voice, I knew the conversation we'd been avoiding was finally here.

" . . . but Margaret's appointment is on the seventh. I've been thinking about it, and I really think I should go with her."

I kept my face blank. *Breathe, Elle. Breathe*, I said to myself. "Okay." My voice was flat, and I saw Barrett's lips tighten and his jaw twitch.

"Okay?" he mimicked, irritated.

"Yeah, that's fine. I mean, you have to go, right? It's your baby and all, and you're going to go anyways." The first punch was thrown, and my petulance was unmistakable. Why did I feel like I had to fight with him? I guess I was still wrapping my head around the whole situation. I knew this was the conversation that could break us. Actually, I was fucking angry.

I saw the frustration transform his face. His brows pinched together and his eyes narrowed. "You know, Elle, it would be a lot easier if I knew you were behind me in this." His blue eyes pierced through my offensive attitude.

Jude flashed across my mind. *Stop it! No*, I thought as the memory of his lips hovering over mine made my spine tingle.

"Barrett, it's not easy for me at all. I already told you how I feel about this situation, and I'm trying to accept it. But it isn't going to happen overnight. Accepting this is compromising a piece of myself, and really, I promise I'm trying to support you in any way I know how, but I'm not okay with this. I'm not okay with another woman having your child. I'm not okay with it being Margaret. I'm not okay."

"What are you saying, Elle?" His voice changed. He was corporate Barrett now. Firm, unbreakable, stoic.

I felt my phone vibrate in my pocket.

> Jude: Elle, call me. Please.

I hesitated. What could this be about? He never texted me out of the blue.

> Jude: Please. It's Mom.

Barrett was glaring at me, waiting for me to answer his question.

"I . . . I don't know. Okay? I don't know what I want," I said, distracted. He scoffed and I held up my phone. "I need to take this, okay?"

His facial muscles tensed, a mixture of shock, confusion, and frustration.

"You can't be serious?" he began, but I was already standing and walking to the bedroom, calling Jude.

"I'm here, Jude." The words fell out of my mouth as soon as I heard his voice on the line.

He was sobbing.

"Jude, Jude, what's happened?"

"My mom, Elle. She passed away this morning." His sobs were messy and raw. I felt the familiar pit in my stomach.

"I'm coming, Jude. Okay? I'm coming. Send me your address."

A few moments later, I had his address and a plan to get to NYC. Barrett, the baby, my future, my book—none of it mattered to me right now. Ava, Jude's mother, had always had a special place in my heart. She'd stubbornly refused to believe her son and I didn't love each other.

I walked into the living room, and with all the power I could muster, I looked at Barrett and held back my tears. "My friend's mother passed away. I told him I'd come." A tear escaped and trickled down my cheek.

Barrett saw my flushed face, and his features softened. "Okay, okay yeah. Where are you going? Do you want me to come with you?"

A small grin crossed my lips. "No, it's okay. I appreciate you offering, though. I'll be okay." Another tear fell. I rubbed my cheek with the back of my hand and sniffled. "We can, um, finish the baby conversation later?" I said, trying to offer an olive branch. "I promise to try harder at understanding, okay?"

He gave me a soft, tired smile. "Okay, yeah. Sounds good, Ellz. Oh, but hey, where is your friend? Are you going to be home tonight?"

"Yeah, I think so. He's in New York. I just don't want him to be alone, ya know?" I crossed my arms over my middle and held my elbows.

"He?" Barrett's ears perked up.

"Yeah, my friend from NOLA, Jude."

Barrett nodded slowly in acknowledgment. I'd never told him about Jude; in fact, I'd never talked about him to Barrett at all.

"I should be home tonight. If not, first thing tomorrow, okay?" I added before going back to the bedroom to pack a bag just in case.

With a resigned gaze, he threw the punch I wasn't expecting. "Elle, you're going to go anyway, right?"

♥

Jude was broken. He answered the door in only his boxers, reeking of whiskey and weed. When his eyes met mine, his upper lip began to tremble. His unkempt hair and tearstained cheeks pierced my heart like a dull blade, so I opened my arms and held him in the biggest hug I could offer. I wanted to relieve the weight of his grief and give him refuge.

By the time he calmed down, it was ten p.m. and way too late to catch the train back. So I stayed. It was like old times, except it wasn't. His mother, Ava, was gone. Our home together was gone. Our bed was gone.

I thought of Barrett as I built a pillow wall down the middle of Jude's bed. *I'm not cheating, I'm not cheating*, I thought to myself as I isolated my side of the bed—the same side as before with Jude. That's when I realized he still slept on his same side of the bed from our relationship.

"Thank you for staying, Elle Belle. I . . . I don't want to be alone," he muttered as he helped me stack pillows in the middle of his bed. His body looked like it was going through the motions of surviving. He resembled a shell of the boy I loved: distant, numb, and aloof.

"Hey, I'm glad I can be the one here for you. It's my turn to catch you, yeah?" I gave him a quick wink and started to fluff my pillow. A large sigh caught my attention, and my gaze went back to Jude. He was sitting on the bed with his hands on his head.

"I love you, Elle." His voice trembled with raw emotion. "I've always loved you, and ahhhh . . ." I could see the frustration swirling in his mind. Our history was so rich, so deep. "I just, I love you and I hate that this . . . *us* isn't possible. I hate it." It was barely a whisper, but my chest tightened with the weight of his words. Each one a bittersweet reminder that I had Barrett at home.

I remained silent as words eluded me. Jude lowered his head in understanding, and two tears traced a jagged path down my warm cheek.

50

Now

Rachel and I met at Bryant Park for coffee and to catch up. "I can't believe you *just* reached out to tell me you were in town, you bitch." Rach stuck out her tongue and laughed as we sat together at a little table with our coffees. "You know you could have saved the awkwardness and stayed with me last night, right?" she said, lifting her brows.

"I know." I groaned. "But you didn't see him, Rach. He's so broken. He literally looks like he's just floating from room to room, hardly aware of what he's doing." Rach's brow furrowed and her face softened with compassion.

"I couldn't leave him alone," I continued. "It was a long time ago, but I remember that dark feeling, and I didn't want him to even think he was alone in this for a moment."

"You're a really good person, Ellz. Forget the fact he's your ex, you are simply good people."

I gave her a lopsided grin, my mouth pulling to the side.

"Do you think he meant it when he professed his love? Or was it like, 'My mom died so I love you' kinda thing?" she asked as we watched figure skaters going around the ice rink.

"No, I mean it was a pretty raw 'I love you.' And he was drunk." I shrugged. "We say what's really on our minds when we're drunk, right? But I felt like a total asshole. I said nothing, Rach. Absolutely nothing." I groaned and pressed my face into my palm.

"Holy shit. That's awkward." She grimaced as we watched a little kid pull his dad down as they skated past us.

"Definitely awkward, but at the same time, I don't know . . ." I sighed and leaned back in my chair.

"Elle, you're with Barrett. Mind you, this is Barrett Henry. You break his heart and you get blacklisted. Cheat on him? Dear God, the horrible possibilities." She shuddered and looked at me with sad, knowing eyes. "It's tough, girl. I know you still love Jude. You've always loved him."

"I told you about the baby, right?" I asked looking away and watching the skaters mindlessly.

"Yeah, that's crazy shit. I can't believe Margaret is suddenly pregnant. What do you think Barrett will do? Is he gonna help her raise it?"

"I'm not sure, I think he's torn, especially since his dad wasn't around. But I told him I don't want children, so that pulls him in two directions."

Rachel considered me for a moment. "Elle, what the fuck are you doing?"

"What?" I was surprised by her sudden shift in tone. "What are you talking about?" I pressed my lips into a quizzical grin and lifted my brows.

"Why are you with someone who is obviously about to be a dad when you don't want to be a mother? The math isn't mathing, my girl."

"It's not that easy," I replied defensively. "I can't just leave Barrett. I love him."

"Okay," she said, "but who do you love more?"

♥

Rachel's question haunted me for two days. *Who do I love more?* It was an impossible question, and she knew it. Unfortunately, since my visit to the city, my relationship with Barrett felt like walking on eggshells; the conversation about the baby was the elephant in the room that neither of us would acknowledge. I think I knew that if we did, our relationship wouldn't survive.

So when he came into the kitchen this morning and reminded me that today was Margaret's appointment, I felt icy jealousy spread throughout my body. I knew without a doubt that I did not want to share Barrett with Margaret. Part of me had been trying to hold on to hope that he would choose me and not her. The other part of me was fairly certain that their child was going to have the best father in the world and I wouldn't get to see it.

"Okay, I'll be back right after the ultrasound, or whatever it is they do. Apparently, they're going to tell her the gender today!" His voice was bright, and he fumbled his keys in excitement.

I tried to be excited for him, but the huge pit in my stomach told me this was the beginning of the end. "Sounds great, let me know what happens." I forced a smile and tried, really tried, to show him I was being supportive. "Louie and I will be here anxiously awaiting your return." I winked and blew him a kiss.

He was out the door before he noticed.

I stared at the door for a few moments, then turned to Louie.

"Who's the bestest, goodest boy? Can you give Mommy kisses?" I snuggled his squishy face and peppered him with tiny, delicate pecks. He graciously returned them with his own slobbery licks. I looked back at my laptop and went to work on the article that was due for Olivia. On another screen, I had a résumé waiting to download from Canva. Ever since I turned in my manuscript, I'd felt more confident in my writing abilities, so I'd started applying for more freelancing opportunities and trying to keep my savings from depleting entirely.

51

Now

Over the past few weeks, the baby was all Barrett could talk about. Seeing its face. Hearing the heartbeat. Whenever Margaret called, he'd step outside and give me a quick glance and mouth, *Sorry*. I hated it but also understood. I knew I needed to be the better person. I knew I needed to support Barrett in this journey—his journey. I'd never forget the happiness that resonated in his voice when he showed me the envelope containing the sex of the baby.

"Elle, I'm having a son! A son, can you believe it? As soon as I heard his heartbeat—oh my God, I can't explain it. I knew in that moment that I was in love with someone I've never technically met. I know that I have to be this little boy's father in the best way I can." His eyes were gleaming. "I wish you could have seen it, Elle. I wish you'd been there."

I tried to smile and reciprocate his joy, but the thought of a baby moving in Margaret's stomach was unappealing to me. The baby was due in June, so only a few more short months until a new baby Henry was bouncing around Boston. I bet he'd inherit the crystal-blue Henry stare too.

I didn't tell anyone my plan. But I knew the day he left for the appointment that I had to end things with Barrett Henry, and I'd spent the past month trying to convince myself otherwise. When he came home full of determination to right the wrongs of his father, I knew my life didn't fit into the equation. Barrett and I had that pure, profound love. Our connection was deep and would forever have an impact on my life. But we were at a crossroads, an insurmountable barrier that neither of us could compromise on without sacrificing a part of our happiness or identity.

He was home in Seaport working when I arrived in athletic clothes with Louie.

"Hey, babe! I wasn't expecting you this afternoon. Did I tell you that Margaret took a video of her stomach moving and sent it to me! I still cannot believe that this is real." He noticed my soft smile and resigned gaze. His smile slowly transformed into a delicate frown and his brow furrowed in confusion. "Elle, you have Louie. Is everything okay?" His voice was a tense mixture of apprehension and calm.

I took a deep breath. "I came to bring him home." My voice cracked as I handed him Louie's leash.

His demeanor changed immediately. The anxiety rolled off his body, and his eyes widened while his breathing came in irregular bursts. "Elle, what's wrong. Let's figure this out. What's wrong?" he urged as he dropped Louie's leash and allowed him to roam through the condo.

"Barrett, I've been thinking—"

"No!" he demanded. "No!"

I gave him a sad smile and continued. "Barrett, I've been thinking, ever since you went to the appointment, you adore this baby. You can't wait to be a father."

"Elle, please." His sobs and cracked voice forced tears to begin streaming down my cheeks. "Please, don't do this."

"Barrett, I love you. You know I love you, but I can't do this. I can't be a mother and compromise that part of myself."

He began pacing, shaking his head and wiping tears from his face. Louie felt the anxiety in the room and began pacing as well. Eventually, Louie stopped by my legs, jumped up with his paws, and scratched at me, telling me to pick him up.

"Elle, stop. Please stop. We can figure this out. I won't have custody the whole time. It'll be fifty-fifty. The baby won't be around that much. Our lives won't really change. I promise. It won't change."

"Barrett, it will change." I walked over to him and reached for his hand. Louie followed. "You are going to be the best daddy that baby could have. He is so lucky to have you to love him."

He looked down, shoulders trembling with every sob. "We can make it work." His voice was barely a whisper as I opened my arms and wrapped them around him. Crying into my shoulder and holding me tight, he murmured, "Elle, I need you. I love you. I'm so sorry I've been distant."

I could feel his tears soaking through my T-shirt, and my own tears were bleeding through his.

"I've been so stressed with work and the baby coming, but I choose you, Elle. I choose you."

We were both crying, the ugly, heavy tears that happen when you can't imagine taking one more breath. This was a heart-wrenching experience I'd never wish on two people. We belonged together, had dreams and aspirations together.

"B, I can't. If we stayed together, we would of course love each other, because I'll always love you, but we would grow to resent one another. It's inevitable. I wouldn't feel fulfilled, and I don't want that. Not with you. I cherish every moment we had together. I cherish our real, very real love. I cherish you, Barrett Henry."

He lifted his head, and his blazing crystal-blue eyes penetrated deep into my soul.

I continued, trying to get the words out before my sobs took over again. "As much as I want to choose you, I choose me."

He tilted his chin down and began sobbing harder. "I love you, Elle. I love you."

"I know." My voice broke and I couldn't hold back the tears. They were flowing down my cheeks, and my heart felt like it had been stomped on by an elephant. "And I love you. I brought Louie back since you were his daddy before there was an us."

Louie was whining on the floor, so I picked him up in my arms and tried to hand him to Barrett.

"No, Elle." A sad, understanding smile flickered on his lips. He stepped back, away from Louie. "If there's anything I've learned together with you, it's that you are a fantastic mother."

Confused, my eyebrows drew together and I narrowed my eyes.

"A fantastic dog mother." He walked up to me and Louie and kissed me on the forehead. Then he leaned down and peppered Louie with kisses.

"You're the goodest boy, okay, Lou? You're gonna stay with Mommy while Daddy figures things out. I love you, little Lou." Barrett lifted his head, and his voice was slightly stronger. "Please keep him. I know we will get through this, maybe not as partners, but I think as friends. I'm sorry, Elle. I fucked up. I really fucked up, but you're the best home for Louie now. Will you keep him for me? In a way, you'll always have a part of us, yeah?"

With Louie in my arms, I leaned into Barrett's open arms. His chest was shaking with his renewed sobs, and I wrapped my free arm tighter around him.

Louie leaned up and tried to lick the tears from his face.

"Yes," I sobbed, "a million times, yes."

52

Now

The weeks after the breakup were bittersweet, and my friendship with Emma was fragile because of all the family politics. Ever since Barrett told his family we called it off, Olivia said she had no more assignments for me. I couldn't believe that Emma would feel the same way. Not only did I lose my relationship with Barrett, but it felt like I'd lost Emma too. One day in Pilates, I saw Emma by the cubbies and decided to check in with her.

"Hey, Em, hope you're doing all right." I smiled nervously.

She looked up from her cubby, gave me a sad smile, and hugged me. It felt so good to be hugged by a Henry again. "I'm all right. You? Oh, and hey, don't worry about Olivia, Elle. Okay? When I'm in charge, you're going to be my number one writer. You got it?" She stepped back and was holding my hand while I tried not to cry. "You're too good a person *and* a writer to dismiss because my brother was a dipshit."

"A loveable dipshit." My bittersweet laugh was joined by tears.

"I wish you the best of luck until we can work together again, Elle. I really do. My brother's a fucking idiot, and I just hope this baby doesn't get caught up in the Henry family bullshit." Disdain dripped from her words.

I held my tongue and stared at her with curiosity.

"Margaret wants to get married; Barrett doesn't." She rolled her eyes and sighed heavily. "But he's going to propose, he told me. He wants to do the right thing by his son and make the family seem whole—blah blah blah." Her phone buzzed, so she took it out of her purse and looked at it.

I felt my stomach drop, but also, I pitied Barrett. He was being forced to do things he didn't want to do because he thought it was right, even if it compromised who he was as a person, a dreamer.

"Sorry, Elle. I have to get back to the office. Let's do coffee or lunch sometime, okay? I miss you. You and my brother broke up, not us." She gave me another big hug. "Hang in there. Oh, I was thinking about it, since Olivia pulled that dick move and blacklisted you, I have some connections with other people in the industry who need freelancers. So let me know if you need a referral, yeah?"

I didn't know what to say, so I nodded enthusiastically as Emma Henry walked out of Align.

♥

A few weeks later, I texted Jude to check in on him. Our conversations still felt awkward, and with the lack of communication, I was scared I was losing him too. I didn't tell him Barrett and I broke up. It was too soon, and I didn't break up with him for Jude; I broke up with him for me.

Rachel called me the other day and told me that she saw Jude recently at an industry event. He'd let his facial hair grow to a stubble, very Clooney. I just needed to give him space, that was all. Space and time, and maybe one day we'd have a chance at something more than friendship if it was still what we both wanted.

I was on my morning run, and while jogging through Harvard Yard and the ancient trees, I felt my watch vibrate. I looked down and saw an email notification.

I stopped under a large oak and tapped the alert. My breath hitched and butterflies erupted in my stomach. It was from the writing competition. It was the announcement of the winners. Hands shaking, I scrolled through the message and scanned once, twice, three times before realizing what in the hell had just happened.

> Dear Elle Watson,
>
> Thank you for applying to the esteemed Literary Times Challenge. It was a pleasure reading through so many inspiring manuscripts! The competition was fierce, and we could only pick one grand prize winner. We are pleased to inform you that you have been selected as our FIRST RUNNER-UP and will receive a prize of $1,000 (USD).
>
> Well done on a finely crafted story, and we wish you the best of success in your future endeavors.
>
> Best regards,
>
> The Literary Times Challenge Team

Oh my God, I was first runner-up. I won money for my writing! My thoughts were hysterical. But I didn't get a foot in the door with an editor. Now what?

I ran back to my house, wondering the whole time if I should be proud or disappointed. I truly couldn't decide. It was winning but not winning. I didn't feel the burn in my legs or the tightness in my chest until I got to my building, panting, with adrenaline bursting through my body. I ran upstairs, flopped onto my couch, and texted my updated group chat.

ME: First runner-up! I didn't win but I got $1,000!

SARAH: OMG, Elle, I'm so proud of you! That's incredible, especially for your first book. Even though you didn't win the competition, I bet you can fix it up and submit it to other publishers, right?

RACH: Fucking congrats! That's awesome. We are excited, right?

ME: I really don't know. Like, I'm happy I did get runner-up, and I did win big money for writing a first draft of something, but like, I really wanted to win, ya know? I didn't get the editor or my foot in the door. Now what? How do I really become a writer?

SARAH: Elle, shut up. You ARE a writer. Don't you get it? You wrote a damn book in just a few months. Your FIRST book.

FINN: Ellz, Ellz, Ellz! OMG, babe! Ahh! Congratulations, my love! Jackson is here and says he's so proud of you too.

RACH: You literally WROTE a book. What else qualifies someone for being a writer? Being published? But that's technical.

SARAH: Rachel, shut up. She could self-publish if she really wanted to.

ME: You think, Sarah?

SARAH: Definitely. You can try the traditional route if you want for a bit, but if that doesn't work, you didn't fail.

ME: I don't think I failed, I think. Not really, at least. I mean, I was runner-up, so that means they liked it . . .

FINN: How many people submitted, Elle?

SARAH: Yeah, how many?

ME: Thousands, I'm sure. It was open nationwide even though it's based here in Boston.

RACH: Holy fuck, ELLE! You placed first runner-up in a national competition. Do you realize how huge that is!?

FINN: Ellz, you are unbelievable. J and I are so proud of you. SO freaking proud.

SARAH: Same here, girl.

ME: But, Sarah, what were you saying about publishing?

SARAH: Oh, just that sometimes, well, don't ask me for stats, but I think a lot of times you can make more money self-publishing because you are more in control. It's just harder.

Rach: When has something being harder ever stopped you, though?

Finn: No comment, ladies. 😑

Sarah: Omg, Finn.

Rach: I can't with this guy.

Me: HAHAHA

Sarah: Elle, clean up your manuscript a bit and submit it. You can feel confident knowing that it's good if it was good enough to beat out thousands of other submissions.

Me: Okay, hold on one sec. I want to read over the rules again in my email and see if they say anything about publishing it in like an anthology or anything. Stand by.

I opened the rules of the competition and began to read. What I read next sent my stomach through the floor. My excitement vanished and anxiety crept through my mind.

Me: We have a problem, Houston. A really big fucking problem.

Rach: WHAT?

Sarah: Excuse me?

Me: The fine print of the competition. They keep the rights to my manuscript.

FINN: NO! Fuck.

SARAH: . . .

ME: I imagined winning so much that I didn't think losing the rights would be a big deal. But yeah, once I submitted it, the competition gets to keep my story.

RACH: So, you knew about that fine print? Elle, what were you thinking? That's awful verbiage. They aren't publishing it without your consent, are they?

SARAH: What the actual fuck?

ME: I don't think so, I could probably get a lawyer or something, but I mean, you guys, it was a shitty first draft, right?

RACH: I don't know, Elle. You slaved over that story. Now you're going to walk away?

SARAH: Yeah, Elle, you can't walk away from that. It's a labor of love.

ME: I'm not walking away from it. I'm going to write something better. Maybe that was the whole point for me. I don't know, maybe it's only for me to understand. Now I know I can do it. I can get paid for my art and my talent. I can win, I can do this. Maybe I can find an agent with the first manuscript I scrapped.

SARAH: The one inspired by your grandparents?

ME: Yeah, it was almost a completed first draft. I bet I can make something happen with it.

RACH: Do you think you'll go back to corporate?

ME: No, I don't think so. I could if I needed to, but I'm not there yet. I was nervous for a bit about my savings depleting, but I've got a steady stream of income from a few clients I do copywriting for. I can't believe it, honestly.

RACH: I don't get it. You could make so much money going into corporate publishing if you wanted to.

ME: Rach, could you ever imagine being a stay-at-home mom? Seriously.

RACH: God no.

SARAH: Thanks, Rach. *Eye roll*

FINN: Sign me up for the stay-at-home dad train. Please. K. Thanks, bye.

ME: See though? Everyone has their own thing. Their own success. That's what makes this so hard to figure out sometimes. It's not one-size-fits-all in terms of life choices.

ME: BTW, Sarah, you're an amazing mom, and I could never do what you do either. It's too hard.

Sarah: Thanks! ❤ I love momming, but James better start making his own doctor's appointments, or I'm going on strike.

Me: HAHAHA

Rach: HAHAHA

Finn: Uh-oh, Jamesie.

Now

I was waiting in the coffee shop for Finn and Jackson for our official debrief of the Academy Awards. We'd had to keep delaying because of my deadlines.

Louie and I were sitting in our usual spot with my latte, and John had gone above and beyond this time by making latte art of Louie himself. I glanced at the door and noticed Finn and Jackson enter the café. When they saw me, they gave a quick wave and got in line to order their drinks.

Once John gave them their orders, they turned to me, and it looked as if they were holding back laughter. Finn's eyes were gleaming, and his lips were drawn inward. Jackson's face was red as a beet, with the occasional involuntary sound escaping his lips. I also noticed Finn had his hand in his pocket and so did Jackson.

I felt an odd tension in the air. Something was off—not bad but off. The boys walked up to the table and Finn grasped my arm, literally jumping to share his news.

"Elle, we have something to tell you," Jackson said, smiling at Finn with an equal glint in his eye.

I had absolutely no idea what was going on other than they were acting bonkers.

They held each other's gazes and then nodded in unison. Together they threw their left hands in my face and yelled, "Surprise!" Both boys had a gold band with diamonds nestled snug on their left ring finger.

The shock rendered me speechless.

"We're engaged!" they yelled in unison. Finn broke into the happiest tears, and Jackson was holding on to his arm while hopping up and down.

I jumped out of my chair and grabbed both of them in my arms. "Oh my God!" I yelled back, and all three of us jumped up and down and babbled like children at Disney World for the first time.

"Oh my God, so beautiful! You must tell me everything!" I looked at both of their tearstained faces.

Jackson was grinning from ear to ear, and Finn was trying to keep up with the tears rolling down his cheeks. The boys shared every detail of their perfect proposal when Jackson asked Finn the question on the Charles River only the night before.

The best part? I was the first to know.

I don't know why I opened the typewriter case to look inside. My grandmother's typewriter had sat untouched on my desk since I moved to Boston. For some reason, though, today I felt like I wanted to touch it. I wanted to use her typewriter and feel her with me. Maybe I'd write a few lines of poetry or just a letter to my future self, telling her how proud I was of her already.

There wasn't any paper in it, and the ribbon was still in the case, so I opened it to find the ribbon, and that's when I saw a tiny piece of aged yellow paper sticking out from a hidden pocket. Well, I guess it wasn't really hidden, but I didn't know it was supposed to be there.

I gently pulled the pocket open and reached for the paper. That's when I noticed it was a thick stack of papers held together with an old, rusted paper clip. I walked over to my bed and sat down, my chest tight, tears rolling down my flushed face.

It wasn't just a vintage piece of paper that I'd found. No. I'd uncovered Grandma Di's competition manuscript. I stayed up all night reading it, and I finally understood why my grandmother had made the decision to forego her independence and get married. Why she'd turned away from something that I thought was her true calling.

It was because she'd wanted to. It was entirely her decision and my grandfather had let her have that choice, just like her main character's love interest let her make hers. She'd wanted to be a mother and a wife more than a writer. That was her true calling.

54

Now

Springtime in Boston was busy, like an emergence from a long hibernation. Flowers were starting to pop up out of the snow, grass was finding its way out of its dormant stage, and the birds were singing sweet melodies.

After gaining a new perspective from my grandmother's manuscript, I rewrote my original story for the competition, the one I never submitted. Then Emma helped refer me to some agents she knew in the area and in New York, and I submitted to them to see if they'd be interested in working with me to make my story a reality.

Unfortunately, I received zero responses. When I reached out to Em, she told me it could take weeks if not months for agents to respond, so I was in limbo. I decided that there was no better time to go to New York for a few days with Louie to see Rachel. She was settled into her apartment in Dumbo, and Central Park had become one of our favorite meeting spots.

♥

Rach was at work, and I was relaxing in her guest room with Louie watching *The Office*, per usual. While scrolling through social media, I had two emails come in back to back.

> Hi Elle,
>
> Thank you for submitting your manuscript. Unfortunately, I'm not taking on any new authors. I wish you the best.
>
> Regards,
>
> Andrew Lenard, Tiff Literary

Well shit, why couldn't he send that weeks ago when he already knew he wasn't going to accept me as an author? I felt my confidence sink a little at the rejection, but he was just one agent. There were still other responses I was waiting for. More emails came through. *It must be query Tuesday*, I thought to myself.

One agent declined outright with no explanation. *That was nice.* I rolled my eyes. Little Lou was snoring at the head of the bed—on my pillow, more precisely. I smiled at my little lovebug. I looked back to my phone after scratching his head and read the last email. Cindy Narland was from Goldengate Lit and said she was no longer looking for romance even though her manuscript wish list hadn't been updated. On the flip side, she did encourage me to keep pursuing my goals, so that was nice.

I felt antsy with the rejections I'd received, so I decided to head into Manhattan. It was a beautiful day to sit in Central Park, and I texted Rach to let her know we could meet for happy hour.

While sitting on a bench close to the Pond, I noticed a man running up who looked oddly familiar—too familiar. He was getting closer, but he had his headphones in and wasn't looking directly at me. The tips of his chestnut hair were sweaty, and his stubble really did look very Clooney. I stared at him as he got closer and closer. When he noticed me, our eyes locked and he shuffled the next couple of yards to my bench. When he stopped in front of me, he was panting and trying to catch his breath. He took his headphones out of his ears, looped them across his neck, and then shook his head like a puppy, spraying sweat all over me.

"You did that on purpose, ass."

"Maybe I did, maybe I didn't." Jude's smirk was devilish.

"Well, I guess you can sit down if you'd like," I said, patting the empty space on the bench next to me.

"We can't keep meeting like this," he said as he took a deep breath and sat down next to me.

I could smell the woody citrus scent of his cologne as his body leaned closer to mine.

"Why are you all alone in Central Park?" he asked as he readjusted his headphones on his neck.

"What are you doing running? I didn't know you still ran?" I asked instead.

"That's irrelevant. I run so I don't have to think. Easy enough," he said, cocking an eyebrow at me. "Seriously, though. What are you in New York for?"

"To see you, of course." I stuck my tongue out at him.

"You've got jokes today, Elle Belle."

"I try." I turned my body to face him. His expression was open, and I couldn't place it. Maybe relaxed? "How are you doing since your mom? I know we've been talking intermittently, but now that I see you in the flesh, how are you, Jude?"

"Thanks for asking." His grin was genuine and effortless. "I'm doing much better. It was rough there for a bit, but I know you get it. Thanks for always responding to my texts. Sometimes I just had to vent, ya know?"

I curled both of my legs up onto the bench. "I know." I smiled gently, then told him what had been weighing heavy on my heart for months. "I'm sorry how we left things last time, Jude. I really am."

His short laugh made the butterflies in my stomach wake up.

"Who knows? Maybe the stars will align one day, Elle Belle." He flashed a quick smile. "I'll be here, though. I meant what I said. I love you and I always have."

He stood up, grabbed his headphones, and placed them in his ears. "If you're in New York for a while, let's grab a bite, yeah?" he asked while brushing his hand through his damp hair.

"I'll text you," I said and waved as he turned around to keep on running.

Just then, Rach messaged me.

> RACH: Ready, Freddie? I can meet you at this bar I want to show you. It's a bookstore and a bar at the same time! It's so you.

> ME: You know me so well! Text me the deets and I'll meet you.

Rachel and I stayed out way too late for thirtysomethings on a random Tuesday night. Who knew you could drink too many espresso martinis while giggling over EmHen's newest book. The next morning, we both sat on a park bench with Louie, nursing our black coffees.

"You know, maybe if you sit here long enough, a runner will stop and ask you to marry them?" she joked as I brought my coffee to my lips.

The park was nice midmorning.

"Been there done that," I said nonchalantly.

"What? Who? When?" She leaned in closer for the gossip.

Louie lifted his head and snorted.

"While I was waiting for you yesterday. Jude was running and stopped to chat for a bit. Only difference is he didn't ask me to marry him." I laughed and placed the coffee back on my right thigh.

"Jesus, Elle. You and Jude run into each other like it's fate or something. Do you realize how big New York City really is? And you see him here?"

"I don't know." I shrugged.

I was wiping away one of Louie's eye boogers when Rachel pointed at my purse with a curious expression on her face. "Elle, I think your phone is going off." I grabbed it and glanced at the number. I didn't recognize it.

"I don't know who it is." I looked at Rachel, confused.

"Answer it, dummy. You never know."

I didn't want to pick up, but she was sitting right next to me and pressured me into it. "Fine," I said.

I took a deep breath and answered my phone. "Hello, this is Elle."

♥

The conversation lasted only a minute, and my body was vibrating. I hung up after repeated thank-yous and stared wide-eyed at Rach.

"Oh my God, oh my God! Who was it? Elle, you look extremely odd. What happened?" Rachel was freaking out and Louie started barking.

"Rach! Rach!"

"Fuck, Elle. What is it?"

"Rachel, I have an agent!"

Her jaw dropped and then she was standing on the bench screaming, "My best friend just got an agent! She's going to be a famous writer! My best friend has an agent!"

The laughter escaped from my lips, and I jumped up on the bench with her, holding Louie of course, and started chanting, "I got an agent! I got an agent!"

When we finally sat back down, Louie's eyes were terrified and Rach was panting.

"Okay, so which agent chose to represent you?" she asked as she cleaned the spilled coffee from her hand and forearm. "So, it wasn't anyone I sent a submission to. It was an agent from the writing competition I entered a few months ago! Her name is Jordan Cline."

"Oh shit! Okay, what did she say?"

"Rach, I can't believe this is real. Seriously. Fuck. Ahh! She said she loved my writing style and my voice and has been thinking about my novel ever since she read it. When she told me she wanted to represent me, Rach, I almost died. Like, oh my God! She wants to represent me!"

Rach leaned in despite Louie's discomfort and pulled me into a warm, firm hug.

Louie was barking like crazy, and suddenly I couldn't stop crying. The happiest tears I've ever cried were racing down my cheeks. "She wants me to send her any other projects I've been working on. I'm gonna send her the manuscript I've been submitting. I think she'd love it. She says she represents mostly general fiction but loves a good romance." My cheeks were hurting from smiling so much. "Oh my God, my chest hurts, I can't breathe." I grabbed my chest and leaned back on the bench.

Louie whined and crawled up me.

"We have to call Sarah, like now!" Rach said.

"And Finn and Jackson. Oh, and Jude," I added.

She lifted an eyebrow and gave me a knowing grin. Rachel dialed Sarah's number, and while she did that, I quickly sent separate texts to everyone.

ME: I did it! I got an agent! I'm on my way to getting published. 🤍

Jackson responded immediately.

Congrats, Elle. Wishing you the best. So proud.

Finn used way too many exclamation points, but all were appreciated.

Let's go, my future bestselling author!!!!

Five minutes later, I had a text from Jude.

I always believed you could do it. Dinner to celebrate? Xo

We all met at a vegan restaurant in Tribeca to celebrate. Rach and Josh, Finn and Jackson, Jude—everyone was there except Sarah, who told us to FaceTime her when we sat down so she could officially be there.

It was a round table inside, close to the bar, and Jude arrived before us. The boys had been in New York for a musical, so they hopped over after their matinee. Greetings were exchanged, and as I went to sit, I noticed an empty seat next to Jude's jacket. I glanced sideways to catch Rach's eye. She nodded and smiled in encouragement.

Jude was standing by me in the bustle of bodies trying to take a seat, so I leaned over and asked, "May I?" I pointed to the empty chair by his jacket. "Or are you saving it for your girlfriend?" I said with a glint in my eye.

He leaned down, his lips brushing my ear. "It's yours."

Goose bumps erupted down my arms and a tingle spread throughout my body. "Good." I lifted my chin and gave him a sly grin.

We all sat down and ordered cocktails to celebrate my getting an agent. As if we were still in New Orleans and as if years hadn't passed, Jude rested his arm on the back of my chair and I placed a hand on the top of his thigh.

Once the cocktails arrived, Jude raised his scotch, and everyone lifted their drinks in response.

"To Elle, for writing not one but two books, getting a lit agent, and doing it all even though she was scared as hell. I told her I was going to give a toast tonight, so she requested some *very* specific words for me to share." He turned to me for a quick pause, smiled, and then looked back to the group. "To the dreamers who dream and the ones who never give up."

55

Now

A few months later, I was in New York for my meeting with Jordan, and we were planning to review the various proposals for my manuscript since multiple publishers were bidding on it. Louie was spending the week with his guncles Finn and Jackson, and I was spending mine with Jude. Emma also texted me a few weeks ago to tell me Barrett had welcomed his baby boy.

> EMMA: I hope you don't mind me filling you in, but I thought you should know.

> ME: Thanks, Em. Seriously. I'm happy for him, and if he wants to be a dad as badly as he said he did, then I'm over-the-moon excited he gets to do that.

> EMMA: He never deserved you, Elle. I'm so happy we are still friends.

As much as I loved Boston, I loved New York too. A part of me had always wanted to come home, even if August in New York was a bit steamy.

I walked by the Bethesda Fountain and embraced the present moment. The wind was delicate against my face, and I felt like there was only one person in my life who I wanted to be with at this very moment. I called Jude.

"Hey, I'm in the park. The fountain. Can you meet me?"

"Be right there."

His office wasn't far, and he'd been grabbing a quick bite from a hot dog stand when I called. We hadn't made anything official, but it was late August and we'd been dating each other for a few months now. I was standing on the edge of the fountain when he strolled up to me.

"Elle, what the hell are you doing?" he teased. He was wearing navy-blue slacks and the Hugo Boss shoes I'd bought for him at Canal Place in New Orleans. His forest-green polo was slim fit and made the golden flecks in his amber eyes stand out.

"I choose me, Jude. I've had to choose me to become a better version of myself and to discover what it was I truly wanted out of my life."

His head tilted. I could see his mind working, and he shook his head and ran his hand through the back of his sun-kissed hair. "Elle, what is this? I . . ."

I raised my voice. "But I also choose you."

He stopped talking, his eyes went wide, and his head shot right back up. "What did you say?"

"I said, 'I also choose you,' Jude. I choose us. If you'll have me." I was holding my breath, praying I hadn't read him—us—wrong.

A little crowd had started to form around us—some tourists, a few runners—and people had taken out their phones to record.

This is going to be embarrassing as fuck if he rejects me, I thought while holding my smile.

He hadn't responded yet, and I could hear murmuring. His ears began to turn red as he looked around at all the bystanders.

Jude was a body length away from me; he was close. I could smell the citrus from his cologne. I could feel his attention now directed only at me. I saw his upper lip slowly rise, and I knew he had me.

I was very aware that I was standing on the edge of the fountain and that his arms were slowly opening. I barely whispered it, but he heard me. "Will you catch me?" I said as I leaned forward.

It was us. Back on that balcony, back in that moment. Except this time, I wasn't lost and it wasn't dark. Pure light radiated around me. My Jude. He opened his arms wider. "Let me catch you."

This time I didn't fall, I jumped right into his outstretched arms.

The crowd broke out into applause. While slightly embarrassing, it was also endearing. They were rooting for us too.

Jude placed me down in front of him, our bodies vibrating with adrenaline and happiness.

"It was always you and me, wasn't it?" I asked, placing both my hands on his chest and leaning into his body. "At least, it's what I've come to think," I said as I lifted my face and he tilted his chin.

Our noses touched and both of us smiled, our lips almost brushing.

His breath went shallow. "Are you mine?" he asked, closing his eyes and pressing his forehead to mine.

"I'm finally yours," I whispered and pulled him into a deep, tender kiss.

EPILOGUE

Two years later

JUDE

stood on our tiny balcony in Dumbo next to Elle's struggling succulents and
took in a deep breath of New York air. It was a warm summer evening, and the
Brooklyn Bridge sparkled while I nursed my scotch. Our version of New York was
magical. It was home. I imagined all the nights we'd sat out here together and I'd
held her body close, our breathing synced while we watched the city lights shimmer.

I took another sip and heard the slow cooker's timer going off in the kitchen.
Another big inhale and I stood up, taking in the city one more time. It never got old.

Once inside, I walked into our little galley kitchen and turned the timer off.
My stomach rumbled as I lifted the lid off of the pot. The aroma of my mother's
red beans with a hint of bell pepper, fennel, and andouille sausage spread through
the house. I thought Elle would be in the kitchen before I stopped stirring, but Louie
came through instead. I glanced down at the little terror and stuck my tongue out.

"Not for you."

He just stared at me with his flat nose high in the air.

"Go away, Lou. Go get Mommy."

He didn't move. That damn dog never listened to me and only moved when Elle moved. The little bastard had his spot between us in bed too, and unfortunately for me, I got the lower, very flatulent half. I'm more than grateful for my sleep apnea mask these days. Fucking Barrett Henry. He had to give her the dog . . .

In all honesty, Lou and I didn't hate each other. We both knew Elle would choose the dog over me in a second, but when she wasn't around, we had an unwritten code between us: Louie behaved and listened up until the moment Mommy walked back through the door. I'd never press it, but the dog really did love me. He just wanted me to earn it in front of Elle.

"Babe, the red beans are almost done. You ready to eat?"

Silence.

"Babe? Elle?"

I waited a few seconds—nothing.

Curious, I tilted my head around the corner and saw her sitting on the couch typing. She heard nothing while her oversized red headphones covered her ears.

Shaking my head, I looked down at Louie and rolled my eyes, looking for some inkling of camaraderie. He mean-mugged the fuck out of me and farted as he walked away. *Typical*, I thought as I went over to the living room.

With a sly grin on my lips, I leaned over the back of the couch to get Elle Belle's attention. She was wearing my old blue-striped boxers she stole back in New Orleans and one of my old college T-shirts. The woman could live in oversized tees and shorts. My eyes closed involuntarily as I brushed by her hair, the smell of eucalyptus and lavender sending a wave of calm through my entire body.

She must have felt me there, because she turned as soon as I leaned over. I opened my eyes and tried to hold in my laugh when her confused stare met mine. It was well established in our house that when she wrote, she forgot herself and hated—I mean hated—being interrupted. Louie was the only one allowed to bother her, and frankly, I was a bit jealous. The little asshole thought he was a king in this house.

She lifted her headphones off of one ear and turned more to face me.

"Hey, babe, what's up?" Her chipper tone caught me by surprise and made my heart squeeze. Her big green eyes sparkled, and her wide smile filled our space with an infectious joy. I couldn't help but give her a big smile and a tiny kiss on the tip of her nose.

She crinkled her nose and squeezed her eyes in that cute little thing she does whenever she's happy.

"I'm sorry, I know you hate to be bothered when you're writing, but dinner is almost ready."

Her eyes went wide with understanding. "Oh my God, I thought I smelled your mom's red beans. Ha, I mean, how could I not. It smells incredible in here. Thanks for cooking." She kissed my cheek with a little peck and glanced back to her computer screen.

"Elle Belle, you want to eat here so you can keep writing?"

"No, no, I'll be right there. I want to sit with you. I can't wait to tell you about this next book!" Her excitement radiated through the space between us, and I knew for the millionth time that this was the woman I wanted to spend the rest of my life with. My mother's ring was at the jewelers getting sized, and Elle had no idea.

"I can't wait to hear." I winked at her, and she playfully rolled her eyes.

"Seriously, give me like, five minutes, okay? I think I know what I want it to say."

Before she could turn around, I caught her chin lightly and whispered, my lips hovering millimeters above hers, "To the dreamers who dream . . ."

She closed her eyes and whispered back, "And to the ones who never give up."

Our lips met in a soft, passionate kiss. Then she pulled away, eyes determined, and put her headphones back over her ears. My lips still tingled with her kiss. I couldn't get enough of her kisses, and I'd let her steal all of mine for the rest of time. Over the years with Elle, she taught me that love is for those who can imagine it and grab hold. And I'd never let her go.

My stomach growled again as I pressed up from the couch, kissed the top of her head, and glanced at her screen. Laser focused, she released a deep exhale and began to type.

I knew death . . .

ACKNOWLEDGMENTS

I had no idea that the day *I* left corporate America, it would be the beginning of *Elle*'s story. I always wanted to be a writer, but up until 2016, I didn't think it was a real path for me. Like Elle, I did all the right things I was told to do and ended up in an existential crisis at twenty-six years old. This book was written at a time when I had no idea how to stand up for myself or my unconventional choices. *Elle* taught me how to do it. By writing her story, I found my voice. I found my strength to live, to write, to be different.

Getting *Unconventionally, Elle* into your hands has been seven years in the making, with plenty of drafts and tears. I still remember writing my first sentence at the Candy Bank in downtown Mandeville in 2018—their nitro coffee gave me the power to start the scariest thing I've ever done.

Additionally, *Elle* wouldn't be here without my talented editors whose expert guidance made me a better writer and *Elle* a better book. They are my A-team, and I'm forever in awe of their expertise and keen eyes. The biggest thanks to Ema Barnes,

Will Tyler, and Jessica Fogleman for getting our girl into the world with only a handful of em-dashes and Oxford commas. Oh, and they let me keep my Taylor Swift Easter eggs, so I'm forever grateful!

A huge thank-you to Sam Palencia for my gorgeous cover—seriously, you created a masterpiece—and to Ashley Santoro for designing the interior of my book baby. Emma Rosenfeld, you are a graphic design queen, and you made me feel like a real author with your logo creation and support.

This manuscript never would have seen the light of day if it weren't for . . . my dogs. Kidding! (But kind of.) Seriously, though, I want to thank my husband, Cain, for always believing *Elle* would find her way into readers' hands. Your unwavering love and support is literally insane. I'll retire you one day, babe. I promise.

Thank you to Grandma Deena for showing me how to be a reader and fall in love with books. Your love of reading was contagious, and your love for me will be in every word I write for the rest of my life. I wish you were here to see *Elle* published, but now you'll live forever in her pages. Also, thank you, Grandpa Joe. Elle found her strength from your words, and so did I. I love you and Grandma - always.

To my beta readers who read *Elle* when she was merely three drafts in—ha ha, have fun reading a completely different book now! I love you guys: Sam, Sloan, Lorelei, Leslie, Mary, Elise, Wendy, Zac, and Janelle. And Shelby Maalouf, my fellow writer, poet, and critique partner, you were my ride or die in the query trenches and make being a writer a lot less lonely.

Oh, and I *must* mention my therapist, Christine Howell. From sitting on your couch in 2016 a depressed shell of a human, to sitting on your couch in 2024 with confidence and a sixteen-page editorial letter, *Elle* is here because of you.

Not to mention your professional advice for Elle herself in the book was greatly appreciated. She was a hot mess too, wasn't she?!

I'd be remiss if I didn't mention the staff at my favorite writing spots. For my people at Tandem, Cured.On Columbia, and Ox Lot Books, I love you with all of my bookish heart. Thank you for being a part of my dream!

Also, thank you to Taylor Swift. You made me feel *powerful* with songs like "The Man" and "Look What You Made Me Do." And let's not forget *Elle*'s first draft was completed listening to *Folklore* on repeat and then edited to *TTPD*. *Elle* was written over many eras, in your music as well as my life.

Unconventionally, Elle was written for the ones who feel lost in life even though they did everything right. The different ones. The weird ones. For the women who are *too* loud and who were made to feel small. To the ones who are stuck in the cogwheel of society but feel like they are made for so much more. For anyone who's ever been bullied for being too smart, too driven, or too much. For the dreamers who dream and the ones who never give up. Finally, for the ones who feel like the darkness of depression will never go away. I believe in you and your magic.

Last but certainly not least, Madi. The Tree to my Tay (even if I'm not the blonde one). Your friendship and love from first draft to final proof have been my rock even in the hardest days. You're one of *Elle*'s biggest fans, and guess what . . .

WE DID IT!

About the Author

JOURDANA WEBBER lives in New Orleans with her husband, four dogs, and an unshakeable Taylor Swift addiction. Lover of the Oxford comma (and em dash), Jourdana is a corporate dropout, an audacious dreamer, and somehow, her family's go-to tech guru.

She hopes to empower readers with her stories but also show them that magic and happily-ever-afters do exist, even when life doesn't go as planned.

You can find her online at

www.jourdanawebber.com

authorjourdanawebber